W9-BGK-077

The
Forms
of
Water

Also by Andrea Barrett

The Middle Kingdom
Secret Harmonies
Lucid Stars

The Forms of Water

Andrea Barrett

POCKET BOOKS

New York   London   Toronto   Sydney   Tokyo   Singapore

A portion of this novel appeared as the short story "The Forms of Water" in *American Short Fiction, Volume 2, Number 6, Summer 1992,* © 1992 by Andrea Barrett.

A fellowship from the National Endowment for the Arts made possible the completion of this novel.

POCKET BOOKS, a division of Simon & Schuster Inc.
1230 Avenue of the Americas, New York, NY 10020

Library of Congress Cataloging-in-Publication Data
Barrett, Andrea.
     The forms of water / Andrea Barrett.
        p.   cm.
     ISBN: 0-671-79521-X
     l. Title.
     PS3552.A7327F66   1993
     813'.54—dc20   92-40644
                                                                                    CIP

First Pocket Books hardcover printing June 1993

10   9   8   7   6   5   4   3   2   1

For Margot Livesey,
who helped me find my way

The cloude passed awaye, and they sawe a ful fayr ylonde, and thyderwarde they drewe. In that ylonde was joye and myrth ynough, and all the erth of that ylonde shyned as bryght as the sonne, and there were the fayrest trees and herbes that ever ony man sawe, and there were many precyous stones shynynge bryght, and every herbe there was ful of fygures, and every tree ful of fruyte; so that it was a glorious sight, and an hevenly joye to abyde there . . . where is ever day, and never night, and this place is called paradyse terrestre.

—from the *Voyage of St. Brendan* (an early translation of the Celtic tale)

Is there then any terrestrial paradise where, amidst the whispering of the olive-leaves, people can be with whom they like and have what they like and take their ease in shadows and in coolness?

—from *The Good Soldier,* by Ford Madox Ford

quotes in the text - from John Tyndall,
The Forms of Water in Clouds and
Rivers, Ice and Glaciers (1872)

Part 1

The Deceitful Heart

1

Henry Auberon, nearing fifty and without a car, sat in a shabby living room that didn't belong to him. The tenant before him had had a cat, which had shredded the armchair and sprayed on the rugs. A water-stained book propped the window open; the gutter above the window leaked and the foundation below it shed chunks of mortar the size of finger bones. Had the house been his, Henry would have fixed these problems instantly. But the house belonged to his sister's ex-husband, who had grudgingly offered it when Henry had found himself with nowhere else to go.

The house was for sale and might disappear from under him at any minute, but Henry refused to think of what would happen then. He sat in his armchair and refused to think of his own lost home or of the wreckage he had made of his grandparents' farm in Coreopsis. He refused to think of the foreclosures, the bankruptcy proceedings, the shame, the failure, his amazing errors; he refused to think of his wife, who had thrown him out; he refused to think of the drunken accident that had cost him his driver's license and reduced him to walking to the temporary job that he also refused to consider, his three-to-eleven shift at the box factory near the Rochester stadium.

Henry refused all this; he refused it absolutely. Instead, on Friday night, just after midnight, aware every minute that he had to rise at six to catch the chain of buses that would take him to the nursing home for his weekly visit to his uncle—instead, Henry closed his eyes and thought of the places he yearned to visit and never had.

He imagined himself in St. Croix, scuba diving along the reefs and following his bubbles back to the surface. He pictured himself in South America, nose to nose with an anaconda; with the gorillas in Rwanda or the Patagonian penguins. Belize, Zaire, Alaska, Spain—until his life had collapsed, six months ago, he'd relaxed at night by reading travel books and plotting how he might get from here to there. Although he had never, except for a few brief trips to Toronto, left the eastern United States, he had planned for years to retire young and explore.

And now here he was, no longer young, trapped in a dead-end job with no future he could see. Having lost his house, his daughters, his friends, his wife, he was left with the travels he could imagine. Caucasia, the Black Sea, the Gobi Desert. The Himalayas and then Bombay. He carried visions of these places to the box factory and held them to him while his machines spewed out sheets of corrugated board printed the wrong colors, slit and scored in the wrong places, glued into improbable shapes. Then at night, in this place he refused to call home, he rolled in his fantasies.

Bujumbura, Madagascar. Apparently he had lost his sister as well. Earlier, as he'd been walking home, a lit storefront window had caught his gaze. In front of a group of people perched on orange chairs had stood a woman who gestured like Wiloma. He had stopped and pressed his face to the glass and cupped his hands around his eyes to cut the glare from the streetlights. That was her, there was no doubt about it: Wiloma, trying to lead another group of people down on their luck to the glories of her newfound religion. In the old days, before her conversion, she would never have ventured into this run-down part of Rochester after dark. Now, he knew, she made these missions twice a week.

He had stared through the window and tried to decipher what she was saying. When her mouth stopped moving, he had tapped gently on the glass. Her face looked so open and animated that foolishly, unthinkingly, he had assumed she would welcome him. Luck had brought her to him, he'd thought; he'd been thinking about her all week, since his last visit to his uncle. Thinking about her and longing to ask her what she knew about their uncle's land. That huge parcel near the Paradise Valley, which Henry had always assumed was long gone but which their uncle still, mysteriously, owned—*half will be yours*, his uncle had said, as blandly as if he hadn't kept its existence a secret for forty years. *After I die, half will be yours, and half will be Wiloma's.*

Wiloma had looked right at the window. She had seen him, he knew she had. Then she had turned her head away and started moving her lips again. He had stepped back from the window, wounded but not entirely surprised. His family sprouted siblings in pairs, as if no other pattern were possible—his father and his uncle, he and Wiloma, his own two girls and Wiloma's daughter and son—but Wiloma had severed their connection and cut him off from the communion he deserved. Since Coreopsis Heights had failed, she'd been very cool to him.

In his dark apartment, among the broken lamps and the rank purple carpets, Henry thought of the land his uncle had kept secret from him and then of Wiloma, cut off from him once by a sheet of glass and then again by her refusal to see him. This pained him so much that he squeezed his eyes shut and sent himself to a beach on Hiva Oa.

A white bird landed in one of the palm trees swaying near

the rocks. Huge waves broke on the shore. The Marquesas were volcanic islands, Henry remembered reading; they rose straight up from the sea. The trees burst into red flowers and lianas trailed to the ground. A flat-faced woman rented Henry a house and loaned him a spotted horse, and as he galloped along the black sand he saw waterfalls thundering down the cliffs and in the distance, bearing down on the island, the ship that visited once each month. He blurred the horse's feet beneath him, blurring with them the fact that he didn't know how to ride.

The ship came, he imagined, to buy the dried coconut meat the islanders harvested and also to deliver mail. On the ship were two letters for him. *Come back,* his wife and daughters had written in one. *All is forgiven. The bank made a mistake— Coreopsis Heights is making more money than you can imagine.* Wiloma had scrawled the other letter on the back of a faded photograph of their grandfather, Da, who had been dead since 1961. *Why did you leave us?* she had written; nothing more.

But Henry didn't want to think about Da. He opened his eyes, went up to bed, closed his eyes again, went to sleep. He dreamed of the day he and Wiloma had first come to Da's farm in Coreopsis. In his dream his parents were still alive and the fields were covered with smooth snow and bore no resemblance to the sea of choppy mud he'd made from them. There were willows, leafless and yellow-branched, down by the water.

He woke feeling very tired. The coffee he bought at the corner was cold and the second bus was crowded. At the stop for St. Benedict's Nursing Home, he had to push his way through a group of young men before he could get off the bus, and then he saw that he was already late. His uncle Brendan, eighty years old, had already rolled his wheelchair down the sidewalk to his favorite perch, next to the stoplight at the intersection of Ashton and West. The brakes on the chair were set and a blanket was draped over his twisted legs despite the warm June sun. His uncle looked like a troll, Henry thought. He acted like a child. He understood so little about the world that he had not, apparently, even realized that the land he owned might have saved Henry from his disgrace.

"Fine day!" Brendan was calling to a woman in a blue Toyota. She was stopped at the light where, every morning, Brendan carried on shouted conversations with people trapped for the time it took for red to turn to green. He sat there even during the winter, bundled in blankets and gloves and a hat, but dependent, then, on strangers kind enough to reach over and roll down their windows.

"Fine day!" Brendan called again. His voice was eager and gay.

This woman's windows were open already, and she was pleasant enough. As Henry watched, Brendan flapped his left arm beside his head in a gesture midway between a salute and a tic. His head was rigid in the brace that supported his weakened neck, and his white hair, grown too long, drifted downily around his skull. Henry told himself that he would not act hurt, he would not complain. He would only, gently, try to lead the conversation back to his uncle's land.

"It *is* nice," the woman called. "Are you having a good time out there?"

"Lovely!" Brendan said.

Henry sighed and walked over to the only person in his family still speaking to him.

2

BRENDAN, WHO HAD A PHYSICAL THERAPY SESSION EACH SATurday morning at ten, had urged Henry on several occasions to come a little later. "Sleep in," he told his nephew. He would have preferred to savor the session by himself. "Relax. Come after lunch if you want."

But Henry showed up tired and bleary-eyed each week, as if he were doing penance. He got off the bus looking pained and put-upon, and then he stood and stared disapprovingly while Brendan chatted at the corner with the passersby. Men poked their hands through the sunroofs and waved; women turned down their radios to say that their peonies were blooming. Children bounced in their seats and squealed hello when their mothers said, "Say good-morning to the nice man," but Henry stood stiff and aloof, frowning until Brendan agreed to go inside.

He acts like I'm crazy, Brendan thought, as Henry wheeled him down the ramps and into the basement of St. Benedict's Home. He knew he looked odd, especially since his last stroke—the left side of his face no longer moved as freely as his right, and his left arm was apt to wander. Lying in bed those first few days, unable to speak while his thoughts hummed at twice normal speed, he'd watched everyone act as if he'd lost his mind and not just his words.

Did he visit me then? Brendan thought. While I was lying there frozen? No. His speech was clear now, completely re-covered, and his mind was as sharp as ever. His friends inside the Home and the people in the cars outside treated him as if he were fine. Only Henry continued to act as if he were senile. He seemed to be unable to tell the difference between Brendan's condition and that of the blank-eyed men who strolled the halls in their pajamas, their minds erased despite their strongly pumping hearts.

Behind him Henry hummed an unfamiliar tune. Brendan poked at his ears with a finger but he still couldn't make out the song. "What *is* that?" he said over his shoulder.

Henry gave a startled laugh and then turned the corner clumsily, bumping Brendan's footrest against the wall. "I don't know," he said. "They play the radio all day where I'm working now, the same songs over and over again, three or four times an hour—they get stuck in my head."

"Doesn't sound like much fun."

"It isn't," Henry agreed. He pushed open the door to the physical therapy room and wheeled Brendan inside, where Roxanne was waiting in the dim light thrown by the cones on the walls. Her hair shone smooth and golden, and she looked so young that Brendan was reminded of how he'd been in the Home almost as long as she'd been alive.

Roxanne unfolded a white sheet and held it up by the corners. She turned her head as Brendan wheeled himself behind it. "Would you like to take a little soak?" she asked Henry, as she did each time he appeared. "Keep your uncle company?"

Henry refused, as always. While Brendan undressed behind

the sheltering sheet, Henry drew a plastic chair to the edge of the whirlpool and sat there uneasily, fully dressed.

Brendan took off the brace that straightened his neck. He handed Roxanne his clothes and then he grasped the sides of the sheet and pulled it around him, hiding his body from her eyes. Roxanne tucked the canvas sling beneath him, dropped the arms of his chair, swung him over the tiled lip, and lowered him into the water.

The sheet came with him, draped over his withered hips and twisted legs, shielding his genitals. He and Roxanne had argued over that sheet at first—"I see naked men all the time," she'd said. "It's no big deal." Brendan had insisted that he keep the sheet in the water. She didn't see naked ex-monks, he'd told her, men on whom no woman had ever gazed. That had silenced her. He'd learned over the years that any mention of his vocation embarrassed people into doing whatever he asked.

The sheet also hid him from Henry, whose eyes skittered like minnows over the flesh that Brendan exposed. The swollen, gnarled, splayed shapes that were Brendan's hands and feet, the huge nodules on his elbows and knees, the scar tissue on his thin chest, the discolorations, the ropy veins, the wattles and wrinkles and creases and pleated folds and sores—he was unsightly, he knew. He'd shriveled up so much that his skin hung on him now like a suit made for two men, one of whom had already died.

Henry's eyes settled on a point an inch or two above Brendan's head. He seemed so disgusted by Brendan's body, so irritated by Brendan's awkward movements, that Brendan wondered why he bothered to visit at all. It was duty, Brendan supposed. Certainly that was more likely than love. But duty hadn't called Henry here during all the years when he was thriving—until he'd fallen into trouble, he'd seldom shown up except on holidays. Now he came every week, and each time he looked at that spot in the air.

"I'll be back in twenty minutes," Roxanne said.

She winked at Brendan, and Brendan let himself think of the long massage she'd give him when she returned. Her hands would be warm; she'd warm the mineral oil. She'd start at his neck and work down to his toes, covering every inch of him except for the small area wrapped in his sheet. Her hands were remarkably strong for such a small woman, and the pleasure they brought him was indescribable.

"Soak," Roxanne said. "Loosen up those joints." Flecks of grass clung to the hems of her pants, as if she'd walked through a newly cut lawn on her way to work. She slipped out of the dim room, her feet silent in spongy-soled shoes.

Brendan would have liked to slip his ears underwater and lose himself in the silence, but he knew Henry would be offended. He sighed and settled himself more comfortably on the ledge, sliding down until the water reached his shoulders. "How's work?" he asked.

"Horrible," Henry said. He launched into the litany of complaints that would, Brendan knew, fill his soaking time and possibly even part of his massage. Brendan closed his eyes and inched over until his spine was centered in front of a whirlpool jet. "And then," his nephew said, "he did, and then he said . . ." Henry moaned about the same things every week, but today his complaints seemed to have an extra, acid edge. He was miffed, Brendan saw, and he meant for Brendan to know it. Brendan smiled and said nothing and nodded occasionally. Henry's mood might prove helpful, he thought, if only he could figure out how to propose his plan.

Next door, in the library, Brendan could hear the people in the prayer group singing a hymn. "Praise the Lord," he heard, over the bubbling water and the drone of Henry's voice. "Praise the Lord, all ye beasts and fishes." There was no keeping that group away—they were based in Pittsford but descended once a month on the Home to hold a healing service. Half the Home's residents were in with them now, holding hands and praying for their afflictions to be healed.

One of the group's leaders had visited Brendan earlier, offering to exorcise the evil spirits plaguing him.

"We'll pray in tongues for you," the woman had said. "We'll do a soaking prayer. We'll soak your being in the love of Jesus until the evil spirits leave you and you're healed."

"You can leave my being be," Brendan had told her. He'd thought of how, after compline, the single lamp that lit the *Rule* for the reader had been extinguished, leaving the monks to chant the psalms in darkness and exorcise the terrors of the night. Compline: the completion of the day. The last of the day's canonical hours, when the sins of the day were reviewed. He'd given that up, he'd wanted to say to the woman. Why would he accept her feeble prayer?

The woman had bowed her head sorrowfully. "The heart is deceitful above all things, and desperately wicked," she'd said. "Who can know it?"

"Who indeed?" Brendan had said, and he'd wondered who could heal him now. He had tumors on his kidneys and in his lungs, others dotting his liver; in his colon, the mass had spread so far that what he swallowed came up as often as it went down. He believed that the seeds of those tumors had come, like the arthritis that crippled him, from the years he'd spent in northern China during the Second World War. Those freezing nights in the abbey's dormitory, which had swarmed with ticks; the even colder hours in the choir, listening to the Chinese novices wrap their tongues around the Te Deum; the months in the Japanese internment camp—those were the things that had made him sick, and if those were evil spirits, they were not the sort that could be chased away.

He closed his eyes and gave himself over to the swirling water. Then he opened them again, aware that Henry's flow of complaints had stopped.

"How are you feeling?" Henry asked. "Really, I mean."

"All right," Brendan said. "About as well as you'd expect."

And that was as much concern as he could get from Henry, who sank back into his own worries instantly. "This man I know," Henry said, "just like me except he built office parks instead of residential developments, he got arrested last week in Buffalo for robbing a bank. I saw it in the paper. The police said that this was his fourth one. There's so much office space standing empty now that he couldn't lease a single square foot, and he had a family and cars and a big house and a summer place and he couldn't make the payments on anything, so he started robbing banks. . . . You can't believe what it's like out there. You don't have any idea."

Henry's voice trailed off again, and as it did the voices next door rose in a sudden, excited babble that sounded to Brendan like "wa-ka-*wa*-ke, wy-a-*wee*-no, ko-*tay*-nu, ko-*ba*-lu, *way*-lo, wa-ka-*wa*-kee . . ." Of course it didn't make sense, it wasn't supposed to make sense. "Praise the Lord!" someone called clearly through the babble. "Praise his works, his ways, his days." In his beloved abbey in the Paradise Valley—not the one burned to the ground in China, not the austere one in Manitoba nor the inhospitable one in Rhode Island but his first abbey, his true abbey, which had lain beneath the Stillwater Reservoir for half a century now—he had praised the Lord seven times daily, his voice blending with sixty others in a cry that rose up from the choir like smoke.

Henry stared into the whirlpool. "They're going to send him to jail," he said. "That guy. I played *golf* with him. I met his wife." He shifted his eyes toward Brendan, as if checking to see what effect his story had had, and Brendan knew he was thinking about the land and what it might be worth.

The land was worth nothing, in Henry's terms; it had no price, it could not be turned into money. On a wooded ridge in Massachusetts, overlooking what had once been the Paradise Valley and was now the Stillwater Reservoir, lay the only remnant of their family's land that hadn't vanished underwater. Frank junior—Brendan's brother, Henry's father—had built a cabin there after the evacuation of the valley, and Henry and Wiloma had lived there until the accident that killed their parents. Brendan had held on to the piece that passed to him until Henry and Wiloma were grown. Then he'd held on to it longer, fearing Henry's greed and Wiloma's impulsiveness.

The mess they'd made of Coreopsis had proved his decision was right, but now the doctors had told him that he was running out of time. And so last week, first during Henry's Saturday visit and then again, on Sunday, when Wiloma had come, he had finally revealed what he meant to leave them. They had stared at him as if he were mad.

"That was Da's land," Henry had said. "Da sold it after the accident, to help pay for raising me and Wiloma."

"Half of it," Brendan had explained. "He sold *half*. He made a will before you were born and left half to your father and half to me. After your parents were killed, he sold the part where the cabin was. But I still own the other two hundred acres."

Wiloma had been equally puzzled. "In the valley?" she'd said. "How can you own land in the valley? There *is* no valley, it's all gone. I thought the place where you grew up was underwater now."

"It's *near* the valley," Brendan had told her, feeling tired and exasperated. Sometimes Wiloma was as dense as a tree. "Near the valley, adjoining the valley, the land your grandfather owned on the ridge—you lived there. Don't you remember it?"

She'd stared at him blankly. "I was eight," she'd said. "When Mom and Dad were killed. You expect me to remember everything?"

"Something—don't you remember anything?"

"I remember the cabin, sort of. I remember Mom listening to the radio and acting stranger and stranger. I remember the day Dad came home from the war." She had paused and looked at the wall. "I remember the night they were killed. You were gone."

She had paused again, and the pause had opened into the hole that swallowed him whenever he let himself think of his brother's death. No one had been able to tell him how that accident happened, because no one had been around; there had been no other cars on the stretch of empty road and no survivors. In place of Wiloma, sitting across from him, the accident he'd envisioned so many times had flashed before his eyes again.

The inside of the old gray Plymouth is steamy and the windshield keeps fogging up. Frank junior has both hands on the wheel and drives silently while Margaret chatters about the friends they've just seen at the VFW dance. The road is slippery and rain pounds on the roof of the car. Margaret's dress is white. They are almost home; they are on the last curve of Boughten Hill before it dips into the valley and rises again to the ridge. Margaret says something to Frank junior, and just as he begins to answer, a deer flashes across the road. He taps the brakes once and then again. The deer bounds safely into the woods. But the brakes lock, the car skids, Margaret shrieks and he wrenches the wheel. There is no guardrail on this stretch of road and the rain has turned the shoulder to mud. The car lurches, tips, falls heavily onto its side and then rolls, over and over and over, to the base of the ravine.

"Uncle Brendan?" Wiloma had said, and the vision had vanished and he'd seen her face again. He'd been in China, in a hospital bed, when that accident had happened: waiting to be shipped home and unaware that he had no home. He hadn't seen his brother for twelve years. He'd never met his brother's wife.

"It's our family's land," he'd told Wiloma, who stared at him as if she blamed him for his long-ago absence. "It'll be yours when I go—yours and Henry's."

She'd smiled and changed the subject; she was so focused on her own strange plans that his news hardly seemed to sink in. But Henry—Henry's eyes had flared and his whole face had glowed. "Two hundred acres?" he'd said. The number had rolled on his tongue like a truffle and was hiding behind his lashes now. He would bulldoze each acre, Brendan feared, unless he could see a reason not to. "Jesus," he'd said.

In the library, Brendan heard someone cry, "Jesus, protect us and save us." Henry looked over Brendan's shoulder and said, "What's going on in there?"

"Some kind of healing service."

"Who are they healing?"

"Me." Brendan smiled sourly. "They asked me to come this morning, so they could cast out my evil spirits and make me well. When I said I was busy, they said they were going to pray for me anyhow."

"Couldn't hurt," Henry said. Which reminded Brendan of Wiloma, whose plans could hurt him, and were about to hurt him, unless he could convince Henry to help him first.

3

SEVERAL WEEKS AGO, WHEN BRENDAN HAD TOLD WILOMA what the idiot doctors meant to do, a vision had sailed into Wiloma's head. Brendan had told her, over and over for years, that he was happy at St. Benedict's. He had friends there, he'd said. He liked the routine. She'd believed him because it was convenient to believe him. But the vision of him hooked up to tubes and pierced by needles had finally convinced her that it was time to bring him home.

"The spare bedroom's empty," she'd told him. "There's plenty of room, it's what I want to do. And now that the doctors are acting so irresponsibly, we can't afford to wait."

"It's just a little chemo," Brendan had said. "They just want to try."

"A little chemo," she'd replied. "A little *poison*. They want to poison you, they think you're dying."

"We're all dying," Brendan had said, and then he'd rolled his eyes at her behind his glasses. She had known what he was thinking—the same thing her children thought, the same thing her unconverted neighbors thought. That she'd been brainwashed by the Church of the New Reason; that she was fanatical, out of control. When it should have been obvious to anyone what the Church had given her.

On this Saturday morning, Wiloma fluffed a pillow in her spare room, straightened the bedclothes, and adjusted the bedside lamp. Brendan could roll his eyes all he liked, but no one could stop her from signing him out and bringing him home. Most likely no one would even try. The staff at St. Benedict's had given up on him and avoided his room as if he were already dead. And so of course he was dying, they were drawing off his life force. The drugs they wanted to give him would quench the last of his Spirit.

She imagined Brendan's Spirit glowing with renewed energy from the new sheets and blankets, the egg-crate mattress she'd bought, the furniture she'd moved, and she thought proudly of all she'd done in the past three weeks. She'd called St. Benedict's and set the paperwork in motion. The social worker there had suggested she hire a daily nurse, but she'd done something better: she'd engaged Christine Emerson, the Church's local spiritual neuro-nutritionist. Christine had told her what else she needed to do. She'd filled the small bookcase with Church literature, as Christine had directed; she'd placed her well-thumbed copy of the Manual within easy reach of Brendan's bed. On the wall she'd hung the framed linen square she'd cross-stitched herself. *Nothing exists external to our minds,* read the motto on the square. *Things are thoughts. The world is made up of our ideas.*

When she'd completed her detoxification, almost two years ago, that motto had been the raft on which she'd floated to safety. The detox team had pulled her bad memories from her one by one, her bad attitudes, her dichotomous taxonomies, her negative and judgmental faculties and her desires for sickness and pain. They'd left behind that motto and the other sayings in the Manual, and they'd helped her understand that her husband's desertion of her for Sarah, his book-keeper, had been for the best.

The team had enabled her to see how Waldo had impeded her spiritual growth and kept their children from the Light. He had *had* to leave her, she'd learned, so that she could flower into the Spirit. And he had *had* to marry Sarah, and Sarah had *had* to become pregnant with Courteney. Just as she herself had *had*, shortly after Courteney's birth, to suffer a pain so sharp and startling that she would slip over the edge at the sight of her children's misbehaviors and crash into a wall of darkness. The Church was big on things that *had* to happen; you had to drown, she learned, before you could be saved.

All of that had been necessary, she'd learned, all that wallowing in the fog of pain her own mind had created. It had been necessary that she go away for a while, necessary that Waldo take Wendy and Win and refuse to return them to her until she had, as he called it, "straightened out." And if her new serenity concealed things of which Waldo might not approve, that was none of Waldo's business now.

She'd had her children back for eighteen months and they were doing fine. Several weeks ago, at Wendy's high-school graduation, she'd been able to sit calmly with Waldo and Sarah and Courteney. Win, looking handsome in a new navy suit, had sat beside her and held her hand while Wendy went up to receive her diploma. Wendy had walked smoothly up the stairs and smoothly down. And afterward, when they stood in a row outside the auditorium and Wendy had kissed them one by one, Wiloma had been able to smile and bless the Spirit in Courteney when Wendy had lifted her into the air.

There is no pain, she'd told herself then. *There is no guilt. There is no blame. Life is what you believe it is.*

She felt happy now, perfectly clear. And all she wanted to do was share that clearness with Brendan, so that, if this was his time to die, he went smoothly into the Light. Not pickled with drugs; not hazy-headed and pricked by needles; not bound by the tired religion that had crippled his life and almost captured her. A clear transit: the best she could offer him, less than she owed.

She checked her watch—ten-thirty already, and Waldo had promised to bring the kids back right after breakfast. She felt a prickle of fear, which she quickly suppressed. Sometimes, when she grew lazy and lax, she couldn't push away the thought that Waldo might steal the kids back for good. Behind that came the thought that he had stolen them once; and behind that the sense that they had sealed off parts of themselves during her absence, and that Waldo had had as much to do with their withdrawal as with their reformed behavior.

But she knew these thoughts were only true if she believed in them, and she pushed them down and buried them like stones. She reminded herself that Waldo was always late; that his tardiness was a part of him and that he wasn't in control of his deeper self. As soon as she thought this and calmed herself, she heard the kitchen door open and her children clatter in.

"Mom," Win called from downstairs. "Mom? Did you wash my soccer stuff? I have a game today, I have to get going. . . ."

"Up here," she called, but it was Wendy who came up the stairs and into the spare room. She was wearing nice clothes, expensive clothes that Sarah had no doubt picked out and paid for: high-waisted sage-green pants, a mustard shirt with large pearly buttons, a broad belt, and pretty sandals. Wiloma looked down at her own faded skirt and old blue blouse, and she noticed for the first time that her skirt had a large stain below the right pocket. Part of the hem seemed to be coming down and her ankles looked callused and dry. She knew she dressed badly. She had often, since Wendy had started dressing so well, meant to clean herself up. But she had so little time to pay attention to her clothes, and even when she tried it seemed as if nothing she owned really went with anything else. She suppressed a sigh, and with it the thought that she missed Wendy's old clothes, the drooping skirts and men's jackets worn over tired T-shirts, the leggings and army boots and old hats studded with pins.

She watched Wendy take in the soft armchair, the bright pillows, and the throw rug she'd transported from the living room. "It looks good in here," Wendy said. "Grunkie's going to like it."

The nickname came from a time when Wendy, at the age of three or four, had been struggling to fit her mouth around "Great-uncle Brendan" and had come up with those two childish syllables instead. When she said them now, she sounded eight rather than eighteen, but there was nothing childish in the way her smile disappeared when she saw the cross-stitched motto on the wall. "Do you want that in here?" she said. "Really?"

Wiloma nodded. "Really," she said.

The scorn in Wendy's voice annoyed her—surely anyone could see how the Church might heal Brendan, after all it had done for her. It was different, entirely different, from the other disciplines she'd sampled between Waldo's departure and Courteney's birth. She'd experimented with Zen, hours of sitting on a round black cushion and listening to the great drum and the ping of ceramic bells. In a Gurdjieff group she'd learned some of the movements; in the latihans of Subud, she had growled and cried and sung. Then one day she'd driven past a convent, which was hidden behind a wall and a row of trees, and she'd remembered how, when she was just a girl, she'd asked Brendan what he'd felt like when he'd first entered his abbey. *Peaceful,* he'd said. *Clean. Whole. Happy.* Feelings that, in those first few months after Waldo's departure, she couldn't imagine ever having again. She'd never been inside a Catholic church. Her parents had died before they'd settled the issue of which faith, Presbyterian or Catholic, would claim their children, and her grandparents had given up on church completely. But she remembered the light in Brendan's face when he talked about his youth, and she wrote the Sisters and asked if she could visit them.

The Sisters mailed her a blue pamphlet with a text hand-printed on coarse paper. Inside were prayers and a daily schedule and a number of photographs: women in calf-length white dresses and black tunics and short white veils, women in work clothes and boots and glasses and scarves that hid their hair. Women milking cows, fixing tractors, cutting melons into quarters; praying, eating, baking, doing useful work. The pictures were hugely appealing and the note clipped inside the brochure said that Wiloma was welcome anytime for a weekend retreat.

She hadn't gone; she'd shown the brochure and the note to Brendan, sure that he'd approve, and he'd suggested, gently, that perhaps she work up to a retreat in steps. Find a church you like, he'd said. A priest you trust. Join a prayer group and see about some religious training. He had asked her what she knew about the Catholic Church these days and she'd had to admit she knew almost nothing. "It's a big commitment," he'd said. "Starting from scratch at your age."

She had gone twice to St. Mary's, a mile from her house, but the services had made no more of a dent in her distress than had her other experiments. The convent was worlds away, she'd seen. Even a visit was years in the distance. And then her Manual had arrived in the mail, in response to a coupon she'd forgotten she'd filled out, and its quiet voice had begun to speak to her.

Spirit is real; matter is unreal. Truth is real; error is unreal. Light is real; darkness is unreal. The voice was simple, the voice was clear. It spoke the words she'd been yearning for. She had fallen into the Church's warm embrace and had never turned back—not when Brendan had expressed his dismay, not when her own family mocked her.

Now she watched her daughter frown and change the subject. "Soft," Wendy said, as she sat down on the edge of the bed and tested the egg-crate mattress. "Sort of strange."

"How was your visit?" Wiloma asked.

"Also strange," Wendy said. Stranger than usual. Sarah made cassoulet—she said it had taken her two days and she was upset when Win didn't like it. But it tasted a lot like baked beans to us. Win gave Courteney some of his, and Courteney threw it in the fireplace. Dad and Sarah got into an argument over some bills. Then after supper Dad took us into that den of his and started showing us maps of this place in Massachusetts. Some of them were topographic maps, those green ones with the lines. Then he had these old ones, not really old but copies of old ones, that he said he'd ordered from the Geological Survey people in Washington. He kept us in there looking at them for an hour."

Wiloma looked at her sharply. "What was that all about?"

"Grunkie. I think. Dad showed us, on the old maps, this place where Grunkie used to live. And then he showed us the new ones, and how that place had been covered by a reservoir. He said there was a big hill or something at the edge of it that Grunkie still owns, and that you and Uncle Henry had been born there."

Wiloma stared at the armchair and tried to sort out what Waldo might be up to. She had mentioned the land to him casually, when he'd stopped by to drop off some papers just after her visit to her uncle. It had seemed like an interesting fact, a drop of oil to smooth their awkward conversation, but she'd known as soon as she mentioned it that she should have kept quiet. "Don't you dare go giving that to the Church," he'd said, as if he had any right to tell her what to do. "Don't do anything with it until I have a chance to get it appraised."

She had shrugged off his comments, thinking them just another example of his reflexive attempts to meddle in her financial affairs. But she couldn't imagine why he'd gathered those maps, or why he'd shown them to the children.

"It was interesting," Wendy said. "How come you never told us about that? This huge area, all these villages being drowned—isn't that amazing? I mean it's awful, in a way, but still . . ."

"I never saw those places," Wiloma said. Her stomach was beginning to ache. "The reservoir was filled before I was born."

"Dad says Grunkie lived there, and that your grandparents had a farm there before they had the place in Coreopsis. It's so amazing—do you think Grunkie remembers it?"

"Of course he does," Wiloma said. "He just doesn't like to talk about it." She didn't either; she had heard the story so often during her childhood that she couldn't stand to repeat it.

"They *stole* it from us," Da used to say. He'd held her and Henry captive for hours at the table in Coreopsis, telling and retelling his tales of the Paradise Valley as if he could bring his dead son back with his words or recover his lost life. She'd known, even then, that those tales were what kept him from functioning as any kind of surrogate father. "Those men in suits, those Boston men—it was Curley and his gang, all that Boston gang, they stole the ground out from under our feet."

On and on he'd gone, about the engineers and the politicians and the cover-ups and the lies; about the woods chopped down and the buildings razed and the bodies exhumed from the cemeteries. And then about what had happened to the twenty-five hundred people who'd been displaced at the height of the Depression—how some, such as Wiloma's father, had migrated to the nearby towns on the boundary of the watershed, while others, such as he and his wife, had left Massachusetts altogether and wandered through western New York until they found someplace where they felt safe.

"Someplace *cheap* enough," Da had said. "Not just safe enough, *cheap* enough—those bastards hardly gave us anything. Farms that had been in our families for generations, and what did they give us? Jack shit." Wiloma had heard those tales so many times that she almost knew them by heart, but she never thought about them anymore. The detox team had pulled them out by the roots, disarmed them so they'd never haunt her again. When her uncle had mentioned the land, she'd been able to let the pictures he'd called up roll right past her.

It'll be yours when I go, he'd said. *Yours and Henry's*. She'd smiled at him and ignored his words and focused her healing energies on his chest. And now Waldo had crept up behind her with this, using Wendy to prick her unprotected flank. He knew the kids came home and told her what went on at his house; sometimes he said things to them that he was afraid to say to her face, knowing the message would reach her. But she wasn't sure what he thought he'd gain by prying at this part of her past.

"I've got to go to work at noon," Wendy said. "Want me to do anything before I go?"

"Maybe clean up your room? I want the house to look nice for Grunkie tomorrow."

Wendy nodded and left. Below her, Wiloma heard Win humming. All day long his head bobbed to the signals of the Walkman his father had given him. He mowed the lawn with it clipped to the back of his pants and fell asleep at night with the tiny black pads still shooting messages into his brain. He was sixteen, he was going through a phase. He hummed with no sense that his humming was tuneless. Sometimes Wiloma dreamed of slipping one of her *Life in the Spirit* seminar tapes into his machine when he was asleep.

She gathered herself together and visualized her list for the day. Vacuum the living room, she thought. Wash the windows. Buy groceries. Go to the dentist—she knew she shouldn't, but a filling had fallen out and she couldn't pray it back into place. Last night, while she'd been lecturing, her whole left jaw had ached. She had looked into the window behind her group and seen her face, twisted with pain, reflected back to her. Her mirrored image had so resembled her brother's unhappy face that she'd thought for a minute that he was there. *Don't think about Henry,* she ordered herself. *Don't think about Waldo. Don't think about Uncle Brendan's land.*

She pictured each of these thoughts as a virus, crystalline and threatening, and then she surrounded each virus with the clouds of red and green particles that were her mental antibodies. She saw each thought sink into darkness, rendered harmless by the healing powers of her mind.

4

FOR TWO WEEKS, WENDY AND WIN HAD BEEN HALFHEARTEDLY trying to get the yard back into some sort of shape for Grunkie, whose new room overlooked the entire unkempt length. Win had mowed the grass three times; she'd weeded the flowerbeds and trimmed the shrubs. Both of them had worked to move the matted drifts of old leaves toward the fence at the rear of the lot, and neither of them had said much about how furious they were. Another person to take care of, another person to whom they'd have to lie. The heap of leaves was already enormous.

All that smiling, Wendy thought now, as she left her mother and bypassed her messy room and fled to the waiting pile of leaves. The pallid compliments she'd offered on Grunkie's new room, the way she'd left the Church motto untouched when what she really wanted was to tear the linen in half and then scream at her mother, *Don't bring him here! Don't we have enough trouble without him? Can't you leave him alone?*—her lies had made her face feel as stiff and deceitful as a Chinese mask.

She seized the pitchfork with relief and attacked the compacted leaves on the ground. As she lofted them to the top of the pile, she heard Harmon Bayer working on the other side of the fence. Snip, she heard. Harmon was edging the grass along his neat beds of ivy. Snip, snip, snip, and then a sneeze, a snuffle, and a wheeze. Harmon had allergies and his breathing was almost as loud as the sound of his shears. She wished him swollen eyes and a streaming nose. Harmon had built the ugly six-foot barrier between their yards, where once there had been only a knee-high hedge as porous as a sieve. When the Silverstons had lived in Harmon's house, Wendy and Win and the Silverston children had flowed through the hedge like water.

Wendy paused and dropped her lower jaw and stretched her mouth until her face began to relax. Then she attacked the leaves again and tossed wads of them over her shoulder. She was rewarded with the pleasure of hearing the snips subside and the wheezes increase on the other side of the fence. Harmon, she knew, was acutely aware of her but would never acknowledge her presence. She whacked leaves against the boards and remembered how Harmon had bought the Silverstons' house during her freshman year in high school, not long after her father had left them to marry Sarah and her mother had started flirting with bizarre religions.

The yard had been beautiful up until then—a long row of roses trained on a trellis, smooth beds of myrtle around the silver maple, shrubs and ferns and rhododendrons and clumps of iris and daylilies. The lawn had stretched like a piece of velour from the flowerbeds back to the low hedge. Then her father had taken her and Win for a stroll by the lake and sliced their lives in two.

They'd been walking. The wind had been blowing. The waves had rolled gently on brown sand scattered with roots and weeds. They'd been chatting about everyday things and then her father had said, "I have to tell you something important," and had severed the sinew and bone of their lives so cleanly that she'd felt no pain at first. He'd gone on talking, heaping one sentence on another until his message was clear, but only weeks later, after he'd packed and moved and introduced them to Sarah, had she understood that the first words of his first sentence held the shape of the rest of her life.

She bent down to pick the twigs and leaves from the myrtle on her side of the fence, thinking of that horrible time when her father had first left and her mother had drifted so far away. She and Win had turned wild almost overnight, drinking and smoking and slinking around as if they'd been possessed. They'd become expert at cheating and lying and hiding, and for a while they'd occupied themselves by setting fires. That stack of old wood by the lake, Wendy thought, remembering the pale, unstoppable flames. And then she remembered the clothes she and Win had stolen, and the notebooks and records and cigarettes, and the way everything they did had seemed to flow past their mother like smoke. They'd found her sitting cross-legged on her narrow bed one day, poring over a pamphlet that had come to her in the mail.

"What is this?" Wendy remembered asking. She could still hear the words that signaled her mother's seduction by the Church of the New Reason.

"It's a way to make sense of things," her mother had said. "Nothing exists external to our Spirits. Things are thoughts. The world is made up of our ideas. So if we change our ideas, we change the world—I'm working on changing my ideas. I'm reprogramming myself."

"But what's the point?" Win had asked.

"The *point*," their mother had said, "is that there has to be something to life besides missing your father and raising you. I hate the way I feel. Our family's falling apart. And there's nothing I can do about any of it."

Wendy and Win had redoubled their efforts to be bad, as if this might somehow bring their mother back to earth. But the extent of her self-deception was amazing. They told her the teachers who sent home angry notes were insane, that the clothes that appeared in the absence of money were gifts, that it had been Wendy's girlfriend's mother who had pierced Wendy's ears four times.

When they lied about their crimes, their mother closed her eyes and said, "Fine. Whatever you say." Then she retreated to her dark room, which was empty by then except for her bed and her new books. She vanished from their lives, and their father, preoccupied with his newly pregnant new wife, seemed to vanish as well. When their mother took off on three-day retreats with her fellow believers, Wendy and Win skipped school and filled the house with stray classmates, falling deeper and deeper into trouble that neither of them enjoyed.

A few weeks after Courteney's birth, their mother had come home early one day and found the garbage cans smoking with pillows they'd accidentally set on fire, and the upstairs bathroom window smashed, and a twelve-year-old friend of Win's throwing up on the living room rug. She had gazed at the overflowing ashtrays, the soiled walls, the broken records, and half-filled cups, and then she'd smiled strangely and said, "This doesn't exist."

She had walked out the door; Wendy and Win had found her, hours later, sitting against a tree in the woods at the end of their street. They'd had to help her back to the house. They'd had to watch helplessly when the two men from the Church arrived for the evening's planning session and found Wiloma on the floor repeating, *I have nothing. Nothing is mine.* The men had made phone calls while Win and Wendy watched. They'd arranged for Wiloma to visit the Church's Healing Center in Boston for a few months, and they'd offered to board Wendy and Win in the home of a local Church family while she was gone. Both men had eyebrows so pale and fine as to be almost invisible.

Wendy had called her father then, not knowing where else to turn, and he'd taken them into the horrid house he'd built for Sarah. He'd been furious with Wiloma at first, blaming her for her weakness; then, as he began to discover all that Wendy and Win had done, furious with them. He missed nothing. He smelled smoke on their hands, beer on their breath, lies on their tongues. He told them that even if their mother got better, they couldn't live with her again unless they straightened out. They had looked at each other and gone underground as smoothly as snakes.

He was firm, not cruel, but they couldn't bear living with him. All that attention, Wendy remembered, as the mound of leaves rose up to her waist. All those eyes. Sarah had monitored their meals and grades and friends, counting their clothes when she did the laundry and wanting to know where this blouse had come from, how Win had torn those pants. Waldo had named the baby Courteney, setting her off from the matched set of *W* names he'd found so charming the first time around. Courteney reminded Win and Wendy daily that they had no part in their father's new life.

They'd dreamed of escape almost constantly during the four months their mother was gone; they'd dreamed, too, that she was in danger and needed their help. They did whatever their father and Sarah asked, hoping to convince them that they'd changed. Win signed up for soccer league and let the shaved sides of his head grow out. Wendy wore the prissy clothes that Sarah bought her. They shed their dangerous friends and brought up their grades and prayed that their father would accept their offerings and fail to discern what churned inside them. When their mother returned from Boston, smooth-faced and clear-eyed and seemingly sane, they sat down with their father and told him they wanted to go home.

"I want you to be happy," he said. "I want you to live where you choose." He made a show of being reluctant to let them go, and of acting hurt over their decision, but in the end he'd given in without much fuss. Wendy recalled how she and Win had both felt, secretly, that he'd let them go so easily because he wanted to be alone with his new family.

"Remember," he said when they left. "Any trouble and you're coming back here."

And because of that threat, and because they felt so guilty over their role in their mother's collapse, they'd kept up their good behavior even after they moved back. Which meant, thought Wendy now, pretending to accept the Church and pretending not to be embarrassed by her mother's friends and by what her mother had become.

Harmon Bayer, snipping away on the other side of the fence, didn't have to pretend about anything; Wendy almost envied his easy, self-righteous rudeness. He had built a small deck off his back door the summer after he moved in and then found that he objected to the view from his newly raised seat. He objected to the ragged lawn behind Wendy's house, which was full of weeds and seldom mowed. He objected to the trellis, which had shattered during a storm and never been repaired. He objected to the unraked leaves and the rusting lawn furniture, but most of all he objected to the people from the Church of the New Reason, who sometimes gathered at the house on weekend afternoons.

Thin men in oversize shirts, overweight women in droopy skirts, all of them sitting cross-legged in the long grass and sipping herbal tea while they took turns reading passages from their Manual—it was shabby, Wendy thought. It was infuriating. Of course Harmon had objected. She objected herself, she hated it, but she never dared say a word to her mother. That was the price of peace, and she and Win paid it so their mother wouldn't crack again and so they wouldn't have to return to their father. But on the day the fence started going up, she had wanted to slip through what was left of the hedge and tell Harmon she understood how he wanted to wall them off.

She wondered, now, if she'd made a mistake not saying anything to her mother. The lives she and Win had lived these last eighteen months had been as false as the lives they'd lived at their father's, and the strain of trying to act like angels had told on both of them. They backslid, now and again; Wendy knew that Win had started drinking beer with his friends, and she'd stolen a few things she hadn't meant to, when her hands had reached out as if they'd had minds of their own. So far, they'd successfully hidden these acts from their mother. Win did well in school now and appeared in photos in the local paper with his legs kicked high as he shot a soccer ball toward the goal. No one would guess that he'd once started small fires all over town. And she'd gotten into college and had a decent summer job, and if she could just manage not to be trapped by this thing with Grunkie, she'd be gone in three months.

All was quiet on Harmon's side of the fence. Wendy scrambled up the heap of leaves and peered over the boards. Harmon was gone, at least for a while; the grass he'd been clipping was so neat it looked like AstroTurf. She dropped back down and stretched full length in the pile of leaves, letting herself sink into them until she was almost buried. Tomorrow, when Grunkie arrived, everything was bound to change. A dying man in their spare room, with her mother bent on converting him—it made her queasy just to think of it. She liked her great-uncle and longed to spare him from her mother's interference, but that was only part of the reason she dreaded his arrival. Buried below that was the fear that he might take months or years to die and that her mother wouldn't be able to manage him alone. And below that was panic at the prospect of being trapped here, balancing her mother's fragile equilibrium and her great-uncle's desire for peace while her own life remained perpetually on hold.

5

ROXANNE'S HANDS SLIPPED GENTLY OVER THE BONES OF BRENdan's left wrist, moved with long strokes up his forearm to his elbow, cradled the distorted joint, and then sailed along his upper arm and tapped and squeezed the shoulder blade under the fragile skin. When she paused at the back of Brendan's neck, aligning her thumbs on his spine while her fingers embraced his weakened neck, Henry feared he might faint.

Her hands were glossy with oil. Her nails were short and rounded. Through her white pants and her short white smock, Henry could see the outlines of her underwear. When she pushed the heels of her hands against Brendan's shoulder, the flesh rose and gathered in bloodless peaks. Henry narrowed his eyes and shifted on his seat. As Roxanne moved from Brendan's neck to his right wrist and then wrapped his arm in her hands, Henry imagined his own arm encircled and caressed.

He felt the thumbs moving up the skin of his forearm, the fingers approaching the sensitive armpit, the first touch on his rib cage. He felt her breath on the back of his head. He felt the tips of her nails against his earlobe, their quick run down his neck, the pressure of the mound at the base of her thumb against his spine. And then, most delightfully (he had lost sight of Brendan completely, no longer saw his ruined flesh, no longer remembered that Brendan was in the room or that he, Henry, was not lying beneath Roxanne but sitting with crossed legs on a hard plastic chair), he felt Roxanne's legs on him, her whole length pressed against his back. He imagined the feel of her breasts. He imagined how she might take her hand and grasp him, gently. . . .

"How's that feel?" she asked, and Henry opened his eyes and drew a breath he knew she heard. She was talking to Brendan, not to him. She was working gently over Brendan's painful kidneys, lifting up the heels of her hand and using only her fingertips.

Brendan mumbled, "It feels okay," but he kept his eyes tightly closed and Henry wondered what he was thinking. On Hiva Oa, Henry imagined, Roxanne's slender figure would be incandescent in bands of pale green and her feet would sink in the sand until her toes were buried. He could spin scenes around her golden hair and pale hands, the way that, when he'd been at his peak, he could envision neighborhoods rising from the featureless countryside. She was lovely, and he couldn't keep his mind off her, and he couldn't talk to his uncle while she was around.

Roxanne began telling Brendan about her old job. She used to work at the baths in Saratoga Springs, she said. In the summer, half her clients had been Hasidic women from Brooklyn, who came to take the waters. They had arthritis, she told Brendan, that would make his seem like a joke; the lack of food in the Polish and German camps had done obscene things to their joints. They came every day, sometimes twice a day, and lay in the hot, effervescent water groaning with relief. Later, when she rubbed their twisted bones, they told her stories. She had heard things, she said, that she couldn't have imagined. She had heard things she'd never forget.

Brendan nodded thoughtfully at Roxanne's tale and told her—not for the first time, Henry knew—about his stay in the Japanese internment camp in China. Henry closed his ears; he'd heard that story before. He studied Roxanne's fingers, which continued to work while Brendan spoke. Roxanne moved her hands down to Brendan's legs and Henry's thighs tingled. He tried to think of other things—of his upcoming court date, of the money he owed his wife, Kitty, and could not possibly pay; of the fact that Kitty would have to leave their house very soon. Roxanne raised Brendan gently until he was sitting up on the white-draped table. Then, after averting her eyes while Brendan struggled into his pants, she transferred him to his wheelchair. She looked at Henry directly for the first time that morning.

"Would you help him finish dressing?" she said. "Would that be okay? I'm running late this morning."

Henry nodded, unable to say a word. She had strong, shapely arms and legs, and when she turned the lilt and tilt of her walk reminded him of his mother. When she'd heard that his father was returning from the war, she had shed her hunched posture and unclenched her hands and danced with Henry and Wiloma in the kitchen of their cabin. She had balanced Wiloma, who couldn't have been more than four, on her feet, so that Wiloma's toes rested on her own insteps and Wiloma's hands were clasped about her knees, and then she had danced as lightly as if she were not lifting Wiloma's weight with every step. On the night of the accident, when the gray Plymouth had sailed off the curve of Boughten Hill and into the ravine below, she had been wearing a dress as white as Roxanne's smock. White shoes, coral earrings, a coral belt and purse. There had been a frill around her neckline, Henry remembered—some sort of ruffle or flounce that fluttered when she moved. The coffin had been closed at the funeral and he'd never seen that dress again.

Henry knelt and eased his uncle's socks onto his twisted feet. "I can do that," Brendan said, and his voice was so crisp that Henry winced.

"I know," Henry said. "I was trying to help." All morning he'd failed to work the conversation around to the land, and now he realized that there was no point to this anyway. He had no money, no credit, no way to develop it. His uncle would hold on to the land as long as he lived, and Henry would go on visiting him each week. Since his own accident, when he'd felt his car lift off the ground so that he had, before the tree greeted him, flown the way his parents had, he'd felt a powerful need to cling to this last connection to them.

Brendan's left foot sat in his hand like a broken basket. The big toe, huge and distorted, splayed almost perpendicularly across the others, which rose up, curled back on themselves, and formed a knot. The arch humped up sharply, the heel spread swollen and callused; a lump larger than an ankle marred the back. Henry eased on the other sock and then the terry-cloth slippers. He tried not to watch Brendan's hands, as useless as paws, struggling with his shirt. The shirt closed with Velcro squares, which Brendan thumped into place.

"You should try a massage," Brendan said. "Really. It feels pretty good."

His left hand flailed at his neck brace, and Henry bent over and fastened it properly. "Maybe next time," Henry said. The weekend stretched before him, bleak and unpromising. He had forty dollars to carry him through to next Friday and nothing in his checking account. The bank had snipped his credit cards to bits.

He stood behind the chair, released the brakes, and began wheeling Brendan out of the room and along the halls. Near the recreation center Brendan said, "There may not be a next time."

"What?" Henry said. "Why not?"

"Because Wiloma's planning to take me home with her.

Didn't she tell you? She's going to set me up in her spare room and bombard me with positive thoughts until I'm cured."

"She didn't tell me," Henry said, thinking of the way Wiloma had averted her face last night on the far side of the storefront window. "She didn't even ask me what I thought. But it's not like she ever tells me anything."

They passed a man in another wheelchair, sitting perfectly still with his chin mashed against his collarbone and his hands drawn up over his heart. The hall smelled faintly of urine and disinfectant. "Would you rather stay here?" Henry asked. "Would you rather have the chemo?"

"Of course not. But that doesn't mean I want Wiloma's heathen healers all over me. They're not even Christians, never mind not being Catholic—as far as I can tell, they think they're all part of some amorphous spirit. Like the cells in a big sponge, or something. I can't believe she believes in that."

Near the solarium, along the hall that led to Brendan's room, Henry stopped at the niche in front of the picture window. "So what *do* you want?" he asked.

Below them the park stretched rolling and green, and a wedding party decked out in shades of lavender posed in front of some shrubs. A very large woman, perhaps the mother of the bride, shouted something Henry couldn't hear at the driver of the limousine. Brendan's left arm drifted up from his chair and hung in the air for a minute.

"What *I* want?" he said. "What do *I* want?" His hand drifted back down to his lap, and then he said, "I want to go to Massachusetts. I want you to drive us there, so I can show you the land I'm leaving you and Wiloma. I want to see the reservoir. I want to see where your parents lived."

For a second, Henry saw the cabin in which he'd spent his first nine years. He saw the rough pine paneling and the wood-burning stove; he saw his mother bent over the kitchen table, snipping war reports from newspapers and magazines. He saw the map of the Pacific she kept on the wall and the pins dotting the islands where battles had raged, with and without his father: New Guinea, Makin, Eniwetok, Saipan. He heard his mother's voice telling him how he'd leapt in her womb during the 1938 hurricane, which had started on the same day Hitler invaded Czechoslovakia and so been ignored by almost everyone. *Calamitous days,* she'd told him. *I carried you through calamitous days.* His spirits soared with his uncle's request and then promptly crashed.

"How can I take you?" he asked. "You know I don't have a car."

Brendan stared out the window and flapped his arm tensely in the air. "We could get one. Those vans in the parking lot, the ones with the wheelchair lifts—we're allowed to borrow them."

"Come on," Henry said. "You're kidding."

"I'm serious," Brendan said. "I could go talk to the administrator, sign one out, get the keys—it's as easy as that. I could sign one out for the weekend, we wouldn't even have to tell anyone where we were going. . . ."

"Really?" Henry thought of a smooth road, a few days of freedom, the pleasure of knowing that his uncle trusted him, even if no one else in his family did. Then he remembered that he didn't have a license. The police had handcuffed him after the accident, once they'd pried him out of the car and decided he wasn't hurt. They'd hauled him to jail and made him appear in court in his dirty clothes, and then they'd taken his license away. "I'd do it," he said glumly. "I'd love to. But I can't. They suspended my license."

Brendan spun around so Henry could see his face. "Fine. Worry about a piece of paper. Maybe once I get to Wiloma's, I can talk Waldo into taking me. *He'd* be interested in seeing that land, I bet—I bet he can talk Wiloma into letting him do something with her half."

Henry's stomach knotted. "Waldo knows about the land?"

"I imagine," Brendan said coolly. "I imagine Wiloma told him. You know she can't keep anything to herself."

Henry could just imagine what Waldo would do. He'd pry that land away from Wiloma somehow; he'd always been able to manipulate her. And then he'd cover it with pretentious houses on three-acre lots, all of them looking exactly the same although they were supposed to be unique. Which was not at all what he had in mind himself; he had big ideas. A vacation complex complete with tennis courts and a health club and cross-country skiing trails, condominiums tucked in the trees, tax credits and depreciation allowances. The units would be small but elegant, energy efficient, cunningly designed. That was the difference, he thought, between a developer and a builder like Waldo: a developer had vision, a developer could *see*. And if he could see it, he could figure out how to finance it. If he could explain it to Brendan, he could get Brendan to go along.

"Forget about it," Brendan said. He spun his chair around again, so that Henry was looking at the back of his head. "I can make my own arrangements."

"No," Henry said. "I'll take you. What could happen? We'll drive slowly, no one will stop us. Are you sure you can get us a van?"

"Wait here. I'll be back with the keys."

Before Henry could stop him, before he could even catch his breath, Brendan rolled down the hall toward the elevator.

6

F ROM THE "LETTERS TO THE EDITOR" OF THE *PARADISE VALLEY*
Daily Transcript:

February 12, 1922
Dear Sirs:

*The report of the Metropolitan Water Commission is deeply
disturbing, recommending as it does "the construction of a
great reservoir in the Paradise River Valley, and of tunnels
sufficient to transport said water to the Metropolitan area."*
*At the town meetings of Pomeroy, Winsor, Stillwater, and
Nipmuck, funds have been approved to hire legal counsel to
represent our interests in Boston. These men, as well as our
elected representatives, have spoken strongly at the hearings
held both in Boston and here. But I note with some distress
that many of their comments have addressed practical details
of the plan. Selectman C. J. Wheeler presented a request that
any land required for the proposed reservoir be taken by pur-*

chase, rather than by eminent domain. Representative Hall-man argues that the land assessment procedures are poorly described in the proposed bill. X. J. Swanson, counsel repre-senting the businesses of Pomeroy, expressed his concerns that delay over a final decision has been detrimental to commerce in the valley. All excellent points—but are these well-meaning men, in their efforts to safeguard our economic interests, truly expressing our desires?

Is not our deepest desire that there should be no reservoir? Does it matter how our property is assessed, how we are paid for it, or when we are told that we must leave—when we do not want to leave? Has not the grinding pressure imposed on us by the Commission worn down our resolute opposition and caused us to think only how we might best profit from this situation, when it is the situation itself that we must resist?

We must keep in mind that this group of engineers and politicians from Boston have one ambition only: to invade our valley, to destroy our towns, to trample on our rights as citi-zens. Compromise with such blind aggression is untenable.

Frank B. Auberon, Sr.
Pomeroy

Part II

One
Old Man
Vanished

7

BRENDAN THOUGHT HE HEARD SIRENS. IN THE PARKING LOT, before they'd even left the grounds; at the spotlight where, sitting high in the van, he overlooked his patch of sidewalk; on West Street, as they finally rolled away from the Home. He expected police cars, motorcycles, announcements on the radio—because of course the Home had no policy of loaning out its vans, and he could not believe that Henry had believed him.

All week he'd been wondering how he might approach Henry. He'd planned a campaign of pity and guilt: *The end is near, my boy. Would you deny a dying old man his last, modest wish?* Something along the lines of that, which would twist Henry's ears with shame. But in his desire to see the valley once more, in his mad passion to gaze at the water beneath which his first abbey lay, he had forgotten that Henry no longer had a car. His heart had almost stopped when Henry had reminded him. Then he'd looked out the window and seen the vans and plucked his scheme from the air like an unripened quince. It was weak, there was nothing behind it. It depended on luck and on his last-minute appeal to Henry's greed and need to master Waldo.

He had not seen the administrator. He had not spoken to anyone. He had wheeled himself into the basement room where the janitors kept their tools and their coffeepot and the pegboard on which hung the keys to the vans, and then he had directed Fred Johannson, who sat drowsing in his chair, to the whirlpool in the other wing. It sounded funny, he'd said. Like it might be overflowing. Fred had lumbered off and Brendan had leaned up against the board and knocked down the keys marked "Medical Transport Van No. 1." A minute's work, except that the keys had fallen to the table and Brendan's hands had banged against them like hooves. He had thought of the way the dogs they'd kept at the abbey had scooped up bones, pressing the pads of their paws clumsily together. No fingers, no thumbs; he had scooped up the keys in a similar fashion and dropped them into his lap.

He had wheeled himself back to Henry as fast as his chair could carry him, and then he had tried to look calm and unworried as Henry dawdled over the closets and drawers and gathered together the scraps of clothing Brendan needed. "Not in the suitcase," he'd told Henry sharply. "Use that plastic bag." They'd slipped through the halls, out the door, and into the parking lot, and he'd prayed that anyone looking out the windows might think they were going for a walk, that the row of oaks shielding the vans would conceal them, that the van would start, that the lift would work, that no one would run shouting after them as they drove away.

He hadn't prayed so much in years. Consciously, guiltily, he had employed what his abbot used to call linear prayer. Prayer that moved the way things move in the world: point to point, step by step, effects following causes and building into a plan—his abbot had spoken of that as something to shed, to be replaced by the deep prayer that sank wordlessly into the mystery of the world. "We have been given everything," his abbot had said. "But we fail to understand that. Deep prayer is the way we recognize that we already have what we seek."

But deep prayer wouldn't get him a van or set him on the road, and so he'd resorted to the kind of prayers made by old women bowed before banks of candles. Pleas, promises, bargains—they were undignified, almost sordid. They were hardly any better than Wiloma's superstitious rituals, and yet for the moment they appeared to have worked.

In part, he knew, they'd worked because he'd laid the ground for his disappearance. He hadn't known when he was going, but he'd spent the week saying good-bye to his companions. "My niece is taking me home for a visit," he'd said—which, until a few hours ago, might easily have been true. He'd said good-bye to Ben and to Charlie and to Kevin; to Judson, who hadn't recognized him or anyone else in thirteen years, but who had once played gin rummy with him every day; to Parker, who rasped his words through an electronic box in his throat. He hadn't managed a farewell to Roxanne, which he regretted, but he had let go of the rest of the Home.

Twenty-nine years, he thought, tilting uncomfortably as Henry took a corner too fast. Twenty-nine years of a routine as regimented and reassuring as that of Our Lady of the Valley. He could still remember his first days at the abbey, when he'd watched forty men file silently into the church and begin the chants of the Office, bowing and rising and singing in unison. When he'd entered the Order, in 1927, the old rules had still been in effect. The monks wore the old habits, brown for him and the other lay brothers, white draped with black for the choir monks. They lived by the old schedule, chanting matins in the dark of the night and then the other hours as the day unrolled, celebrating Mass after terce, working outside between none and vespers, retiring just after dusk.

In those old days before the war and the reservoir, before he'd sailed to China, every minute had been full to overflowing and the ten years he'd been granted had passed like a long and busy day. In his memory it was always mid-April there, a month his father had hated for the mud and the frenzy of work but which he had come to love within the abbey's sheltering walls. The gray stone of the buildings shining palely as the sun rose over Hollaran Hill and illuminated the morning mist, the haze of green in the orchard as the branches broke into bud, the reddish shoots of the peonies breaking through the winter mulch along the warm south wall—the colors were sharp at dawn and gentled as the day progressed, and when it rained the pond to the east of the garden was black and tranquil. Ducks paddled in the dark water and laid their eggs in a tangle of juniper. He had worked in the kitchen after he first took his vows; a few years later he'd been assigned to the greenhouse and the garden. The flowers that graced the altar each day had been his.

There was no garden at St. Benedict's, and he wasn't allowed in the kitchen. His years there had passed like a single sleepless night, but still he'd had discipline, routine, certain meals appearing at predictable times, and a sense of community if not of common purpose. It had been like joining another Order: that of the old and crippled and confined. He and his companions had not taken formal vows, but they'd practiced them all the same.

Poverty—they owned nothing; chastity—the women lived in a separate wing and mingled with the men only at meals. Obedience—the administrator ruled their lives more firmly than any abbot. Stability had been easy, they lived and died in the Home. And then there had been fasting—who could eat the food?—and the discipline of silence: to whom could one talk in the endless nights? Corporal mortification had come without effort, courtesy of their decaying bodies, and although Brendan tried to don street clothes each day, many of his companions lived in bathrobes as shapeless as habits.

The van sped past Cobbs' Hill as Brendan thought about the life he was leaving behind. Thousands of people had stood on that hill in their Advent robes, his friend Judson had said, back when he could still speak. A century and a half ago, they had stood there waiting for the Second Coming and prepared for their own ascensions. All day and all night they stood, waiting for a miracle that never came. And when the ground didn't open and swallow the sinners, when the saints didn't leap from their graves, the faithful had climbed down from that hill and trudged home brokenhearted.

"They held their arms over their heads," Brendan remembered Judson saying. "As if they were going to start flying any minute." Judson had held his own arms in the air as he spoke, his pale blue bathrobe dropping away from his wrists and his eyes sharp with amusement. For thirteen years now he'd been as good as dead, and on the grass where the faithful had once crowded hip to hip, a group of teenagers were sunning themselves and tossing bright plastic disks to their dogs.

Henry drove past the hill, past the park, down the ramp that led to the highway, and nothing happened. Perhaps they haven't noticed yet, Brendan thought. Perhaps they don't care. One old man vanished in one old van, which surely the people at the Home understood had been borrowed, not stolen, and would be returned. The tires hummed on the pavement, and Brendan saw billboards, road signs, digital clocks flashing white numbers, cranes, drains, a half-built bridge, cars, weeds, chicory growing in blue profusion, litter, grass, sky, storefronts, the back of a church, a lit cigarette spinning end over end, a dog running behind a fence, a flock of pigeons rising all at once, a canoe strapped to the roof of a truck, rocks, gravel, trees, clouds.

Lord, he thought. Thank you for springing me. And he was about to be grateful for the ease with which they'd escaped when Henry turned left at the snarl where the highways intersected.

"Wrong turn!" Brendan cried. They had to go east, not west, along the path of the Erie Canal to Massachusetts. Henry was driving too fast, and they were not even launched on the Thruway yet, and already they were lost. Brendan's wheelchair was parked behind Henry's seat, and he couldn't lean forward far enough to tap Henry on the shoulder. His left hand flapped uselessly in the air. "You're going the wrong way!"

"I have to make a few stops. Pick up a couple of things before we head out." Henry turned on the radio and hummed along with the tune that suddenly filled the van.

"We don't need *things*," Brendan said. He was amazed that Henry couldn't feel the urgency, the absolute importance of leaving town that instant. "What do we need?"

"A little road food. A couple of thermoses, lots of coffee, some blankets, maybe some sleeping bags—you know. Stuff for a weekend trip."

Henry hummed and drove, seeming each minute to be in a better mood. Behind him Brendan lapsed into silence and tried not to sulk. He had never, in his long life, made a weekend trip; he was in Henry's hands and could do nothing without him and it was useless, he knew, to resist. Better to let go of his own will and to find some joy in surrender. He gazed at the maple trees lining the road, with their soft green leaves spread out like flounces. He peered into the windows of the passing cars and marveled at the faces. He thought how, at the Home, the aides would be loading the lunch trays and Roxanne would be finishing her third old man of the morning. He still felt the warmth of her hands on his back, and he knew that his success with Henry was due in part to her. Henry's lust and longing had filled that room like a cloud and rendered him incapable of thought.

Henry turned off the highway, drove down a road Brendan had never seen, and pulled into a strip of stores built so recently that the trees along the sides were no more than stems propped up by sturdy poles and wires. They grew melons here, Brendan thought. When I was Henry's age. And potatoes and onions and cucumbers and squash.

"I'll just be a minute," Henry said, and then he hopped

out and vanished behind the bright facade of a 7-Eleven. He returned a minute later, frowning. "Do you have any cash?"

"Me?" Brendan's clubbed hands beat at his pockets. "Maybe ten dollars," he said, considering what might be left of the thirty dollars he received from the Home each month. "Look in my coat."

Had they brought his coat? Henry frowned again, picked up the plastic bag containing Brendan's clothes, and then threw it down without looking. "We're a little low on funds," Henry said. "We'll have to think of something to do about that."

Brendan had given no thought to money at all, but he had assumed Henry would take care of whatever came up. Now he saw that their trip was going to require wits as well as luck, and for some reason this cheered him. They could move across the state like friars with their begging bowls, living on whatever came to them.

Henry vanished into the store again and returned a few minutes later with a small bag and two huge plastic mugs that smelled of burnt coffee. He handed Brendan one of the mugs. "Here you go. This'll charge you up for the trip."

Brendan bent his palms around the mug, which was capped and seemed to be insulated. He sipped through the tiny opening in the lid. The coffee was scorched and doctored with milk and sugar; he usually drank it black and he was prepared to dislike it. But the muddy fluid was hot and sweet and tasted wonderful.

A police cruiser entered the lot behind them and nearly clipped the bumper of the van. Brendan bowed his head and sipped from the mug. It's over then, he thought. Over before we've even begun. He'd had this coffee, different from any he'd had before, and a decade's worth of sights from their brief drive. Those would have to be enough. He sang a psalm to himself and waited for the rap on the window, the head stuck inside the door. Henry started the engine and drove past the cruiser as if it were only another car.

"One more stop," he said, and Brendan lifted his head in amazement. The policeman seemed unaware of them. He had rolled down his window and was talking to a girl in a halter top. "One more stop," Henry said, "and then we're on our way."

8

HENRY HAD ALMOST FORGOTTEN HOW DELICIOUS IT WAS TO BE behind a wheel. The van handled well despite its size; the steering was tight and the highway was as smooth as a woman's leg. He sped down the stretch between the plaza and the turnoff to Irondequoit, and when he caught the light at Titus he cornered with a small but satisfying squeal and then slowed when he heard his uncle gasp. Through the broad curving lands of his old neighborhood, past the culs-de-sac and the handsome houses and the islands planted with magnolias and bulbs, he drove smoothly, rhythmically, enjoying both the feel of the van and the sight of all he'd created in what had once been a melon field. Kitty used to tell him that he loved this first development of his the way another man would love a first child, and he knew, looking at the smooth green lawns, that she was right.

His sense of well-being vanished when he saw Lise's car parked next to Kitty's in front of his old house. Lise, his oldest daughter, wasn't speaking to him and wouldn't answer his calls. More than her younger sister, Delia, she seemed to be unable to forgive him. She might have accepted his failure and financial ruin—she had made it through college, she had a job, she was safer than the rest of them. But when Kitty, on the night she'd cursed Henry and thrown him out, had called both Lise and Delia and told them it wasn't just the way Henry had trashed their futures, nor the way he'd gambled everything on his foolish project and lost, but the lying, the cheating, the girlfriends—Anita, most of all—the girls had turned their backs on him.

Anita, Henry said to himself, and he nearly groaned aloud as he parked the van and lowered his uncle to the ground. Useless for him to try to explain that Anita had also abandoned him. Lise and Delia had turned away from him, sped to their mother's side and embraced her cause completely. Kitty, who wore the role of wronged wife as if she'd been born to it, hadn't spoken to Henry in more than a month. He had hoped to find the house empty today.

He wheeled Brendan up the flagstone walk he'd laid so carefully when the girls were young. "Does she know we're coming?" Brendan asked.

"No," Henry said. His heart skipped several beats. The pachysandra around the beech looked ratty and dry and the lawn was riddled with grubs. The screens still leaned against the garage where he'd left them. One wheel of Brendan's chair caught the corner of a stone thrown up by frost, and the fact that Kitty hadn't had the stone replaced annoyed Henry enormously. His house was falling apart already, and by the time the bank auctioned it off it was bound to look hollow, haunted, unloved. Whoever bought it would have only contempt for the man who had let this happen.

Brendan said, "Why don't I wait out here?"

"Come in with me," Henry pleaded. "You haven't seen Kitty in ages." He rang his own doorbell and then stood behind the wheelchair, hoping his uncle's presence might neutralize Kitty's venom.

His dog, Bongo, yelped and yowled inside the house. His daughter opened the door, stared at him, and then said, "Grunkie," after a moment's poisonous silence.

Lise had cut her hair, and within its smooth brown frame Henry saw his own face reflected. She had his bumpy nose, which looked craggy in his face but was too strong and large in hers. She had his jaw, a bit too square, and his pale blue, almost lashless eyes. It pained him that she wasn't more attractive, and he wished that Anita, or someone like her, would take her aside and teach her how to dress and wear makeup. She was almost aggressively homely, and in her refusal to decorate herself, in her blunt manners and sensible clothes, Henry saw his own stubbornness. Delia, dainty and feminine, so much resembled Kitty that he felt he'd had no part in making her. But Lise was his, so much like him that he both rejoiced and despaired.

Lise stared steadily at him and then slipped her eyes to Brendan's neck brace. "What a surprise," she said.

"Lise," Henry said. "It's good to see you." His voice sounded false even to him and he winced as she helped Brendan over the threshold and into the house without another glance at him. Bongo hurled himself at Henry's knees, sixty pounds of spotted mutt with a floppy pink tongue, and Henry scratched Bongo's ears as Lise and Brendan chatted. Then Lise called, "Grunkie's here!" as if Henry didn't exist. Henry's heart shrank and withered and burned.

"Lise," he said again, but she looked at him scornfully and moved away. When she was a tiny, bony child, she had sometimes looked at him in just that fashion. She went to her room and hid in the back of her closet whenever he punished her, and when he went up later to coax her out, her eyes glittered so coldly that he found himself apologizing and forgetting her misdeeds. She stood at the shelves near the staircase now, slamming books into boxes. The floor was littered with them, he saw—boxes of books, of pictures, of crystal and china and clothes. He had thought Kitty still had a few weeks before she had to move.

Kitty came out of the kitchen, wrapping a goblet in white paper and saying, "Brendan! What in the world . . . ?" in the low, rich radio voice she'd developed when she went to work at the PBS station. Henry could remember when her voice had sounded like anyone else's. One afternoon, during the summer that he'd turned twenty and had been working with a construction crew, he'd looked down from the roof of a cottage on Canandaigua Lake and seen on the beach below him a young woman with two little girls in tow. The girls were blond; the woman, hardly more than a girl herself, was black haired, creamy skinned, delicately boned. She looked like Henry's mother, whom Henry could hardly remember. She spread out a blanket, settled the girls and the dolls they'd brought with them, and arranged a meticulous picnic: sandwiches cut neatly in half, grapes and peaches wrapped in a napkin, homemade cookies in a lidded box, and miniature versions of everything for the dolls. A baby-sitter, he'd decided, watching as she solemnly poured liquid into the dolls' cups. Working for one of the wealthy summer families. The charmed circle she and the girls had formed on the sand looked like everything he'd missed in his own life. He had climbed down from the roof and dropped his hammer and told his foreman he was taking a break. Drawn by an envy so strong that it was already almost love, he had introduced himself to Kitty and her charges.

"Is that your house?" she'd asked, and he would have given anything to have been able to say yes. The sweet, bland surface of her life enchanted him. She had two parents, two brothers, a dog and a cat; as he courted her, with a frenzy that excluded both his sister and his ailing grandparents, he saw a chance that he could escape his ragged childhood and make a stable family for himself. His dreams had worked out just the way he'd wanted. He'd married her and moved into the city and left Coreopsis behind; they'd raised two daughters and had picnics on beaches and vacations in the mountains. All along, until that wretched radio station had captured her, he'd thought she shared his contentment.

And then one year, when the girls were half-grown and he was working day and night building the fortune he'd thought they both wanted, she'd signed up for some night courses and made friends with a group of women he disliked. She'd started volunteering at the radio station when Lise entered high school, and then somehow, when his back was turned, she'd become a stranger with a tangle of black hair and too much eye makeup and this voice—this husky, rippling voice—that rained over the city five times a week.

There'd been times, in the last few years, when he'd been driving along the back roads searching for land and had heard her voice purring from the radio. Then he'd imagined that he didn't know her at all and that he could go home and fall into bed with this frightening, exciting stranger. He'd imagined creeping up the stairs and coming upon her damp from her shower, her hair glistening with steam and her voice caressing him. But she kissed him absently when he approached her and then put a load of laundry in the drier or a chicken in the oven. She set her glasses on her nose and said she had papers to read, or she complained about his friends or his hours or his bills. When he made love to her, she looked out the window or twined her fingers in the fur of Bongo, who came and stood by them and sniffed and whined. She had pushed him away—on purpose? By accident? He'd never been sure—and then used the women to whom he'd gone for comfort as an excuse to push him out.

Her face soured when she caught sight of him. "Oh," she said. "You."

"Kitty," he said. She looked dry, self-possessed, incapable of yielding. And yet he could remember a time, before the voice, when she'd lain down with him in the fields of Coreopsis.

"Are you here for a reason?" she said.

He stood behind Brendan's chair and waved his hands over Brendan's head, meaning, *Don't humiliate me. Don't do this in front of my uncle;* feeling, behind his hope, the weight of all the hard words she'd heaped on him the past six months.

"We're busy," she said, disappointing but not surprising him. "We have things to do. I'm *moving,* in case you've forgotten."

Brendan cut smoothly and gently into her angry speech: "Where to?" he asked. He might have been talking, Henry thought, to one of the strangers at his stoplight.

"Where to?" Kitty said mockingly. "Lise was able to find me an apartment in her complex. Two stories, a little patio with a bit of grass all my own. I'm sure I'll be very comfortable."

"Twin Oaks?" Henry said. "You're moving there?"

"You have a better idea?"

"Let's go in the kitchen," Henry said. "Please? We need to talk."

He strode off, hoping Kitty would follow. Behind him Brendan said, "Henry? You know we ought to get going," and then, as Henry turned the corner, "We can go in a minute, I guess. I'll just sit here and talk to Lise . . ."

Kitty followed Henry. "What are you doing here?" she said. "I asked you not to come . . . and what in the world are you doing with Brendan?"

Her voice was so biting that he realized he couldn't safely tell her the truth about anything. She twisted his words; she twisted his every move. She hates me, he thought with surprise. He couldn't remember anyone ever hating him before.

"I'm bringing him over to Wiloma's," he lied. "She and the kids wanted to see him. Then we're all going out to dinner. The Home loaned us the van." He hoped Kitty wouldn't remember that he wasn't supposed to be driving. She glared at him, waiting for something more. "I thought I'd just swing by here, since I was out," he said lamely. "I need to pick up a couple of things, some extra blankets, some clothes I forgot . . ."

Kitty wrapped glasses silently. She had always been able to wait him out, wait until his nervous voice filled the silence and he hung himself. He forced himself to change the subject: "How are the girls?"

"Like you care."

"You know I do—you know this is killing me. You think I like seeing you forced out of our house?"

"*Your* house," Kitty said bitterly. "*Your* house, *your* development, *your* stupid, stupid projects—when was any of it ever *ours?* When did you ever think about what the girls and I might want?"

This was so manifestly unjust that Henry stared at her. He had always, always, done everything for her and the girls—all his work, all his buildings and projects and plans and dreams. "That's not fair," he said. "If Coreopsis Heights hadn't failed—I was trying to make something for all of us, make enough money so that you and the girls would be really secure, so you could do whatever you wanted." He had said this before, he thought. Or something like this—he had told his sister, years ago, that he couldn't stay in Coreopsis while Da was sick because he had to go make enough money to save them all.

"And Anita?" Kitty said. "What was that?"

"A mistake. I made some mistakes. Can't a man make a mistake now and then?"

"I heard you're working at a box factory. Another mistake?"

"It's just temporary. It's what the employment agency had. It's just until I get back on my feet and we get all of this straightened out."

"Don't kid yourself," Kitty said, whacking silverware into a box. "*We*—we aren't straightening anything out. *We* aren't a *we* anymore. I'm moving Wednesday, and once I get out of this place and the lawyers finish up, *we* aren't going to see each other again. Not if I can help it."

Henry backed away from her, wondering when she'd gotten so mean. "I'll just go get what I need," he said.

"You do that." Kitty tore open another cabinet and began stacking dishes furiously. Henry tried to imagine her in one of the apartments at Twin Oaks: shoddy construction, low ceilings, flimsy stairs and walls. The closets were shallow and all the windows jammed. He knew the man who had built that complex: Dominic, who had skimped on every phase of the construction. Kitty's belongings—*our belongings,* he thought with a pang of loss—would be hopelessly out of place.

In the living room Lise was listening absently to Brendan. "I'm fine," Brendan told her. "Fine, never been better." Lise glared at Henry as he passed her and fled up the stairs. More boxes, more disarray. His shirt felt heavy on his shoulders and he started to sweat. Without thinking, hardly seeing, he pawed through the closet he had once shared with Kitty. Blankets—fine, he thought. Two. A short-sleeved shirt and his long-billed Red Wings cap. Sneakers—I thought I had those. I thought they were at the apartment. The briefcase Da had given him when he'd left Coreopsis, with the sheaf of yellowed newspaper clippings and papers inside; the framed picture of his parents at the Farewell Ball, where, his mother swore, he had been conceived—don't look at that; a stack of ties the girls had given him, which he had never worn but always saved. He crammed these things into an empty box he found lying near the bed. He hadn't taken much when Kitty had thrown him out—it hadn't seemed necessary, he'd thought he had plenty of time. But now he was seized by the fear that Kitty might get rid of everything.

When he came downstairs, Brendan said, "Things you need?" Kitty came into the living room and said, "Good. Get that junk out of here."

"We ought to go," Henry said to his uncle, who nodded. Lise wheeled Brendan out the door and then stood by him near the van, saying something that Henry couldn't hear from the living room. He touched Kitty's elbow, the elbow of this woman who had once been his wife.

"I'll call you Monday," he said. "We need to talk."

"Don't bother. We don't."

Henry cleared his throat. "Listen. I know this is a little strange—but do you have any cash you could spare?" He had to ask, although it tore at his stomach; he and Brendan had fifty bucks between them. "I get paid next week, I'll pay you right back. . . ."

Kitty laughed at him. She called Lise to her and eased Henry out the door; as he passed Lise, she looked over his shoulder as if he were nothing to her. He thought of the time he'd lost her at Midtown Plaza, when she'd been three or four and small enough to blend into the forest of knees and thighs. He still didn't know how it had happened. He had taken his eyes from her for just a minute, just long enough to examine the posters filling the travel agent's window with palm trees and blue water and stretches of white sand, and when he looked back for her she was gone. The plaza was packed that week before Christmas, a sea of dark coats and scarves and jumbled legs and lines of children waiting to sit in Santa's lap and ride the mechanical reindeer. Lise hadn't made her way to the other children or the tree hung with gifts or the tired men costumed as elves. She wasn't at the candy counter or the ice cream stand. He had climbed up on the concrete planter ringing one of the potted trees and looked down on the crowd, but still he hadn't been able to see her. For the next half hour he'd run around in a fog of panic and guilt.

She turned up in the arms of a security guard at the information desk, and when she caught sight of him she burst into angry tears. "You *left!*" she shrieked. And while he knew he hadn't, that he had stood unmoving in front of the window while she trotted away, her accusation had stung him. He'd forgotten her for a minute and it came to the same thing.

Kitty closed the door behind Lise, shutting out Henry and Brendan and also Bongo, who had slipped out behind Brendan's wheelchair and was chasing a squirrel around the yard. Henry walked slowly toward the van, carrying his box of useless objects. When he opened the van door, Bongo leapt inside before Henry could finish raising Brendan's chair. Henry looked at his dog, flop-legged and pink-tongued and uncomplaining and eager, and he said, "Fine. You want to come, you come."

"Henry," Brendan said from his perch behind the driver's seat. "This maybe isn't a great idea."

Henry closed his door and started the engine. "He's *my* dog," he said, and the three of them drove off.

9

ANYTHING WE CAN CONCEIVE OF DOING, WE CAN DO, WILOMA READ. *In our dreams we can do anything, and the same is true of our waking lives.*

Wiloma was sitting at her kitchen table eating cottage cheese, although she would have preferred a tuna sandwich. She'd eaten tuna for several years after she stopped eating meat, but then she'd read about the dolphins; now she ate bland white curds doused with tamari and sprinkled with sunflower seeds. In between bites she tested her new filling with her tongue and felt guilty about her visit to her dentist.

Her tooth felt smooth and whole again. She knew that if she'd been able to visualize it strong and healthy it would have healed itself, but each time she'd closed her eyes and called up a picture of it she'd seen it cratered and crumbling, the dark interior leading to a ribbon of pain. She had failed; she could admit that. She found it harder to admit that she had looked forward to seeing her dentist and enjoyed her visit to him.

Her dentist had a warm, burred voice and a lovely neck. The chair in which she lay tilted so far back that her head was under his chin, and when she looked up, she saw the beard beneath his white mask and his shaved neck and the soft skin behind his ears. His hands were gentle and strong, and the way he cradled her head with them made her wonder how he'd hold the rest of her. While she lay there, her mouth stretched open and filled with a rubber dam and a drain and thin metal bands, she took her mind off the pain by staring at his eyes and his skin. She told herself that the fantasies she wove in that chair were not so terrible—she hadn't made love to anyone since Waldo had left her, and it was natural, normal, that she should be attracted to this man. What was not so normal—what went, really, against the grain of everything she believed—was that her teeth acted up more these days than they ever had before, and that she couldn't put the energy into healing them that she knew she should. And that was, she suspected, because she didn't really *want* them healed; healing them would mean missing those gentle hands.

It was ridiculous, embarrassing. She was forty-eight and knew she ought to know better. She turned back to her Manual, which she'd propped on the table behind her cottage cheese, and she read both to prepare herself for Brendan's arrival and to stiffen her resolve not to let her mouth rule her mind.

Heal the Spirit and the body will heal itself, she read, from the chapter on nutrition and healing.

Drugs are a diversion and a distraction and work only by suggestion; how can that which is material, and thus unreal, influence that which is Spiritual and real? Healing occurs only through strengthening of the Spirit. However, certain foods can aid healing, through transmission of qualities of Spirit which are diminished in the Subject. These foods are curative not through any corporeal property, but because of the Spirit manifested in all things which grow from the earth.

Spiritual nutrition is an art, which we discuss in detail elsewhere; it requires the full collaboration of the Subject and a trained neuro-nutritionist for the best results. However, even an unwilling Subject (one who has not accepted the omnipotence of the Spirit, or who has lost all will to command the Spirit) may be aided by a neuro-nutritionist who designs a diet based on the following guidelines:

• *Roots (e.g., potatoes, onions, beets, turnips) nourish the muscles and are useful in cases of muscle wasting, paralysis, sprain, strain, or spasm.*

• *Leaves (e.g., lettuce, spinach, cabbage, dandelions) cool inappropriate passions and heat and are useful in cases of fever, sleeplessness, mania, and consumption.*

• *Shoots (e.g., asparagus, fiddleheads, green onions) stimulate circulation and brain activity and are useful in cases of excess fluid, depression, and coma.*

• *Flowers (e.g., broccoli, cauliflower, nasturtiums) have an affinity for the eyes and ears and are useful in cases of blindness, infection, and in certain disorders of emotion and behavior, which are actually disorders of perception.*

• *Fruits (e.g., apples, oranges, melons; also such vegetables as eggplants, peppers, tomatoes) soothe and regulate all disorders of the skin and upper digestive tract.*

• *Barks (e.g., cinnamon, birch, slippery elm) purge and purify the bowels and liver and are useful in cases of constipation, diarrhea, gallstones, liver congestion, and tumors of the digestive tract below the stomach.*

• *Seeds (e.g., grains, peas, beans, nuts, sesame, poppy) stimulate and cleanse the generative organs and are useful in cases of barrenness, impotence, disordered menses, enlarged prostate or prostatic tumor, ovarian cyst or tumor, difficult pregnancy, and both lapsed and excessive desire.*

There was more, much more, but Wiloma skipped to the end of the list and read the last paragraph: *Keep in mind that these are only guidelines. The neuro-nutritionist will modify them as needed, based on the dialogue of his or her Spirit with the Spirit of the Subject.*

How, Wiloma wondered, was Christine, her neuro-nutritionist, going to establish a dialogue with Brendan's Spirit, which he kept hidden and caged? Although he'd left his Order when Wiloma was still a child, although he hadn't set foot in a church since Second Vatican, she suspected he wouldn't relinquish his Spirit to anyone but a priest. But Christine was cunning, and if anyone could break through to Brendan it would be her.

Wiloma had known Christine since her return from the Healing Center in Boston. She hadn't introduced Christine to Wendy and Win, but she'd seen her often, surreptitiously, for the minor ailments that continued to plague her despite her efforts to drive them out. These ailments shamed her, but Christine was very pragmatic about Wiloma's lapses. The Spirit Scale was just that, Christine said—a scale, along which we proceed by steps. It takes time to shed our old thoughts and old habits, and even when we move along the Scale a few degrees, some backsliding is inevitable in times of weakness or inattention. And although Wiloma should not, she said, ever resort to drugs, the proper foods and herbs and minerals could aid the flow of energy along the body's channels.

Christine had given Wiloma extracts of bryophyllum leaves for her anxiety attacks and infusions of yarrow and silver for her insomnia. For her migraines, she'd concocted a mixture of iron, sulfur, myrtle, and honey. She gave Wiloma infusions of young birch leaves when her eczema broke out, and nasal sprays of lemon juice and mucilage of quince for her allergies. All these things had been comforting and some of them had helped; certainly none of them had harmed her.

She was sure that Christine could help Brendan in similar ways. The plan she'd worked out for Brendan included blackthorn and stinging nettles and strawberry leaves, colloidal flint and lily of the valley, turmeric rhizomes and horsetail and infusions of elder blossoms. These were meant to strengthen his worn organs, but the heart of the treatment, Christine said, was mistletoe, which was known to be helpful in cancer and other catastrophes of form. And if it was too late for a cure—as, Wiloma had to admit to herself, it almost surely was—still, mistletoe given in the context of a full Healing Ceremony was guaranteed to help Brendan's Spirit detach from his body fully, painlessly, and quickly. He'd merge into the Light like an arrow, Christine had said. Like a bird winging free from the earth.

Wiloma was pondering this, and wondering how she could pry Brendan's Spirit free from the guilt and dogma that bound him, when the phone rang and scattered her thoughts. The administrator from St. Benedict's announced himself and asked if Brendan was with her.

"Of course he isn't." Wiloma thought of Brendan's room, clean and almost ready for him, and she reminded herself to vacuum the screens so the sun could flood the bed. "We arranged that I'd pick him up tomorrow."

The administrator drew a deep breath. "That's what I thought. But we were hoping—you know, your brother visited your uncle this morning."

"It's Saturday. That's the day he always visits."

"Your uncle's gone," the administrator said. "So's your brother. So is one of our transport vans. We were hoping there had been some confusion and that maybe they were with you."

"I'm sorry," Wiloma said. "Say that again?"

The administrator repeated himself. "They were both with your uncle's physical therapist earlier," he added. "Someone else saw them leave the building and assumed your brother was just taking your uncle out for some air. But then your uncle wasn't back in his room when the lunch trays were delivered, and one of the janitors discovered the missing van, and another one said your uncle was seen in the vicinity of the key case. And we're afraid they took off together."

Wiloma focused the full power of her detoxified intelligence through space toward him, marveling at the way a grown man could allow his thinking to be so clouded by fear and confusion. "That's ridiculous. There must be some mistake. They're probably on the grounds somewhere, enjoying this beautiful weather. Couldn't one of your own people have taken the van? Maybe someone forgot to sign it out. Henry would never do something like that. And my uncle—he was all set to come here. Surely you can see that there are other explanations?"

"I hope you're right." The administrator's voice sounded sour, as if his stomach were troubling him, and she wanted to encourage him to eat some fresh fruit. Something sweet, something cleansing. "But I'm afraid we may have a serious incident here. If you see either of them, if you have any news at all, would you call us?"

"Of course. But I'm sure you're mistaken—they'll probably walk in any minute."

There is no pleasure in evil or error, she reminded herself as she hung up the phone. *All Spirit ultimately acts for the good.* She took six cleansing breaths through her nose, closed her eyes, and focused on the spark of serenity centered between her ears. It was not possible, she told herself, it could not be possible that Henry had kidnapped Brendan. No matter how depressed and disturbed he was, he could not have stolen Brendan away without telling her—not now, when keeping

Brendan away from Christine for even a few more days might mean the loss of his Spirit.

And yet she could picture Henry stealing into the Home, luring Brendan out, maybe drugging him or binding and gagging him, stuffing him into a stolen van. Henry was lost, he was past salvation. There was nothing he wouldn't do. The hardest thing she'd learned at the Healing Center was that she had to write Henry off. *There are people*, her teacher had said, *so deeply corrupted that no human heart can save them. Only by divine intervention can the seeds of the Light take root in them*. When she heard those words, she had thought about the way Henry had tricked her out of her share of the land in Coreopsis. She'd made her peace with that land by then; the auction after Da's death had drawn the poison from it, like venom from a wound.

After the tractors and balers had vanished, and then the furniture and the dishes and the clothes and the books; after the house had been boarded up and she had moved and married Waldo, she had come to see that plot of land as a place like any other. Not just the spot where she'd mourned her parents' deaths and grown up lonely and afraid, not just the spot where she'd nursed her grandfather through his last illness—but also a *place*, some acres of land. A pretty place, in fact; a spacious, rolling bit of country where she could picnic with her children.

She had learned to see the pond as a place where her children could swim, the hill as a place with a beautiful view. And then Henry had come to her, his hands bristling with papers and his mouth dripping honeyed words, just when she'd begun to worry about sending her children to college. A loan, he'd told her. The movement of a few words on paper, purely to satisfy the bank; if she let him hold the land in his name for just a few years, he promised he'd make both of them rich. Half of all the profits would flow to her, he'd said. He'd never said she risked losing everything.

And she had let him get away with that. She had put aside

all his broken promises and let him fool her one more time. Her teacher had said, *When someone does wrong and you excuse him without helping him confront the wrong deed, you only enable him to do more wrong.* She'd turned a blind eye toward Henry's deeds for years; he was all the family she had left except for Brendan. Only when it was too late had she learned to see how Henry had betrayed everyone. He'd left her alone in Coreopsis when their grandfather was dying. He'd turned on Waldo, with whom he'd once worked; he'd neglected Brendan until he was desperate, and he'd abandoned Kitty and his girls.

During her detoxification, her teacher had made her write Henry's name in huge green letters on a piece of paper and list all Henry's crimes below in red. Then he'd read the list back to her in his slow, careful voice. *Did your brother do this?* he'd asked after each item. And then, *Did you permit it?*

Yes, she'd answered, and *yes.* The list was appalling; the relief she'd felt when they'd burned it in the Crucible of Crimes had been immense. Henry's deeds had turned to ashes. Since then she'd treated her brother as a stranger. She was polite to him, no more. When he wasn't around she never thought of him.

But Henry hated her involvement with the Church, and her teachers had also told her that the enemies of the Church were resolute. She had talked to witnesses and read some of the testimonies. Misguided people, the sort who dread Moonies and Krishnas, had been known to mistake the Church of the New Reason for one of those evil cults and to hire deprogrammers to kidnap their family members and purge them of their new beliefs.

If she could picture Henry doing such a thing, did that make it possible? He might have gotten wind of her plans for Brendan and determined to disrupt them; there was nothing he wouldn't do. She paced the kitchen and meditated silently for a while. Then she wondered guiltily if her inability to keep from imagining Henry engaged in horrible acts might not have caused those acts. Some thread of confusion in her longed for her teeth to fall apart so she could see her dentist; her teeth complied. Maybe a similar thread wanted Henry to act badly so he could be punished for his errors. Maybe she had somehow made him do it?

She directed her attention toward Brendan's Spirit, hoping to locate him. When she found nothing but blankness she telephoned her daughter for advice.

10

At the Henrietta McGovern Museum, Wendy sat sorting dolls. Two huge cases of them stretched down the walls of the room, and at her feet lay another, uncataloged array. Farther down, and in all the rooms upstairs, more cases held lead soldiers, stuffed bears, cloth-bodied dolls with bisque hands and heads, rocking horses, dollhouses, board games, trains—a complete collection of nineteenth-century American toys, overwhelming in their profusion. The toys, as well as the books and china and furniture and costumes and pictures made from dead people's hair, had all come from the jammed rooms of Henrietta McGovern's mansion. She had lived to be ninety, Wendy knew; she had lived alone except for these objects. When she died, it had taken six people five years to sort what was worth keeping from what was not, and then another year to move the crates to the new museum building. Some of the collection had been shelved already, but the storerooms were still full of unopened boxes and each box was full of surprises. Wendy's job, which she'd stumbled into almost by accident, was to sort through and label the contents of the boxes the assistant curator brought to her.

As she pulled dolls from the boxes, she fantasized about her escape. Fall would come, she thought, if she could just survive this summer; and then she'd enter college and be on her own at last. She'd have a room, a roommate, interesting classes. She could live any life she chose. In her closet at home, folded into a pile of sweaters, she had a huge sheet of paper on which she'd written all the rules by which she meant to live. She had a plan, a program, ready to kick into action the minute her real life began. She set aside a blond baby doll and then sank so deeply into her dreams that she hardly paid attention at first when her mother called and told her the news.

"Grunkie?" she said, when her mother's words began to make sense. "Grunkie's gone? How can he be gone?"

Then she heard the manic hum behind her mother's words and realized what was going on. Her mother seldom allowed herself to worry these days, but when she did she pulled out all the stops and could build elaborate conspiracies from the slenderest of threads. The only way to manage her in one of these moods was to let her talk herself out.

He wasn't gone, her mother hypothesized—he and Henry had taken a long walk, and the administrator was hysterical. Or he was gone, and Henry—"You know how your uncle's been. He's been unbalanced. He hasn't been himself"—Henry had kidnapped him to keep him away from the neuro-nutritionist she'd engaged.

Wendy groaned. She'd taken a matched pair of rag dolls from her open box, a boy and a girl dressed in calico with bright button eyes and yellow yarn hair and red floss smiles. She rested these dolls in her lap, one on each thigh. Then she laid her forehead on the desk and placed the phone receiver next to her ear, with the mouthpiece pointed away from her. While her mother spun her theories, Wendy talked to the dolls.

"*Blah*-blah-blah-blah," she whispered to them. "*Blah*-blah. *Blah*-blah."

The dolls stared back and her mother rambled on. In her lap, Wendy danced the dolls to the rhythm of her mother's words. "Foolish," she whispered. That was one of the rules on the sheet of paper buried in her closet: *I will not act foolishly.*

"What?" her mother said sharply, and Wendy lifted her head from the desk and moved the receiver toward her mouth.

"Nothing." She brought the dolls up from her lap and laid them down on the desk. "I was just saying it's such a nice day, maybe Uncle Henry took Grunkie out for a picnic." Every day will be like this, she thought. Once Mom gets Grunkie home.

"You know what's going on with him," her mother said. "Grunkie hasn't had any appetite in weeks."

Wendy had forgotten that. But there was surely some reasonable explanation for his absence, something different from her mother's wild theories. "Maybe he just wanted some sun." She looked into the open box at her feet and saw lead soldiers tangled in wigs made of human hair, kidskin hands splayed across wooden legs. She wondered who had packed the boxes so carelessly.

"Maybe," her mother said. "You're probably right. They'll show up in an hour or two and won't know what all the fuss was about."

"Uncle Henry's okay. He's back on his feet, he's got a job."

"He does," her mother agreed. "And so do you—you've got things to do and here I'm bothering you with this."

Wendy turned the calico dolls facedown on her desk. Her mother always turned to her when she had these lapses of pessimism; she spun her fantasies and let Wendy calm her down, and then she apologized until she'd convinced herself she hadn't thought her dark thoughts. But this was the first time she'd called Wendy at work. Wendy wondered if her mother would call her at college. She'd imagined herself cut off completely, except for occasional visits home. She hadn't considered how the phone lines might bind her and her mother like an umbilical cord.

Her mother grew quiet, seemingly reassured. "I have to go now," Wendy said. "I have to get back to work."

"Okay," her mother said. "I'll see you for supper. I'm sure this will all work out. But it's just, you know—I'd feel better if the administrator hadn't said that thing about how Grunkie was down in the room where the keys to the vans are kept, and how he sent the janitor off to fix a whirlpool that wasn't broken. And then how when the janitor came back, Grunkie was gone and later he noticed that so was this set of keys— do you suppose Henry *forced* him somehow?"

"What?" Wendy said. "Did you tell me that before?"

"I don't know. Weren't you listening?"

"I was," Wendy said. "I am." She cut her mother off before she could tie up another half hour. "Don't worry. I'm sure everything's fine. I'm going to hang up now."

Afterward she couldn't concentrate on her work. The kidnapping idea was crazy, she knew, but that bit about Grunkie and the keys to the van, the bit her mother had dropped so late, so casually—that sounded real, and for the first time she wondered if Grunkie might actually be gone. She felt a brief buzz of elation at the idea that Grunkie had slipped through her mother's hands, and in so doing guaranteed her own freedom as well. Then she began to wonder what might have happened to him, and how her mother might respond to the loss of him, and if her own desire not to have him at home had somehow caused his disappearance. *Think a thought and you make it true,* her mother had warned her time and again, and certainly she had wished fiercely enough for her great-uncle not to join them. But that was her mother's twisted thinking, not her own, and she pushed it aside.

Her mother had said that Grunkie was eager to come to them and be Healed, but she knew that couldn't be right: he thought the Church of the New Reason was beyond contempt. He couldn't be Healed in the way her mother had because he didn't accept the same things. And so perhaps he'd fled?

She thought she was considering these possibilities calmly, but when she looked at her hands she saw that each one still held a doll and that the dolls were dancing frantically on the desk. This family, she thought. When am I going to be free?

After she and Win had gone back to live with their mother, their father had told her to call him anytime. "I'm here to help," he'd said. "If something comes up you can't handle alone." She hadn't called him often; she had feared that if she asked for help he might take them back. But a handful of times, when she'd been overwhelmed, she'd called and he'd helped her deal with the real problems and dispel the imaginary ones. She called his office now and told him everything, expecting him to laugh and sympathize and dismiss this the way he'd dismissed her mother's other strange imaginings. But he listened to her in silence, and when he spoke his voice was very grave.

"They're gone? Both of them?"

"Well, that's what Mom said the man from St. Benedict's said. But you know Mom, she thinks everyone's conspiring against her. And Uncle Henry would never—"

"Damn," her father said. "Damn, damn, *damn*—I bet I know just where they've gone. Don't worry, I'll take care of it. I've got to run."

He hung up, and Wendy stared at the phone as if it had suddenly sprouted fangs and a forked tongue.

11

IN THE FIELDS THAT STRETCHED ALONG THE HIGHWAY, CORN WAS growing, and clover and grass, and purple loosestrife in the hollows. There were red-winged blackbirds perched on fence posts and skimming over the fields, and hawks—Henry saw five of them in as many miles—standing in the trees. Normally he saw nothing when he drove; he drove too fast, he always had, and while his hands steered, he plotted and daydreamed and schemed. He'd always done his best thinking on the road, his mind focused by the humming wheels and the blur of passing scenery. He'd never had Brendan sitting behind him, commenting on everything that passed.

"Look at that hawk!" Brendan said. "What a beauty! To your left, Henry, over there—see where the blackbirds are clustered in the cattails? Woodchuck, in that dip; woodpecker—no, sapsucker; look at that hill, at those trees on the top, those birches; those are juncoes; are those goats? Look, there's the exit for Phelps. We're so close to Coreopsis . . . Henry?"

"What?" Brendan, back there pointing and naming next to the sleeping dog, made Henry aware of the flowers and trees and hills and clouds. The sights made him aware of his hands, his hands made him aware of the van; his awareness made him wary of the trucks roaring past, which had never bothered him before. His old car, the one the bank had repossessed, had been low and slinky and fast. This van sat so high that the truck winds rattled it, and he overcompensated, veering from right to left. When Brendan pointed out another hawk, chasing a mole through the cropped stubble at the base of the trees, Henry lifted his foot from the gas while he looked. The car behind him honked and passed him angrily.

"Let's get off at the next exit," Brendan said. "We're so close to Coreopsis, it's hardly out of our way at all. I want to see what you did."

"You don't," Henry said. "It's such a mess—I don't want you to see it."

"I do," Brendan said. His voice was firm and carried the force of an order. Henry, who had already bent his day toward his uncle's wishes in such an unexpected fashion, bowed and bent a little more.

He paid the toll and turned left on the narrow road that led to Coreopsis. They were forty miles from Rochester and hardly more than that from Syracuse; an easy hour's commute from either city. He had made the trip a hundred times and it puzzled him, still, that his potential customers had found it too long. He drove past Kriner's farm, past the fenced fields dotted with cows and the ring where Cory Kriner taught pigtailed girls how to ride. He drove past the van Normans' dairy farm, past the fields of turnips and corn, into the village of Coreopsis with its red-brick Presbyterian church and the white town hall and the beauty parlor and the string of failing stores, and then he drove out the other side and turned left onto a smaller road and left again onto one still smaller. He stopped at the huge red-and-white sign announcing the failure of his pride.

THE FORMS OF WATER

"Coreopsis Heights," read the sign. "An Exclusive Community of Executive Homes." It pained him like a knife in his ribs. Before him lay the curves of his elegant roads and the lots marked off by orange-flagged stakes. Green lawns surrounded the two finished models, with their thermal glass and Jacuzzis and white-finished kitchens, their tall stone fireplaces and airy stairs. Beyond them lay the shells of the others, dotted across the acres of corrugated mud.

Henry's eyes registered the roofs that hadn't been finished, the holes waiting for windows and doors, the empty foundations and piles of lumber and shingles, but these were not what he saw. His mind added all that was missing, and he saw the sewer pipes, the electric cables, the phone wires buried underground. The homes, each different and handsome, the streetlamps with their shapely globes, the driveways lined with green shrubs, the tubs of flowers paired on the steps and the children playing in backyards—the picture was so clear that he couldn't understand how it had failed to materialize.

Anyone might have done it, he thought, surveying the wreckage of his dream. The site had been so promising and the economics had seemed foolproof. The land cost nothing—he and Wiloma had inherited it from their grandparents. The taxes were low, and it had cost so little to tear down the house and the barns, remove the fences, uproot the trees. The survey had gone so smoothly, the design had been so distinctive, the planning board had been so obliging when he'd proposed the subdivision—who could blame him for signing that promissory note? He'd been so sure the project would fly that he'd signed his life away.

The builder had bled him dry and everything had cost too much: road bonds, utilities, building permits, taxes. Still, if he'd sold just a few of the houses, he could have stayed afloat. But the buyers had refused to come. He'd imagined executives from Kodak and Xerox, well-fed men in new cars who'd be willing to drive just a little bit farther to live in this unspoiled countryside and raise their children in this fresh air. He'd thought those men would see how the crumbling village and the ramshackle schools would be transformed. New schools would spring up from the flood of new property taxes; charming shops would open to satisfy the new owners' needs—surely those men could understand that services followed money, money fertilized growth. A little faith, a little vision, and Coreopsis would have been a new place.

But the men hadn't come. Instead, during those bleak Sundays when Henry had paced his model homes, local families had driven up in rusted cars and trucks held together with baling wire. Men whom Henry remembered as boys, the boys with whom he'd gone to school before he fled, had driven up with their wives and children and gawked at Henry's project as if it had been an amusement park.

"How much do you want for these?" they'd asked. *"How* much?"

When he'd told them—a hundred and a half for the smallest, two twenty for the four-bedroom with two and a half baths; a bargain, a steal, compared with similar houses in the suburbs closer in—they'd laughed. The friendly ones had laughed; the others, the older ones who remembered Henry's grandparents and the farm that had been there for generations, had cursed him and called him names. Those same people had bought everything that was not nailed down at the auction after Da's death.

They had felt sorry for him and Wiloma then. "It's a terrible thing," they'd murmured, fingering drapes and roasting pans and wooden-handled tools. "Losing both of them so quickly." As if they'd forgotten that Da and Gran were not Henry and Wiloma's parents; as if they'd forgotten that Henry and Wiloma had already lost their parents and had come to Coreopsis against their will. Those neighbors had sat on the lawn in the cool, bright air and munched sandwiches and cookies while the auctioneer gabbled on the front porch. Vultures, Henry remembered thinking. The men hoarded tools and the women clutched at gravy boats and silverware, driven, as far as Henry could tell, half by lust for a good bargain and half by a sudden, sentimental pity for the two young people they suddenly saw as orphans. Wiloma had just finished high school that year; Henry had recently married. The neighbors who had never asked how Henry and Wiloma were doing, trapped on a farm with their ancient grandparents; who had looked on placidly while their own children teased the newcomers—suddenly they'd been full of concern. Four different families had offered to buy the farm outright: "Get you out from under those taxes," they'd said. "Give you a little capital to get started somewhere else." Even then, Henry had had enough sense to hold on to the land. But those neighbors had proved useful in their own way; the proceeds from the auction had helped set him and Wiloma on their feet.

The place looked hellish now, bulldozed and littered, no longer farm but not yet neighborhood. The fault lay, he thought, with the narrow-minded people who'd failed to recognize his vision. With the bank, which had declined to extend his payments; with the lawyers and accountants who'd persecuted him so relentlessly; with the other developers who'd overbuilt the land nearer the city and caused the market to sag. The idea had been sound—in a few years, someone else would make a killing here. Someone, but not him. The bank owned the land now, as well as the buildings; Wiloma's share as well as his. Wiloma was furious with him.

All this passed through his mind before Brendan said a word. Henry hovered at the sign with his foot on the brake, unable to make himself drive down the roads the bank had stolen. He turned and saw Brendan peering through the windows, one hand flapping and the other on Bongo's neck.

"But where's the house?" Brendan said.

There were houses, or shadows of houses, all around them, but Henry knew what his uncle meant. "We tore it down," he said. "The house, the barns—everything."

81

"It's *gone?*"

"Gone," Henry said, and when he saw the expression on Brendan's face, he felt his loss—not the loss of his project, but the loss of his old home—for the first time. The cool green porch where he and Wiloma had sat, polite and frozen, when Da and Gran had first brought them here; the shadowy dining room, where they'd gagged on unfamiliar food and absorbed Da's bitterness; the barns where they'd done their chores. The pastures where the cows had grazed, the sheds where the tractors and balers loomed, the orchard and the grove of willows by the creek where he'd kissed Sally Kiernan and ground his pelvis against her thighs; the bedrooms in which he and Wiloma had lain, never talking about their dead parents, never sharing their dreams of escape; the parlor off the dining room, where Henry had first met Brendan. And the meadow crowning the small hill, where, long after he and Wiloma had grown and left and married, they'd gathered with their children and spouses a few times each summer, for picnics overlooking the abandoned house. Wendy and Win and Delia and Lise had run through the grass catching fireflies, and he and Kitty and Wiloma and Waldo—this was years ago, before things had gone sour for any of them, and before he'd even thought of Coreopsis Heights—had chattered aimlessly over grilling meat.

Gone, he thought. All of it. And as he continued to look at his uncle's face, he wondered if Coreopsis Heights had not been, all along, simply the only way he could find to destroy the memory of his childhood there. The glee he'd felt when the house had fallen and the bulldozers had taken their first bites from the land had felt justifiable at the time: the thrill of starting a new project, pride in his audacity. Now he wondered if what he'd felt had been only the joy of destruction. All the grief he'd felt for his parents, all his isolation and loneliness; the muddy, complicated mixture of gratitude and revulsion and affection and resentment he'd felt for his grandparents—all those feelings had been swept away by the falling trees and the vanishing fields and the neat, artificial curves of the roads. Perhaps, he thought, the auction hadn't cleansed the place for him as thoroughly as he'd once believed. Perhaps, during those summer picnics, his old life had haunted him more than he'd been willing or able to admit.

But it wasn't like Henry to brood this way, and when Brendan said, "Let me out. I want to get out," Henry snapped himself back to the present. He stepped down from the driver's seat, slid open the side door, and lowered Brendan's wheelchair to the ground.

Bongo jumped out behind him and then stood sniffing at the mud, and Henry, who felt hungry, reached under the seat and pulled out the paper sack holding the sandwiches he'd bought at the 7-Eleven. Brendan rolled slowly down the smooth black road away from him. Henry had to trot to catch up with his uncle, and when he rested his hand on Brendan's chair and said, "Wait—where are you going? Why don't we find a place to sit and have some lunch?" Bongo, leaping and prancing, snatched the sack from Henry's hand.

"No!" Henry shouted, running after his fleeing dog. "Bongo, goddamnit, Bongo, you come back here!"

But Bongo bolted for the mound of soft dirt surrounding one of the foundations, and while Henry stood gasping, panting for breath, Bongo dug a deep hole and dropped the sack neatly into it. He pushed the dirt over the sack with his nose and then ran back toward Henry, head high, as if he were proud of his foresight.

12

"Y OU TORE DOWN THE *HOUSE?"* BRENDAN SAID, BUT HENRY was too far away to hear him.

When Brendan had entered the abbey of Our Lady of the Valley, he had made one vow with an easy heart. Poverty, chastity, obedience—those had troubled him, they had broken saints. But stability, the extra vow of his Order, was what had called him in. To stay in one place always, under perpetual enclosure; to call one place home for the rest of his life, the way the Irish monks had adopted their landfalls as they'd climbed stiffly down from their boats—that had appealed to him.

One home, one family in the brothers who had welcomed him. One liturgical year, repeated endlessly; one niche in the wall behind the main altar where, before retiring, he and his brothers had turned toward the Blessed Virgin and sung the *Salve Regina*. When he'd first come as a postulant, he'd stayed in the guesthouse and been put to work washing dishes and waxing floors. The novice master visited once in a while, but otherwise Brendan had seen the monks only at a distance until the day when he'd finally been received. He'd gone into a room and turned over his clothes and his personal belongings; then he'd donned his new robes and passed through the door that led into the cloister and the novitiate wing. When the monks welcomed him, he'd believed he would never leave.

In his ten years there he had never gone beyond the walls. His family had visited once each year, and between their visits he'd kept silent. He'd spoken only to Father Vincent, his abbot, and to Father Norbert, the novice master; outside of chapter, he and the other brothers never talked, communicating in the archaic sign language peculiar to their Order. Despite that, he'd come to know his fellow monks more intimately than he'd ever known anyone else. Because they didn't converse, he couldn't know where they had come from nor why they'd entered the Order; he couldn't know, directly, what hurt or inspired or disappointed them. But he'd learned to read their faces and eyes and to see their moods in their movements. They'd become familiar to him; they'd become his family. He expected to die among them and rest his bones beyond the orchard.

But then the abbey had been dissolved and his vow had vanished with it. He'd been peregrinating ever since, going forth into strange lands and waiting for another home to reveal itself to him. The abbey in China might have held him if the war hadn't come, but after the internment camp, after the trial and the march and the massacre, Our Lady of Consolation had been burned to the ground. And then he'd been tainted, a displaced person, a monk without a monastery; he'd lost one abbey to water and another to fire and he'd lost his faith as well. The abbeys that had sheltered him upon his return, in Manitoba and then in Rhode Island, had been guesthouses, rest houses, never more than that. When he'd left the Order and come to stay with his parents in Coreopsis, he'd promised himself that this would be his final home.

He'd forgotten that his parents were old. His mother died, and then his father, when he first became ill, had said, "I'm leaving this place to the children, Brendan—you'll have the land in Massachusetts, and there's enough money in the bank to pay the taxes until you decide to sell it. I want the children to have this."

He'd had to move again. He had tried not to resent the decision—he was so badly crippled by then that he couldn't take care of himself and couldn't have stayed in Coreopsis even if the farm had passed to him. He'd moved into the Home and imagined his niece and nephew at peace in the old house. But neither Henry nor Wiloma had ever lived there again. They'd boarded up the place, they told him. Sold all the movable goods. For years he'd dreamed that one of them might move back and raise a family there.

And now Henry, stumbling after his dog, had done this. Brendan rolled himself down the road, heading toward a cluster of half-built houses that stood where his parents' house might once have been. One shell rose slightly above the others, absorbing the sun and reflecting the breeze in a way that seemed familiar. The land was shattered and scarred, stripped of its trees, built up falsely in some places and falsely hollowed in others, but this place looked as if it might be as hot in the summer as the old house had been.

He wheeled himself up the driveway until he reached the garage, and then he turned and gazed past the ruins at the gentle patchwork below. There were the woods covering the back part of Thompson's place. There was the pond, there Niedemeyer's corn, there the silos and pastures of the Cummings' place, the muddy creek that dried up in the summer, the low hills that rose in the distance—the view, or very near the view, that he'd seen from the parlor where he'd slept. He had first met Henry there, when Henry was fifteen. Henry had walked into the room where Brendan lay, and Brendan's mother had said, "Henry, this is your uncle Brendan."

She'd looked at Brendan then, clearly uncomfortable with

her words. "Brendan?" she'd asked. "You're sure that's the name you want to use? Not Ambrose?"

"Brendan," he'd said, holding a knotted hand out to his nephew. "That's what people call me." These people, anyway: this family. Brother Ambrose was the name he'd taken when he'd entered the Order; he'd left it behind with his robes.

Henry had been thin, freckled, stringy from farm work. His hair had been cut too short around his ears, exposing a pale line where his tan broke off. The skin around his nails was gnawed and torn, his pants were too small, and his shirt, although clean, was worn. His eyes were guarded, troubled, distant, and he ignored Brendan's outstretched hand.

"You knew my father?" he said—the first words Brendan ever heard him speak.

"I'm his *brother*," Brendan replied, startled and hurt. He frowned at his mother and she twisted her hands.

"I told them," she said. "I told them all about you."

Henry had ignored her. "You're too old," he said. After a minute, Brendan had figured out what Henry meant. Frank junior had been thirty-four when he'd died five years earlier; Brendan, at forty-five, had known he looked sixty. "Brendan's the oldest," his mother said, as if that explained everything.

Henry looked at her with a weary disappointment that told Brendan more than he wanted to know about how the children had fared since their parents' deaths. Then Henry turned his gaze on him. "If you're my father's brother," he said, "how come I never saw you before? How come you didn't help him? How come you didn't help us?"

"I wasn't here." Brendan had tried to sit up, but his back had been as frozen as his hips and his hands and his knees. He'd never been so debilitated, before or since, and he'd been useless, flat on his back, a mass of nodules and pain. "I was in China," he said. "I went there before your parents even met each other. I was still there when they were killed. We couldn't get mail. I didn't know."

Henry had treated that excuse with the contempt it deserved; he'd stared steadily out of his narrow eyes and then walked away. I didn't know, Brendan thought now: and that was true. But he also knew he might not have responded differently even if he'd heard the news. He'd renounced his family, renounced the world, left all he'd loved behind so he could lose himself in what had seemed, then, like a higher love. And if his brother lost his way, if his brother's children were orphaned and forced to live with grandparents too old and bitter to care for them properly, had that been his concern?

It had, he thought. Or it should have been. He and Henry had felt their way, after that bad beginning, toward a tentative friendship that hung on Brendan's reminiscences of his childhood with Frank junior. Henry had been starved for news of his father, grateful for the scraps that Brendan could give; later, he'd become interested in Brendan's China tales and how those fit in with what he knew of his father's war. Henry's bedroom walls, Brendan remembered, had been covered with maps of the Pacific. There were pins stuck into the islands on which Frank junior had fought.

The strained, pained boy of Brendan's memory bore almost no resemblance to the clumsy man who galloped across the mud tugging Bongo by a length of blackened rope. Henry's eyes were blank, his cheeks were flushed. Brendan couldn't imagine what went on inside him. He never talked about his mother; long ago, when he married Kitty, he'd stopped talking about his father as well.

"Sorry," Henry said. "Bongo stole our lunch. You want to see the inside of this place? It's one of my favorites, it's almost done. You can almost see how it was supposed to look."

A plywood ramp led from the driveway up the missing steps to the door. "Sure," Brendan said, thinking it couldn't matter. His parents' house was gone and nothing could bring it back. Nothing could bring back the childish Henry whom Brendan had grown to love, or the young Wiloma either—they were grown now, past grown, they were middle-aged. He realized with a shock that both of them were older now than he'd been when he'd first come here. They were old, and he was ancient. His kidneys twinged and his bladder cramped.

Henry tied Bongo to a concrete block and said, "Stay. You can't come in. Your feet are too dirty."

He spoke as if the dog understood him. "This is the kitchen," he said, giving Brendan's chair a push that bumped him over the threshold. Behind them, Bongo barked. "We were going to have slate-blue Italian tiles on the floor, and more on the backdrop below the cupboards. Gray countertops, black appliances, recessed lighting . . ."

Brendan tried to imagine it, but all he could see was plywood and Spackle and tape. In the old kitchen, in the old house, his mother had kept her own mother's dishes in a glass-fronted case. "The dining room," Henry said, wheeling Brendan on. "Aren't those windows great?" They were tall and narrow and pointed, like windows in a church; they were crisscrossed with masking tape and dotted with decals, which carved the view into kaleidoscopic shapes. The old house had had a bay window, full of dusty geraniums. Brendan's bladder cramped again as Henry bent and peeled back some brown paper and exposed the half-laid wooden floor.

"Is there a bathroom down here?" Brendan asked.

"Two," Henry said, missing the point completely. "A full bath in the guest suite and a powder room here." He flung open a small door and pointed out the mango-colored fixtures and the mirror framed in mock bamboo. Brendan eyed the toilet, which was low, oval, and padded on its cover and seat. It bore no resemblance to the toilets at St. Benedict's, nor to any toilet he'd ever seen.

"Does it work?" Brendan asked. Henry, who was stroking the sink, turned and looked at him blankly.

"What?" Henry said, and then his brain—where does he go? Brendan wondered. When he drifts away like that?—seemed to snap back into focus. "Oh," he said. "You have to go? The water's not connected—you could just go outside. There's no one around."

Brendan made a face and kicked his heels against his footrests. "Oh," Henry said again. "Right. What if I found you a jar or something? Could you use that?"

Brendan nodded, humiliated; he hadn't considered the details of being away from the aides at the Home. They had routines there, for washing him and transferring him into and out of his chair, for helping him to relieve himself so that they could all pretend nothing was happening. Drapes, discreet containers, averted heads. He followed Henry through the dining room, the living room, back through the kitchen, into the hall. They found nothing.

"Shit," Henry muttered. "You'd think there'd be a paint bucket, or something . . ." He threw open another door, into the wing he called the guest suite, and then he froze so suddenly that Brendan ran into the backs of his legs. "What the fuck?" Henry said. Outside Bongo barked on and on.

Brendan craned his head around Henry's hips. On the floor, in the corner, lay a nest of flattened cardboard boxes and paint-spattered tarpaulins. Three people crouched there on a sheet of blue plastic: a man, a woman, and a boy. The boy was gnawing his thumb and had pressed himself against the man's side. The woman looked at the floor; the man stared at Henry and Brendan and then slowly raised his right arm and brandished a length of two-by-four.

"Don't come any closer," he warned.

"The hell," Henry said. "I *built* this place—what do you think you're doing here?"

"You don't live here," the man said sternly. "Do you."

"No," Henry sputtered. "But . . ."

Brendan reached out and grasped a fold of Henry's pants, restraining him. The family, if it was a family, seemed to have been here for some time. A few clothes were stacked in a corner, along with a handful of dishes, a jug of water, a basin, and a pack of cigarettes. A cluster of black-eyed Susans stood in a jar.

"Well, we do," the man said. The woman reached for the jar of flowers and slid them silently behind her. The man said, "That camp where they put the other berry pickers is such a dump. And this place was abandoned, so we claimed it. You have a problem with that?"

Brendan kept hold of Henry's pants; he could feel Henry tensing himself to say or do something unforgivable. He craned his head to the side and spoke before Henry had a chance. "You pick berries?" He'd picked berries himself, at the abbey. They'd made them into jam. "Strawberries?"

"All berries," the man said warily. He lowered his arm and looked around Henry to Brendan. "Strawberries, raspberries, blueberries. Also peaches when it comes to their time, and then apples. Then we move south for the Georgia harvest, then we hit the oranges in Florida." He paused. "What happened to your legs?"

"Arthritis," Brendan said. "How long have you been doing this?"

"A while," the man said. "Suellen and me hooked up nine years ago. Then Lonny came. Can you walk at all?"

"No," Brendan said. The boy had raised his head at the sound of his name and now Brendan saw his eyes. They were distant, troubled, guarded; they looked the way Henry's had, when Brendan had first met him in the vanished parlor. "Mister," Lonny said, "is that your dog outside?" Bongo's howls rose to a frenzied pitch.

Henry nodded stiffly.

"You gonna let him bite us?"

Henry said nothing, so Brendan spoke. "Of course not," he said, tugging steadily at Henry's pants. "This used to be our place, but it isn't anymore. We're leaving now."

The man nodded and cupped his hand around the back of

Lonny's neck. "If you could," he said quietly. "If you would . . ."

Henry made a strangled noise and then bolted, leaving Brendan alone with the family. "I had a dog," Lonny said softly. "In South Carolina, once. Where'd you get that chair?"

Brendan looked at him, unable to think of anything to say. At the Home, where everyone talked all the time, his words had turned into something frothy and useless and polite, a foam of social chatter that flowed from surface to surface and never cut deeper. He lifted his right hand and spoke to Lonny in the sign language he'd used in the abbey.

He rested his forefinger along his upper lip—the sign for *black*—and then pressed that and his middle finger together and touched his forehead with them in the sign for *abbot*. *Black* and *abbot* signed together like that stood for *St. Benedict;* he followed with the sign for *house,* joining the tops of both hands in a peak like a roof. St. Benedict's Home, where his chair had come from. He felt a sudden rush of warmth in his hands, which hadn't signed in years.

Lonny stretched his lips in what might have been a smile, and then he held out his right hand and touched his forefinger to his thumb. Brendan didn't know what he meant, but he flashed back the sequence of signs that had once been his name: *brother* and *A* and *help* and *cook* and *house;* Brother Ambrose who works in the kitchen. Lonny said again, "I used to have a dog." Brendan, having left his old name behind, turned and left the family to their lives.

He thought he might try to talk Henry into leaving his dog with Lonny, but Henry was crouched on the ground outside, with his face buried in the ruff of fur that stood out from Bongo's neck. In that posture he looked hardly older than Lonny; he looked as if he might need Bongo more than Lonny did. When he raised his face, his skin looked weary and lined. "I'm sorry," Henry said. "This was a bad idea. This place always makes me so crazy."

"It was my idea to stop," Brendan said gently. "I'm glad we came." He'd expected rage from Henry, self-pity, destruction; not sorrow, not resignation; while Henry had not dealt with the family well, he'd done better than Brendan could have expected. For the first time he began to feel glad that Henry—Henry himself, not just any person with functioning limbs and a few free days—had been the agent of his escape. His bladder cramped again, and he longed for a bathroom and made the signs for *shame* and *house* without thinking.

Henry saw his movements, or maybe he only saw the plastic cup that lay on the ground between him and Brendan. He picked it up. "Here," he said. Brendan turned his chair away from Henry, tugged open his fly, and let his urine flow out in a slow, painful stream. The relief was astonishing. He emptied the cup when he was done, shook it dry, and wedged it between his thigh and the arm of his chair, not knowing when he might need it again.

"What am I going to do?" Henry said. His voice was quiet and strained, without the brassy bounce and feint that had colored it for years. "Strangers sleeping here—the whole thing's gone, it's ruined. I lost it all."

"You lost it a long time ago," Brendan pointed out. "When you left. Do you want to get going?"

"I guess," Henry said wearily. "I could use some lunch."

"Me too," Brendan lied. He hadn't been able to eat for weeks without throwing up, and even the smell of food often made him sick. But he realized, now that he'd had some time to think, that they shouldn't get back on the Thruway. They needed back roads, small roads, where the people who might be looking for them would never think to go. He remembered the route his bus had traveled, years ago, on his journey here from Rhode Island. "We don't have much cash," he said.

"No fooling," said Henry.

"And the tolls from here to Massachusetts are bound to add up . . ."

"Shit," Henry said. "I forgot about the tolls."

"And we're hungry, and we want some lunch, and I'd like to see some of the countryside. And we've still got most of the afternoon—why don't we go the back way? It isn't really any longer."

The gloom lifted from Henry's face. "We could take 5 and 20. I drove that once from Albany, when I was checking out some land."

"We could eat wherever you want," Brendan said. "We could stop by one of the lakes."

"Better than staying here." Henry buried his hand in Bongo's ruff one last time and then started pushing Brendan's chair toward the van. Brendan knew, without turning around, that Lonny stood at the window behind them, watching them leave.

13

LONNY AND HIS PARENTS STAYED IN HENRY'S MIND AS HE DROVE along the road threading the tips of the Finger Lakes together. That boy who'd looked like a wild thing, an otter or a mink; the silent woman; the man with the stick—they'd made him feel violated in some place the banks and the lawyers had missed, and yet he could see that Brendan was right. The house was theirs now, more than it had ever been his.

He drove quietly. He drove very fast. Brendan, if he was thinking about that family, kept his thoughts to himself, and Henry tugged his Red Wings cap down low and longed for the expensive sunglasses he'd broken in his car crash and hadn't had the money to replace. The cap had a red mesh crown and a cheap plastic tag in the back, but the bill was wide and long and shaded his eyes. He'd purchased it years ago, at a baseball game to which he'd brought Lise and Delia and Wiloma's kids. He couldn't remember why he'd kept it, but he was glad that he'd had the foresight to take it from Kitty's house. When they'd left Coreopsis, he'd plucked it from his box and stuck it on his head, longing for some form of disguise.

The cap, and his perch high in the van, made him feel like a truck driver. He pushed Lonny out of his mind and imagined himself in the cab of an eighteen-wheeler, crossing the bleak flatlands of North Dakota. The cab was air-conditioned and roomy; in the space behind his seat was a narrow bed and on the bed rested the young woman he'd picked up on the highway west of Fargo. Her hair was the color of wheat. She was traveling alone. She said, "I wanted to get away. Don't you ever feel like that? I wanted to leave my past behind me, forget everything I'd ever done and everyone who'd messed up my life. I just walked out and closed the door behind me."

I did that, he wanted to say to her, but Brendan broke into his dreams and said, "You want to stop here? That diner looks okay."

Henry focused his eyes, which had been seeing the road but no more, and let the girl dissolve. They were in Geneva; the diner was old and needed a coat of paint, and he couldn't imagine why Brendan had chosen it but then couldn't see anything better. He parked and lowered his uncle to the ground and maneuvered him inside the diner doors. They left Bongo locked in the van, howling mournfully at the traffic, and they settled themselves at a table by the window.

Henry pushed one of the chairs aside and rolled Brendan into place, but the arms of his wheelchair wouldn't fit beneath the table. The waitress who brought them menus looked from Henry to Brendan and back again and then said, "This isn't any good. You hang on a minute—I'll fix you up." The white plastic pin above her left breast read *Mirella*.

Henry studied her closely as she walked away. Her bottom was broad but solid, crowned by the bow of her apron; her stride was crisp, with a roll to it that sent smooth waves through her flesh. Two small rolls of fat formed a triangle above her round buttocks, and the rest of her seemed composed of similarly simple shapes. Cones, cylinders, hemi-spheres—even her hair was geometric, a mass of round red curls. Mirella, Henry said to himself. The name curled on his tongue.

Mirella returned with a white metal tray that was dotted with yellow ducks. "I know this looks funny," she said to Brendan. "But it works great on high chairs, and if we can just get it in here somehow . . ." The clips on the bottom of the tray didn't quite fit the wheelchair's arms, but she hammered on the tray with the heel of her hand until the clips spread and held. "There," she said triumphantly. She moved Brendan's water glass onto the tray and handed him his menu. "Isn't that better?"

"Very nice," Brendan said dryly. The duck tray over his lap, the white neck brace, and the heavy glasses gave him the look of a sinister, overgrown child.

"What can I get you?" Mirella asked.

"Would you give us a minute?" Henry said. Brendan bared his teeth at her in a grimace that might have been a smile. She tucked her order pad into her apron and left.

"You want to go someplace else?" Henry asked.

Brendan shrugged and his left arm drifted above the tray. "Where? The same thing's going to happen anyplace we go. But these ducks . . ." His hand thumped on the tray.

"Forget about it," Henry said. "Let's just get something to eat."

For a minute they studied their menus in silence. Henry examined the prices carefully: grilled cheese? The hot dog special? He longed for pork chops, chicken, steak, but he kept his eyes resolutely on the sandwiches. Brendan leaned toward him and said, "Everything's so *expensive*. Three fifty for a hamburger—what is this?"

"It's cheap," Henry said, and then he studied his uncle's face. "When's the last time you ate out?"

" 'Sixty-seven. Maybe 'sixty-eight? When the old director was around, they took some of us on a field trip to the lake.

Augie Furlong had a stroke there, just after we had lunch, and they never took us out again. Coffee cost a quarter then."

"Different world," Henry said. He tried to imagine what his own life would have been like if he hadn't eaten out since 1968. Cheaper, certainly—Kitty had hardly cooked a meal once she'd started full-time at the radio station, and for years they'd eaten out or ordered in almost every night. He still missed the elaborate meals she'd cooked during their first years together. Pot roast, creamed chicken, pork loin stuffed with prunes. She liked to cook then, she said she enjoyed it. When he'd come home from work, he'd walked in the door and found the table set with place mats and flowers, the girls scrubbed and dressed in clean clothes, Kitty bearing covered dishes that sent out delicious smells. All that had vanished years ago; what had drawn him to Anita, and to the women before her, had been at least in part the food.

His stomach rumbled and he settled on the hot dog special. Brendan said, "I'll just have some pie."

Mirella came and took their order and vanished again. She had lovely calves, Henry saw, sturdy and full but tapering to shapely ankles. He stared at his hands and imagined a life with her. She'd live in a trailer nearby, on a nice bit of land overlooking Seneca Lake. The hard-packed dirt outside her door would be dotted with bicycles and plastic bats and be-headed dolls; she'd have two children, or maybe three, and at least one would still be in diapers. Inside, the trailer smelled of soap and ammonia and sugar cookies, but although the place was crowded with belongings and beings— a dog, Henry thought, some company for Bongo; two fish in a bowl, a parakeet—it was clean and warm. In her room she had a water bed that rolled when Henry stretched out on it, and at night, after the children slept, she came to him and untied her apron and slipped her uniform up and off, disarranging her curls. Her feet were sore and he rubbed them and then set them gently down. Then he kissed her ankles, which were very fine. Then he kissed her calves. The dogs barked at the moon outside, the children dreamed of rubber rafts on the lake, the fish spun languidly in their small container. He kissed her knees and ran his hands along her hips. Her thighs were as white as her knees and they welcomed him, and afterward she walked naked to the kitchen and made them sandwiches.

Pickles? Kitty used to ask him, back when she'd fixed sandwiches for both of them after a romp in bed. *Do you want whole wheat or rye?*

When Mirella arrived with their plates, Henry managed to brush her arm with his hand. Her smile made him blush and pay attention to his hot dogs. They were grilled, he saw, not boiled, and they tasted good. But then anything would have tasted good after the food in the box factory's cafeteria. He'd been eating there every day because the food was cheap and he couldn't drive anyplace else. Rubbery cold cuts sweating moisture, falsely bright vegetables in yellow sauce, everything frozen and sealed in secret films, salty, processed, microwaved. The young men he worked with said it tasted fine to them.

Brendan's pie sat untouched before him. "You don't want that?" Henry said. His hot dogs were already gone; he could have eaten several more if only they hadn't been so pinched for money.

"I can't cut it," Brendan said levelly. "My hands."

Henry flushed and bent over his uncle's plate, dissecting the pie into bite-sized chunks. "I'm sorry. That was stupid of me. I wasn't paying attention."

"You don't, much," Brendan said. "Do you? You're always wandering off somewhere."

"Lots on my mind."

Henry held a forkful of pie to Brendan's mouth, but Brendan took it from him. "I can *feed* myself. I just can't *cut.*"

"Sorry," Henry said again. The fork in Brendan's fist made its wavering, halting way to Brendan's mouth. Brendan licked a tiny bit of filling from the edge and then lowered his hand to his chest. "Canned apples," he said thoughtfully. He seemed to be chewing that bit of filling, actually mashing the drop around in his mouth before struggling to swallow it. The brace hid his Adam's apple, but Henry could see the muscles working under his chin.

Brendan lowered the fork to the tray and then below it, into his lap. He fixed Henry's eyes with his and said, "Remember the food your grandmother used to cook? When I was a novice, I used to dream about her roast pork and her steak and onions and her tomatoes fried in bacon grease. I was so hungry there, at first. All of us were."

Brendan's hands had been moving quietly as he spoke; Henry hadn't seen him swallow anything, but somehow half the pie was gone. Henry thought of the dreams he had of Kitty's food, the nights he'd wandered around the kitchen while she was off at work or at a meeting. The refrigerator had been full of food and so had all the cupboards, but he hadn't known how to cook any of it and he'd prowled helplessly, salivating, longing for someone to transform those vegetables and cool slabs of meat and containers of cream and butter and stock into something edible. Sometimes Lise or Delia had taken pity on him and made him dinner, but more often they'd shown him the stove, the pots and pans and cookbooks and said, "Here's everything you need." They didn't seem to understand that he could do nothing with those tools.

"Why did you leave home?" he asked his uncle. He did remember Gran's food; she'd been a good cook, although not as good as his mother. "Why did you go in?" He couldn't imagine why anyone would go to a place with no food, no freedom, no women.

"When we were kids," Brendan said, "your father and I used to walk over the ridge near our place and watch the monks working in the fields below us. All those men in long robes, planting and hoeing, never saying anything—I liked the quiet, I think. I liked the peace. And sometimes we'd stand outside the enclosure walls and listen to them chanting in choir, and I loved that. After the first time I visited there, something happened to me—I can't explain it. I just knew it was where I wanted to be. Your father thought I was crazy. But your grandmother was pleased. She would have liked a priest in the family, but this was close enough."

"That's hard to imagine. Her being pleased about anything."

"You only knew her after," Brendan said quietly. "Losing your father really broke her. And to have that come on top of losing her home and all her friends and everyone she'd ever known—she wasn't sad like that when I was growing up. Neither was your grandfather."

Henry thought of the briefcase he'd taken from Kitty's, which was stuffed with all of Da's newspaper clippings. Da had saved everything he could find about the Paradise Valley and the Stillwater Reservoir, from the first hearings through the River Acts legislation and every step after that.

"Gran and Da used to sit me and Wiloma down and make us look at all this old stuff," Henry said. "They had programs from the last school graduations. Pictures they'd clipped from the papers, of the building, the evacuations, the engineers and the work crews—Wiloma and I thought they were crazy."

"Maybe a little crazy," Brendan agreed. "They'd been through a lot. We didn't believe it was going to happen, you know. None of us did."

Henry thought about his grandparents, old and sour and gray. Then he thought about the empty houses of Coreopsis Heights. His grandparents had been dispossessed in the same way, expelled, cast out. He tried to imagine himself in Da's position, his real home, and not an extra house, taken over not by strangers but by water. His whole life uprooted and one of his daughters dead. His stomach heaved and he pushed the thought away. "So where are we going?" he asked Brendan. "Really, I mean."

Brendan's plate was empty. "I'm not sure," he said. "Wherever we want. The dam, I guess—I've never seen it.

And we'll try and find my land, and after that we'll see. We'll do whatever we feel like doing."

"You think the cabin's still there? On the part that used to belong to my father?"

"Hard to say. Your grandfather sold that thirty years ago."

Mirella came by with coffee and hovered as if she wanted to talk, but this time Henry had no eyes for her. He was remembering his mother in that cabin, pregnant with Wiloma when she heard the news of Pearl Harbor, still pregnant when her husband went off to the Pacific, then nursing Wiloma while she listened to war news on the radio. She kept a picture pinned over the rocking chair, and he could just remember how she'd held Wiloma in her arms and sat him on the stool at her feet, pointing to the picture and saying, "See Mommy? See Daddy? That's us, at the Farewell Ball."

That was the picture he'd tossed in the van, the one he'd taken from Kitty's closet and glimpsed again when he'd reached into his box for his cap. His mother had told him the story of the ball again and again while his father was away, and his father had told it when he'd returned, and his grandparents had repeated it later. The night had been warm, his mother had said; an April night in 1938. The forsythia was blooming. The valley was partly torn up by then, the dead exhumed and moved and half the living vanished. The huge dam was almost done and the pipes that would carry the water to Boston had all been laid. The Water Commission had closed the post office, the Grange Hall, the churches and the schools; they'd torn down the big hotel and told the farmers not to plant any crops. The fields were weedy and rough.

Mirella was chatting with Brendan now, but Henry ignored her. *We dressed up,* his mother had said. *We wore black; we knew we had to move by June.* They had walked quietly, in twos and threes, to the Nipmuck Town Hall where the firemen were hosting the ball. A thousand people came, maybe more, and they danced in dazed circles and drank. When midnight came, the band played "Auld Lang Syne" and the people wept. The towns were dissolved a minute after midnight, by order of the governor, but people danced on in that ghostly place.

Your father was so handsome, his mother had said. *So strong.* She'd told him how many of the men, Henry's father among them, had worked clearing brush or digging up graves or driving trucks and dozers for the Commission. It was the Depression, his mother had said. No one had blamed them for taking the work. Henry had been two when his father was called up, and he couldn't remember that—his first memories of his father came from after the war, when he'd returned to them pale and bony and shaken. He tried to picture his father strong-armed, gathering brush and burning it for the engineers. He tried to picture his tanned face, his bold eyes, the way he'd walked up to Margaret Kelso at the Farewell Ball and whispered into her ear.

The old people had gathered in corners and grown sentimental—that was the part Da and Gran remembered, the part they'd always told him about, but he was more interested in the secret part his mother hinted at. *Your father took me outside,* she'd said. *All the people our age were having a party of their own.* In the woods beyond the common they'd built a fire; they'd burned their high-school diplomas, their report cards, the programs and certificates their parents had saved. They drank whiskey the older boys had brought—his father had told him that. They danced their own dances. *We made you that night,* his mother had said, although it had been years before he'd understood what she'd meant and he'd had to imagine the details for himself after she was dead. How they went into the bushes in pairs and emerged owl-eyed, hours later; how they went somewhere, and his mother got pregnant, and later she and his father married.

A few weeks after the ball, Da and Gran had left the valley and headed for Coreopsis. Frank junior had stayed behind with Margaret and built a cabin on a hill just outside the reservoir, on the piece of land Da had bought years ago for timber. The engineers went to work like ants, razing the remaining buildings so that nothing would contaminate the reservoir. *The water had to be clean,* his mother had said. *For the people in Boston.* That was why they'd dug up the cemeteries and moved the bodies; that was why they'd crushed the houses and carted the pieces away, why they'd burned the stubble in the fields. When the hurricane came in September, the wind found nothing to take but trees; afterward, his mother said, the valley looked as if it had been bombed. His father had helped bulldoze the remaining trees and had stripped the hills until they were bare except for the green crests that were supposed to turn into islands. Below these crests, which marked the waterline, the valley was shaved like a skull.

Henry couldn't remember that sight, but he remembered the waters rising after his father had left for the war. His mother had brought him and Wiloma down the hill weekly, pointing out the slow, inexorable spread of water building up behind the dam. She'd meant, Henry knew, for them to see the horror of it, but he'd been five then, six, seven, and he'd never seen the valley when it had held people and buildings. He'd seen scarred land, rubble, desolation, and the water that rose over the ugliness had seemed like a benediction. It had spread, smooth and pure and serene, until it reached the line where the trees still grew. Then it stopped. It looked like a lake. He had wanted to swim in it, but swimming was forbidden.

He shook his head, wanting to clear it. He hardly ever thought about those times or about his parents, and he wondered how much more of this his journey with Brendan would stir up. Mirella was still talking to Brendan, and he tried to focus on her but found that his vision of her trailer had gone cold. She was telling Brendan about her kids—she had three of them, he'd been right. She said, "My oldest, Angeline, she wants to be a dancer. I made her this tutu last month, for her recital. . . . You have kids?"

Brendan blinked at her. "Me? I'm a bachelor."

She turned to Henry. "What about you?"

He thought of Lise and Delia and his heart skipped a beat. "Six," he said evenly, as if the extras were insurance.

"Hell," she said, and then laughed. "*Six*—why didn't you just shoot yourself and get it over with?"

Henry rose and stood behind Brendan's chair. "Nice meeting you. We have to go."

"Stop by again if you're passing through. What's your name?"

"Jack Pomeroy," Henry said, adopting the name of his parents' hometown. "This is my father."

"Does he have a name?"

"Ambrose," Brendan said, which Henry admired. Not quite a lie, nothing so flamboyant as his own, yet good enough to keep her from knowing them. He wasn't sure why he'd lied to her, or why Brendan had played along.

They left her touching her red curls and returned to the van, where they found Bongo standing in the driver's seat with his face mashed against the window. Henry settled Brendan and Bongo in the back and then watched as Brendan took a napkin out of his pocket and slipped something from it to Bongo. Bongo gobbled it hastily.

"A little pie," Brendan explained. "I saved him a bit, for a treat. He's probably hungry."

Henry was pretty sure the napkin had held the whole piece of pie, square piled on sticky square. He moved the box holding the things he'd taken from Kitty's from the back of the van to the empty seat beside him, and he shifted the picture of his parents from the side to the top of the box, where he could see it. Then Brendan hiccuped and they drove off.

14

SIT DOWN," WALDO SAID. "TELL ME AGAIN."

And Wiloma, after a cleansing breath, did. She explained what the administrator from St. Benedict's had said, she explained her theories. Theory, now—the set of possibilities she'd explored over the phone with Wendy had shrunk to one when Waldo had appeared at her door. "Wendy called me at work," he'd said. "Wendy was all upset."

Which could mean only one thing, as far as Wiloma was concerned: Wendy was too sensible to worry without a reason, and so her own darkest fears about Henry and Brendan must be true.

Change the belief, she told herself, and you change the situation. Her Manual was explicit—error is created by wrong thought, error *is* wrong thought. She had never said to herself, "My uncle has cancer," but now she said, out loud to Waldo, "Henry has kidnapped him." The words came out like a sneeze, with a similar sense of relief, and were immediately followed by waves of guilt. She'd said it; she'd thought it. If it was true, it was partly her fault.

"I don't know," said Waldo. He paced across the smooth blue carpet, looking sleek and prosperous. His pants were neatly cuffed and his feet were shod in expensive walking shoes. His hair looked perfect from a distance. Only when he drew very close could she see the delicate grid of plugs across the top of his scalp. "That doesn't sound like Brendan," he said. "Brendan's no pushover."

Wiloma told him what the administrator had said the second time he called. "Someone saw them in Brendan's room. Putting some stuff in a plastic bag. Someone else saw them leave the building together. And after the alert went out, a policeman radioed in from Irondequoit and said he'd seen a St. Benedict's van earlier at the 7-Eleven."

"Irondequoit?"

"That's what he told me."

Waldo adjusted the cuff of his shirt. "So maybe they *did* borrow the van. But maybe they're just headed for the lake, or the park—I don't know. Did you call Kitty?"

"Why would I call her?"

"Irondequoit," Waldo said. "Maybe Brendan wanted to see her, and he asked Henry to take him over there for a visit. Brendan was always fond of her. And I don't think he's seen her in years."

"Oh, *please,*" Wiloma said. She'd come to dislike her sister-in-law immensely since Kitty's transformation. Acting all of a sudden as if the years she'd stayed at home raising her daughters had been hateful, worthless; as if she thought Wiloma wouldn't remember the lazy, laughing afternoons the two of them had shared with all four children. Kitty had been terrific with Lise and Delia and with Wendy and Win as well. But now she said those years had been like being in jail. She'd given up doing "women's work," she said. No more cooking, cleaning, making of parties, no sending of birthday cards or presents. No visiting her husband's aged uncle when her husband was too busy to go himself. That was what had annoyed Wiloma most: that Kitty had stopped visiting Brendan.

"Why would he go see her?" Wiloma asked. "When he could come here?"

Waldo shrugged and picked up the phone. "I'll just check."

Wiloma listened as Waldo casually asked Kitty if she'd seen Henry recently. Something about the apartment, he said, lying smoothly. The ceiling was leaking, he'd scheduled a carpenter, he needed to let Henry know and hadn't been able to reach him. She *had* seen him? Wiloma watched the color seep from Waldo's even tan as he responded to something Kitty was saying.

"Uh-huh, uh-huh, uh-huh," Waldo said. "I know. . . . Uh-huh. I understand." This went on for minutes; apparently Kitty was angry. Waldo turned his back and Wiloma studied the neat curves of his legs. He looked wonderful again, his ex–football player's body only slightly softened. He worked out, Wendy had told her. He went to the gym three times a week. He did this, Wiloma knew, for Sarah, who was only thirty-four—this, and the clothes and the funky shoes, the hair transplants, the sunlamp tan. He'd been balding and overweight when he'd belonged to Wiloma.

"Shit," Waldo said when he hung up the phone. "That *was* them in that van—they showed up at Kitty's a couple of hours ago. She says Henry's in some kind of weird mood—he took a bunch of old stuff from their closet, and he tried to borrow some money from her. She says he said he was bringing Brendan over here for dinner."

"Not likely."

"No," Waldo agreed. "Kitty says they took her dog when they left. Bongo."

"Bongo's his dog, really. Not hers."

Waldo waved his hands in the air. "His dog, her dog—but if they went to see Kitty, maybe there's nothing more to this than a day trip. A little jaunt. Maybe Brendan just wanted a few hours off. Or maybe Henry got it into his head to see Kitty, and he used Brendan as some sort of shield—you know how screwed up they are. She won't even talk to Henry half the time. Not that I blame her—I'm surprised his girls are even speaking to him."

"They're not," Wiloma said. "At least that's what I hear from Wendy."

"Serves him right," Waldo said, but then he winced as if thinking how narrowly he'd escaped the same fate. The difference was money, Wiloma thought: money, which Waldo had by the generous handful and Henry had lost. Waldo's money—and my own weakness, she thought, remembering the months before her Healing—had been enough to reconstitute his doubled family into a workable shape. She tried not to think about what her breakdown and absence had done to her children, or what their lives had been like while they lived with Waldo. Waldo had changed them, in ways she didn't always like, but he'd held the surface of their lives together and thought he was a hero because of that. He shared many of Henry's faults but found Henry contemptible.

"Did Kitty call St. Benedict's?" she asked.

"No. She thought they had permission to take the van. I didn't tell her anything different."

Wiloma stared at the andromeda outside and mulled over a vision of Brendan and Henry at Kitty's house. They had gone there at Brendan's request, they had had tea; they were going to take a drive by the lake and then head back to the Home. Could that be true? she wondered. No. Henry was trying to keep Brendan away from her and the Church. She turned to Waldo, who was watching her closely.

"I don't know why they went to Kitty's," she said carefully. "Some sort of detour, maybe. Or maybe they meant to confuse us. But I know they're headed for Massachusetts. I can feel it. Henry's so desperate, that's just what he'd do. He ruined Da's place in Coreopsis, and now he wants to ruin this."

She paused. Waldo knew she'd been planning to bring Brendan home but he didn't know why, and she wondered for a minute if she should tell him about Christine. She decided against it. Waldo said, "I think you're right. Henry may have talked him into the trip somehow—he's so greedy, he wants that land so bad. I know what he's thinking. He wants your half, too."

Not like you, she thought. Not much. She was aware that Waldo's presence, and his apparent concern, had more to do with Brendan's land than with worry over either her or Brendan. She didn't care what happened to the land; it was only land, and no concern of hers. But she didn't mind using it as a lever to move Waldo. "You think?" she said.

"I wouldn't put it past him."

And then Wiloma said what had come into her mind just that minute, which she recognized immediately as right. "I'm going to go after them. They've only got a couple of hours start, maybe less—I could be there in six or seven hours."

"That's crazy," Waldo said, as she had known he would. "You'll never find them. You don't know where they're headed, and you'll have to stay overnight somewhere."

"I'll find them," she said serenely. If I can think it, she told herself, it must be so. If I need help, help will appear. She looked at Waldo steadily, willing him to step into her silence and offer what was needed. Waldo said, "Hang on a minute. I think I have something in the car."

He strode off, leaving her to think about her uncle. Brendan had meant nothing to her when she was a child; she would have sworn that on her parents' graves, had she known where to find them. He'd been sick and crippled and useless and quiet, a bag of bones with a big head and wispy hair, another old person brought into a house already tilted so far toward old that Wiloma had felt like a fern struggling to grow in a forest of ancient oaks. Someone else to look after. Someone else to wait on. His hands had been covered with blue veins and his reminiscences of China had been as dull as Da's reservoir tales. She couldn't believe Henry had listened to him. She'd never believed Henry's affection for him was sincere.

But then Gran had died, and Brendan had moved to St. Benedict's, and Henry had run off with Kitty and left her alone with Da. And during Da's long illness, when she'd been so isolated, she'd begun to realize how she'd leaned on her uncle without knowing it. The tray she'd fixed for him each afternoon, when she'd returned from the school where she still felt like an outsider—that had anchored her, given her a point around which her days had revolved. Herbal tea, three arrowroot biscuits, a teaspoonful of jam. While she helped him hold his cup and dab jam on his biscuits, he had asked her to describe her day to him.

He was bored, he said. He was stuck in the house and never saw anything. She'd be helping if she told him the details of her day: anything, any small stories. What the weather was like, what her teachers had said, what had happened on the bus. She had sighed but described these things dutifully, shaping each day's events into anecdotes that filled an hour, always thinking she was doing him a favor and wishing she could spend that hour somewhere else, never understanding how much the knowledge that she had to pay attention enough to fill that hour had helped make her days bearable.

Only after her marriage and Wendy's birth had she started to visit him at the nursing home. She'd gone out of a sense of duty, and from a desire to show off her child: *Here,* she'd wanted to say. *Look at this. I did this.* His hands were too twisted to hold Wendy properly, but he'd found a way to rest his elbows on his lap and bend his arms until he could cradle Wendy between his forearms and his chest. "She's beautiful," he'd said. "A regular princess. When your father was born, his eyes looked just like that."

His pleasure had been so genuine that she'd begun to visit him regularly. Before long, she'd found herself storing up the events of her weeks to tell him each Sunday. He had listened to all her ups and downs—Win's and Wendy's childhood illnesses, money problems, broken plumbing; then Waldo's defection, her own struggles, her salvation by the Church. He never passed judgment on anything. He was always glad to see her. He was the only person left in the world who could link her children to her dead parents, and it was impossible to let him go.

Waldo returned with a sheaf of maps; the same ones, she suspected, that he'd shown Wendy and Win. "Where would they go?" he asked. "If they were going someplace in particular."

"Hard to say," she answered. "The land Uncle Brendan told me about, where our cabin used to be—that's outside the watershed altogether, it's in a different town now. But there were some dirt roads that led from there into the reservoir lands, and there was a point that my mother used to bring me and Henry to."

She paused; she hadn't thought about this in years. "The East Pomeroy Common. Or what was left of it—a road lined with cellar holes, some old stone walls, paths that broke off at the water's edge. The reservoir was almost filled by the time my father came back from the war, and he used to take me and Henry down there and try to get us to imagine what his village had looked like. Then he'd start drinking. Then he'd cry."

Waldo touched her elbow with his hand. "How old were you?"

"Five," she said. "Maybe six. Something like that." His fingers sent sharp jets of warmth up her arms and she moved her elbow away.

"Is that a place your uncle would know?"

"I don't think so. I remember Da telling me how they were just beginning to build the dam when Uncle Brendan left for China. He was gone for five or six years before they began to fill the reservoir. And then—I don't know, this is so hard to piece together. We left after the accident, and then Uncle Brendan came back from China a few years later, but he didn't come home—he went to Canada, to some other abbey

there. I think that's what he told us. I don't think he ever
saw the water."

Waldo unrolled one of his maps. "Where are you talking
about?"

Wiloma studied the long, mulberry-leaf shape of the reservoir, and then she brought her finger down on a point on the
northeast shore. "Somewhere around here," she said. "This
point—you see how they have the old dirt roads still marked,
and the gates leading into the state land? We used to go
through one of them, maybe this one." She traced a tentative
path with her finger around a knob that dented the water's
boundary. "Here?" She hesitated and looked at the map
again. The edges of the reservoir were so pocked with points
and coves that she wasn't sure she could tell one from
another.

Waldo unrolled another map, slick and shiny and gray:
some kind of photocopy. It was dated 1940, two years before
her birth. "Does this help?" he said.

She looked at it and then looked again; a map from a
dream. There was no reservoir on this map, no water at all
but a few small ponds and the branches of the Paradise River,
winding through Winsor and Nipmuck and Stillwater and
Pomeroy, East Pomeroy and Lizzie Springs. Her father, and
then her grandfather, had drilled those lost names into her
head.

Waldo stared blandly back at her. She wondered where he
had gotten that map, and she found it unpleasant that he
should know more than she did about the place of her birth.
She reminded herself that her dealings with him had always
required a caution foreign to her. "I can't tell," she said,
although she thought she recognized the point on this older
map.

"But if you saw it, wouldn't you recognize it? And don't
you think Henry might remember it?"

"He might," she agreed. "Better than I do—he was older.
He might bring Uncle Brendan there."

He might; he might do anything. And the more she thought about it, the more reasonable it seemed. He'd bring Brendan right to that spit of land, and there—her imagination failed her, but she didn't care. Henry had stolen Brendan and she was off to rescue him, and with these maps she knew she could track them down.

"Can I take these?" she said. "I'll bring them back."

"I have a better idea. Why don't you let me come with you? I could help with the driving—we could take my Saab, instead of your old clunker. And if Henry gives you a hard time, I'd be there to help."

Waldo's face was smooth as a hazelnut. She knew he was interested in her uncle's land, not in her uncle, not in her, but despite that she felt a great surge of exhilaration and hope. Overnight, she thought. Just me and Waldo; no Sarah, no kids. He might think he was joining her for one reason but that reason might change into another: if they were alone together all day and all night, and if she thought clearly and didn't nag about money or harp about her church, and if he left just a crack in his mind open, a channel through which she might seep—anything might happen. Anything. And even if nothing changed, even if he was only civil, only kind, he was good with maps and directions and he had a nose like a bloodhound's. He thought like Henry; he'd be able to shadow Henry's trail and that would lead her to Brendan.

"That would be lovely," she said. "If you wouldn't mind." He smiled and she smiled back, letting him think he had tricked her.

15

THE NOTE WAS STUCK TO THE REFRIGERATOR WITH A MAGNET shaped like a butterfly.

"Your father and I," Wendy read—*your father and I?* When was the last time her parents had linked themselves like that?—"have gone to Massachusetts. We think that's where Henry took Uncle Brendan. We'll be home sometime tomorrow. Make sure Win takes a shower when he gets back from soccer. There's broccoli casserole in the fridge for your dinner. I want you both to stay in tonight—I know I said Win could go to that party, but I don't want him out while I'm away. You take care of him and be a good girl. I'll call."

Wendy looked at her watch. Five-thirty—they couldn't have been gone for more than an hour. How could they have gone without calling her first? She kicked the corner of the refrigerator and swore under her breath, cursing not only her parents but herself. If she hadn't called her father, if she'd kept her worries to herself and gritted her teeth and told her mother not to worry, this never would have happened.

Her mother's car was still in the driveway, which must mean they'd gone off in her father's fancy Saab. The two of them trapped in there for hours, sniping at each other—it was ridiculous, it was bizarre. They couldn't have coffee together without fighting. They were still in and out of court all the time: Wiloma wanted the deed to the house and Waldo refused, claiming she'd only donate it to the Church. Wiloma wanted more child support and money for college tuition; Waldo said she'd give away whatever he sent. Which was true, Wendy knew: her mother gave half of whatever she had to the Church, and the family-court judge always ended up agreeing with her father. He paid the mortgage and their medical bills, bought them clothes and books and bikes, but he never sent money and they had to ask him, item by item, for the things they needed. He never said no, but Wendy found the process humiliating. Why should her mother have to ask for gutters, or Win ask for running shoes? Why should she have to ask for a pin or a purse? The best thing about her job was the privacy it bought; she had fifty dollars in her pocket right now, which no one knew about.

Somewhere along the Thruway, she knew, her mother would be accusing her father of being stingy, as if she'd never given him reason to think she did odd things with his money. Her father would be accusing her mother of being obsessed with the Church, as if he'd never abandoned her and driven her to it. They'd be arguing as if all the years they'd spent together had never existed, and there was nothing she could do about any of it except wonder why her father had bought into her mother's delusions, and why Sarah had let him go, and why none of them could seem to see that whatever Grunkie was up to was his own business. She picked up the phone and called her cousin Delia.

She didn't call Delia at her dorm in Syracuse, where Delia was supposed to be; she knew that, although Delia was enrolled in summer school there, she secretly took the bus back to Rochester almost every weekend. Delia had a boyfriend named Roy, whom she'd been seeing since her senior year in high school and whom her family hated. Roy worked in a furniture warehouse, loading delivery trucks; he'd been on his own since he was seventeen. He had a beat-up car and a ponytail, an Irish setter and a worn mattress tossed on a floor littered with cans and clothes. Delia had told her family that she and Roy split up when she left for college.

Only Wendy, who had bumped into the two of them at the lake one Sunday afternoon, knew that Delia had managed to keep seeing Roy these past two years. In the cottage Roy shared with his friends, on a street behind the row of shops and bars that fronted on the beach, Delia and Roy had taken Wendy into their confidence. Their secret affair seemed romantic to her, and sometimes, when her own life seemed particularly empty, she visited them just to remind herself of what might be possible if she ever escaped.

Roy answered the phone and said that Delia was in the shower. Wendy imagined that rusty metal stall with the tattered curtain and the stained walls and was impressed by Delia's devotion. "You want me to have her call you back?" Roy asked.

"I'll hang on," she said, and they chatted for a few minutes. Roy's parents had, like Wendy's, been divorced for years. When Delia had raged and cried over her family's disintegration, Wendy and Roy had comforted Delia together and smiled at each other ruefully. Wendy had thought, but not said, that Delia was acting like a child.

"Here she is," Roy said, and then Wendy heard her cousin's voice.

"What's up?" Delia asked. "You want to come over here tonight? We can go out, maybe hear a little music . . ."

"I can't. My mother went away overnight and I have to watch Win." Wendy didn't explain what had happened; she could hardly sort it out herself and figured she'd tell Delia the details later. "I was wondering if maybe you guys wanted to come over here. I can't stand sitting around all night by myself."

"No problem," Delia said.

Wendy hung up and then went to change her clothes. She hated the neat things her father and Sarah had bought her, but she knew why she wore them: these were the clothes that had said, *I won't cause any more trouble, I promise,* when her mother had returned from the Healing Center. They'd said, *Dad and Sarah don't have to guard me anymore. I can make a new life, I can behave,* but what they said to her now was, *asleep.* She was seized with a craving for the outfits she used to patch together during the years when she'd run wild. Men's suit jackets and overcoats, rhinestone pins and feathered hats, black high-tops and torn long underwear flirting beneath skirts so short they were almost belts—she wanted her old clothes back. She wanted her old life. She wanted the time before her mother had caught them at their party and then cracked, and the minute before she'd made the mistake of calling her father this afternoon.

She dug out a pair of jeans, a clean shirt, and the list of rules she'd folded between her sweaters. The list began:

1. I will stop stealing
2. I will stop lying
3. I will learn something useful
4. I will make some friends

But there was no point in reading on, she'd already broken the first two rules. On her way out of her basement office, her hands had almost absentmindedly brushed the two rag dolls on her desk into the embroidered sack she used as a purse. She was furious that she'd taken them, and she dreaded the lies she'd have to tell to protect herself. She comforted herself with the thought that the rules were for her other life, her real life, which could not begin until she got away.

Everything was spoiled, she thought, as she dressed and then tucked the list back into her closet. Grunkie was missing, her mother was crazy, her father was involved. Her father was involved because of her. She flopped down on the bed her father had made her, a raised, carpeted platform with a hollow in which her mattress rested. The surface of the mattress was level with the surface of the platform; sleeping there was as safe as sleeping on the floor. Her father had made this for her because, years ago, she had so much feared falling out of bed that she sometimes fell. She'd never had the heart to tell him that now she longed for a proper bed with legs.

Below her she heard the kitchen door crash, and when she went downstairs she found Win bouncing up and down on his toes in front of the refrigerator, reading their mother's note as the yellow plugs of his radio poured music into his ears. "Hey," she said, but he couldn't hear her. "Win!" she said more loudly.

He plucked the note from the refrigerator and turned to her, slipping the headset down until it hung like a collar around his neck. "Take care of Win?" he said. "What is this? You think I'm ten? What's going on?"

Wendy tried to bring him up to date. "Grunkie took off. Or something." She explained about the phone calls—the administrator's to their mother, their mother's to her, hers to their father—and watched as Win's face changed from disbelief to disgust. They hardly talked at all anymore. Since their father and Sarah had cleaned them up and remade them, they'd been strangers to each other. They never discussed what they used to do; they never spent time alone together. Win was wrapped in a web of lies at least as dense as hers, and when he looked at her now his eyes shot off to the sides.

"So they went chasing after him? Why don't they give the old guy a break?"

"I don't know," Wendy said. "Mom's real worried about him—you know that healer of hers is supposed to start on him tomorrow. She sounded like she was losing it again. I shouldn't have called Dad, but I thought he'd just talk to her or something—calm her down. You know. I didn't expect him to come over here. And I don't know how she talked him into driving her to Massachusetts."

Win opened the refrigerator door and stuck his head inside. "She threw a fit," he said. His voice was muffled by the metal. "That's how. Just like she always does. Except she did it in front of him instead of us."

Wendy came up behind him and peered into the coolness. Low-fat milk, some old pears, bread, cottage cheese, carrots. Broccoli casserole as promised, the stems swimming milkily under a scattering of whole-wheat crumbs. Their mother skimped on the groceries; that was one of the ways she tricked their father. She sent his food allowance to the Church and fed them all on the slim checks she got from teaching workshops to the new recruits. "Mom thinks Uncle Henry kidnapped Grunkie," Wendy said over Win's shoulder.

"Mom thinks the world is out to get her," Win said. "Mom thinks everyone is as crazy as her, and that if she doesn't watch everyone all the time, they'll nut out on her when her back is turned. She *makes* people crazy."

He slammed the refrigerator door. "There's nothing to eat. You want to order a pizza?" He had a girlfriend, Wendy knew. When their mother went out, he slid a dark-eyed girl a year younger than him into his room. She was almost sure they were sleeping together. Win and his girl, like Delia and Roy, meeting secretly but at least meeting. Whereas she—and Lise, Lise was always lonely and always complaining about it—had been left with no one. She wondered if this meant that she and Lise were somehow alike. It was Delia she wanted to mimic, Delia with her thick, red-gold hair and her arm draped around Roy's waist.

"Pepperoni," Wendy said. "And sausage." At least she could eat.

"Great. Then you can make sure I take a shower. Then you can *watch* me."

"She didn't mean it that way."

"The hell she didn't. She wants you to sit in a chair and stare at me all goggle-eyed, the way she does—*Are you happy? Are you well?*" The way he mimicked their mother's voice was uncanny. "I swear. I swear—I'm going to that party."

"Don't," Wendy said before she thought about it. "Couldn't you stay in tonight? Keep me company? Delia's coming over later with a friend of hers—you could have some people over too, if you want. I'd feel better if you were around."

Win made a face. "Guilt, guilt, guilt—you sound just like Mom. *Oh, take care of me, I need you.*"

"I'm sorry. Do what you want. But I know she'll call, and if you're not here, I'll have to lie."

"And we wouldn't want that," Win said. "Would we? Not from us, the truthful twosome."

Wendy laughed despite herself and Win looked into her eyes for the first time in ages. "You'll be out of here in three months. I'm stuck for another year and a half. You want to take me with you?"

"I would if I could." Their shared past hung in the room like a mist. "When we're twenty-five," she said, "this will all seem funny. We'll be able to laugh about it."

Win picked up the phone and dialed the pizza parlor. "I won't remember it by then," he said. "I'm not planning on remembering any of this. When I'm twenty-five, I'm going to be in another country."

16

F ROM THE "LETTERS TO THE EDITOR" OF THE *PARADISE VALLEY Daily Transcript:*

July 6, 1927
Dear Sirs:

 Our fate has been sealed with the passage of the Paradise River Acts. Although we have been left up in the air as to when we must leave our beloved valley, and what parts of the valley we must leave, and how we shall be compensated for the loss of our land, our homes, our livelihoods, and everything we hold dear—leave we surely must. But we need not leave yet.

 Already, many residents have requested real estate appraisals from the field offices of the Commission. Many, in fact, have left the valley; at the last Nipmuck town meeting, it was reported that 200 residents had already departed, and that those remaining were finding the tax burden intolerable. Two of the summer camps in Pomeroy have closed. The Merri-weather School and the Sweet Hill Hotel have shut their doors. Stores are leaving all of our valley towns. Can we not maintain at least some semblance of dignity, some shadow of our former lives? The Commission assures us that it will be some years before the start of serious construction, and many more years before construction is complete. By leaving now, by collapsing and admitting defeat, we only aid and abet the destructive plans of our occupiers. Should we not stay here as long as we can, and live what remains of our cherished lives here as fully and richly as we can? Each family that leaves now tears a permanent hole in the web of our community life. No new neighbors will come to replace those lost: we are the last people who will live here, and we must band together. Let us leave only when we must. Let us leave together, at the end—not piecemeal, in panic and terror, at the beginning.

Frank B. Auberon, Sr.
Pomeroy

Part III

The Country of the Young

17

HENRY AND BRENDAN DROVE EAST ALONG THE FINGER LAKES, past brick buildings with flat roofs, white churches, stone Masonic Halls, gas stations, red lights, convenience stores. Brendan drank the sights in eagerly. The towns looked much as they had in 1954, when he'd traveled by bus from Rhode Island to Coreopsis, but the spaces in between the towns had changed. Low-roofed shopping centers and garden stores dotted what had once been stretches of field.

They passed an old woman in Waterloo scattering bread to some pigeons, and a row of swallows perched on the telephone wires in Cayuga. The sun caused complex patterns of shadow on a yard in La Fayette. In Cazenovia, a dog with brown eyes caught sight of Bongo and chased the van wildly for a while. Henry was silent, his face hidden in the shadow of his Red Wings cap. *Look,* Brendan wanted to say. *Here. Look at all this.* But instead he let Henry drive unmolested.

The van broke down south of Herkimer, within sight of

another small town. There was a noise, first, which pulled Brendan's eyes from the window; then there was smoke. Then Henry said, "Damn—the fan belt," and then, "Hell. The power steering just went." While Brendan watched, helpless but interested, Henry wrestled the van to the side of the road and then coaxed it into the parking lot of a service station next to a church.

Brendan let out his breath, aware only then that he'd been holding it. "Lucky for us," he said.

"Lucky?"

"That it happened here."

Henry shook his head, and when he hopped out of the van, it appeared that they were not so lucky after all. Quarter past six on a Saturday night—the station had just closed and there was no one around except for a boy with a lazy eye and a gap between his front teeth. Brendan opened his window as Henry approached the boy.

"Nope," Brendan heard the boy say. "Can't help you. All the mechanics are gone."

"Is there someone I can call?" Henry asked.

"The other stations are all closed. Everyone's gone home. I guess you'll have to wait until Monday."

"Monday? What are we supposed to do until then?" Henry laid his hand on the boy's shoulder and eased him toward the van. "Look at this," he said as he opened the side door. Brendan smiled down at the boy and said hello.

"This is my uncle," Henry told the boy. "He's eighty. He's sick. Can't you just look under the hood?"

Brendan did what he could to help. He let his hands curl into claws and his head loll forward against his brace. He wiped his smile away and let his mouth fall open, trying to look eighty, ninety, on his last legs. The boy was visibly impressed. Behind him, Henry shook his head and smiled.

"Wouldn't do any good for me to look." The boy stepped back and almost bumped into Henry. "I just pump gas. But there's this guy my brother knows—he has a tow truck of his own. Maybe we could give him a call."

"Let's do that," Henry said.

The two of them vanished inside a darkened building, and when they returned Henry looked relieved. "Just wait here," Brendan heard the boy say. "Jackson'll be along—he'll take care of you. I gotta go."

He ran his hand through his long blond hair, and his eyes disappeared as the strands rose and separated and then fell back against his face. He snapped his neck with a gesture Brendan hadn't been able to make in years, which parted the curtain of hair and revealed his eyes again. Then he drove off in a low red car with enormous tires.

"Strange kid," Henry said, and Brendan turned to him. "What's going on?"

Henry climbed back into the van. "We wait, I guess. This guy said he'd come tow us to his shop—he's got a garage of his own, way out in the woods somewhere."

Twenty minutes later Jackson appeared. His hands were grimy and his teeth were bad; he poked under the hood and said, "I can't fix this here. Have to bring you back to my place. That all right?"

"Fine," Henry said wearily.

Henry rode in the truck with Jackson, but Brendan and Bongo stayed in the van, which was tilted up and suspended by a tow bar. Jackson blocked the wheels of Brendan's chair with the box Henry had taken from Kitty's house, and he promised to drive slowly. For miles, out of town and along a quiet road that ran beside a river and then rose up into wooded hills and turned to dirt, Brendan watched the world pass by on a mysterious slant. Bongo barked beside him, excited and confused.

It might feel like this when I die, Brendan thought. His soul might float above the earth, dipping and tilting so that things were skewed from their natural positions. He'd felt like a ghost for months already, parts of his body shutting down one by one until, as the pie he'd tried to eat earlier had reminded him, nothing was working but his head. The tumors inside him had grown until his throat closed like a door when he tried to swallow. He couldn't feel his legs at all; his hands and arms were his only intermittently. His lungs felt as solid as cheese—when he breathed, the air seemed to stop somewhere in his throat. He was solidifying, turning to stone, the organs and tubes that had once been hollow silting up. Sometimes it hurt, but mostly it didn't; he often felt better, in an odd way, than he had in years. His joints, which had once stabbed him with shooting pains, felt as if they'd been packed in sand. His stomach, once a sack of fire, was calm. He was only his head, only his eyes and ears—the wedge of sky that flew by his window was as soft and gold as the skin of an apricot. Letting go wouldn't be hard at all, he thought. The deadness would creep from his chest to his head and then his soul would slip out of his mouth. His brother's soul might have slipped away just that easily.

The inside of the old gray Plymouth rings with Frank junior's laughter. Margaret has just finished telling him a joke she heard at the dance, and Frankie says, "Olsen told you that?" and then reaches down to clasp the hand she has rested on his thigh. The rain pounds down on the roof of the car but inside they are warm and safe: finally, after all this time, almost at peace with their new lives. "We'll go for a picnic tomorrow," Frankie says. "Take the kids someplace nice." And they are busy planning what they'll bring when they come to the last curve on Boughten Hill. Frank turns the wheel easily, casually, but nothing happens; something in the steering mechanism has chosen this minute to break. They sail off the road without a pause and the wedges of night sky fly past their windows in the seconds before they meet the ground. Margaret is wearing a white dress and Frankie still has hold of her hand.

"Frankie," Brendan said out loud. The van made a broad circle and then stopped.

Henry let Bongo out and tied him to a tree, and Jackson lowered Brendan's chair. They were in a clearing, Brendan saw, a rough oval of dirt and grass surrounded by tangled trees. In the clearing sat a crumbling garage made of white-washed bricks, an assortment of broken cars and trucks, a huge stack of wood, and a mound of trash. Off to one side, some tattered lawn chairs surrounded a ring of stones capped with a metal grill.

"You all right, old man?" asked Jackson.

"I'm fine," Brendan said. "I enjoyed the ride."

They never felt it, he told himself. They were flying, and then it was over. He focused his eyes on Jackson's left hand and noticed a circle of white on his fourth finger, where a ring had once been. Dusk was closing in on the clearing and the trees were full of birds. An owl shrieked in the distance and then was still.

"It's nice of you to rescue us," Brendan said.

"Thank me if I fix it." Jackson parked Brendan on the grass near the lawn chairs and towed the van into the garage. Henry followed him, and Brendan watched the clouds of birds gather and swoop and settle down for the night. The light inside the garage glowed yellow against the darkening sky. He could hear the men talking softly, the clang and rattle of tools, the hiss and pop as a car of beer or soda was opened. He lowered his head to his chest and fell asleep thinking about his days in China, where he had been when his brother had died.

On a bitter winter's day in 1937, Father Vincent, his abbot in Massachusetts, had gathered the community together to break the news. They'd have a year, Father Vincent explained, no more, before the valley was flooded. They had to disperse; they had to decide, each of them, where they wanted to go. France, Kentucky, California; there were houses all over the world. Snow covered the fields and icicles hung from the roof of the church. Brendan's companions disappeared one by one as the snow began to melt. The witch hazel down by the pond exploded into silky gold tassels; the crocuses Brendan had planted flowered and the grape hyacinths pushed up their heads. Still he hadn't made a decision. "Brendan," Father Vincent said gently. "You have to choose." When the buds on the dogwoods began to swell, Brendan asked to be sent to China.

The Chinese foundations were shorthanded, he told his abbot. And he was homeless and in his prime. Where else could he be of more use? He looked out at the beautiful hand-laid walls and imagined them knocked to the ground.

"China?" Father Vincent had said.

"China," he'd replied. He'd said nothing about the sense of betrayal he'd felt when his prayers had failed to fend off the water, nor about his need to put half a world between his failure and himself. He had eschewed linear prayer in favor of a deep and loving contemplation of his surroundings, just as Father Vincent had taught him. Now his surroundings were about to disappear.

When the cherries and apples flowered, and the rhododendrons and his special azaleas, he packed his small bag and left the abbey. He crossed the United States by train, the Pacific by boat, the rugged hills of Inner Mongolia by foot and mule. The Japanese warships in the harbor startled him, as did the Japanese soldiers waiting on the wharf at Tientsin. The rough buildings of his new abbey, Our Lady of Consolation, startled him too and then pleased him. They were run-down, primitive; he could work on them forever and never fear that someone else might want them. No orchards, no flowers. His brothers were Belgian, Dutch, and French; the novices and postulants were all Chinese. He communicated with them in ragged Latin until he learned to speak Mandarin.

In the garden behind the refectory he helped raise millet and sorghum, potatoes and cabbage; he grew thin on the coarse food and dreamed of eggs, which were rare. The dormitory, unheated even in winter, was so cold that he slept in two sets of padded jackets and pants beneath his robe. In the hot weather, the mud-brick walls swarmed with lice and ticks. He was homesick, uncomfortable, sometimes frightened, but he told himself that these were the trials he was meant to endure, the tests he was meant to pass. In his heart, buried so deep he never saw it, was the dream that if he surmounted all this, he might return to the Paradise Valley and find his home miraculously restored.

He'd expected hardships, but he hadn't expected to find himself in the middle of a war. In Europe, war was a rumor and then it was real. In China, the war that seemed to have gone on forever just went on and on. Sometimes he could hardly keep track of who was fighting whom. The abbey lay between a Japanese garrison and a ridge held by Chinese Communist troops, and there were weeks when columns of one or both advanced and retreated across the valley, so close he could smell the guns. Japanese officers rested in the abbey's guesthouse after the battles; Communist soldiers demanded money and food and threatened to conscript the young brothers. Wounded soldiers from both sides took refuge in the chapel. He spoke all the time—he had to speak, to tend to the wounded, buy time, buy peace, buy food—and as his silence vanished, so did his ability to pray. Prayer was action, he'd once believed; a group of men gathered together might pray the world right. He prayed for the war to end, and bombs rained down on Pearl Harbor.

In the Japanese internment camp near the coast, where he and the European monks were taken, he shed the last remnants of his cloistered, contemplative life. The *Rules of the Camp for Enemy Nationals* supplanted the *Rule* of his Order; he lived in rooms packed with Protestant missionaries and their families, nuns and monks from other Orders, teachers, customs officers, Russian women, Dutch Lazarists, American businessmen. There was little to eat and no privacy. He kept himself busy nursing the sick and arranging lectures and teaching the children to read, and he tried to convince himself that he honored his vows by serving others. *Laborare est orare,* he reminded himself. To labor is to pray. At night he stood near an isolated section of fence and tossed the money and jewelry he'd gathered from the inmates up and over and into the hands of Chinese farmers, who tossed back forbidden food. Two dozen plums once arced back to him, one precious piece at a time.

He tried to build a life out of what he had at hand. *This is our way,* Father Vincent had once told him and the other postulants. *In this community, with this work, these people, these problems—our vow of stability means that we embrace life as we find it. We accept God's plan.* The abbey where Brendan had made that vow was gone, and he'd been torn from his adopted one, but he tried to see the camp as a new home. Rumors flew through the camp like moths: England was defeated, Russia crushed, Australia conquered by the Japanese. The rumors were so frequent and so often false that he ignored the ones following the first B-29s over the camp. The Japanese were abandoning China, he heard. They were taking the internees back to Japan with them. A Dutchman told him gloomily that they would all be murdered first.

Brendan was standing with a group of Belgian nuns when they heard about the bombs that had fallen on Hiroshima and Nagasaki. "There is no city," whispered the nun who'd heard the news from a guard. "The city is gone." A few days after that, six American soldiers parachuted into the dry field outside the fence, and then they were free. Just like that, the community Brendan had worked so hard to hold together dissolved. The internees scattered; Brendan and his brothers made their way back to Our Lady of Consolation just in time to see the abbot imprisoned and the community attacked.

One war was over, but the civil war had just begun and the abbey lay in an area held by Communist troops. Brendan watched the soldiers turn the peasants against the monks.

The monks were oppressors, the soldiers said. They had stolen the peasants' land. Brendan stood in front of an angry crowd and said, "Have we not shared every crop with you? Have we not fed you during famines?" But the peasants, encouraged by the soldiers, took the abbey's goats and grain and straw mattresses, the sacristy vessels and the firewood. They tore the leather covers off the books. They imprisoned the monks in the chapter room and held trials and meetings, beatings and interrogations. The abbey was gutted; the trials grew more serious. The abbot's head was crushed with rocks before Brendan's eyes. On a December day, after Brendan heard a rumor that Nationalist troops were on their way to rescue them, he and his brothers were marched away from the abbey and into the surrounding hills.

Those were the worst days, the days that had stayed with him for forty years and crippled his joints and burned the holes where his tumors now grew, but when he dreamed it was not so much about the march, or about the huts where they were beaten and starved, but about the slow, perilous journey back to Peking that he and a handful of survivors finally made.

There were only eleven of them. One night, they never knew how or why, the doors to their huts were opened and then abandoned. Emaciated and tattered and sick, he and his brothers had stepped out, looked at each other, and walked into the night. They hid by day and traveled in darkness, slinking through fields and eating rats and weeds while the abbey—they passed it, they saw the fire—burned to the ground and wolves and bugs ate the unburied bodies of those who had died on the march and been left behind. He saw things on that trip he could never describe; two more of his brothers died. By the time they reached Peking he could no longer talk.

He remained silent in the hospital there; silent during the endless travels that brought him to Hong Kong; silent during his ocean crossing. Silent on the train across the prairie, to the abbey in Manitoba that had offered to take him in. But there, in those cool, serene buildings where silence was once more expected and blessed, his silence had cracked when he tried to resume his old way of life. Among those gentle, orderly men, he was seized with a need to say what had happened to him.

He'd spent twelve years in China, thinking he'd never leave, and to end like that, like an animal—it had stripped him of everything. He led men into corners, interrupted them at work and prayer, broke into their meditations. "Listen to me," he said. "Let me tell you this." War, famine, pestilence, death. He broke the *Rule*, again and again; the abbot reprimanded him and still he could not control himself. The silence that had drawn him into his Order now seemed repellent, and when the abbot suggested he transfer to the new foundation in Rhode Island, he went without a fight. He thought he might have something in common with the flood of new postulants there, shell-shocked men returned from the same war in other places, but he found them even more withdrawn than the brothers in Manitoba. Crippled by then, heartbroken, he'd applied for dismissal from the Order and made his way back to what was left of the family he'd abandoned. His brother—his real brother, his blood brother—was already dead.

Near Jackson's garage, he dreamed of his nights in the Chinese wilderness. He dreamed of his silent trips. He dreamed of the days, in Manitoba and Rhode Island, when his hands had reached out for a belt or a sleeve and his mouth had moved, words had come out, but his companions had lowered their eyes as if he didn't exist. They'd looked through him as if he were dead. And they'd been right, he should have died and joined his martyred brothers. He'd had no business surviving. *I am a brother to dragons*, he dreamed. *And a companion to owls.* He was dead in his dream, a ghost in a misty cowl and robe.

When he woke, it was very dark. Light spilled from the

open garage, outlining Henry and Jackson; Jackson wiped his hands on a rag and lowered the hood of the van. "That ought to do it," Brendan heard him say. English words, an upstate accent. Cool, calm, quiet. His brothers had been dead for forty years and China was half a world away; he was not a monk and hadn't been for years. In the dim light his hands formed the signs for *bitter* and *blessing*.

"That's great," Henry said. "Lucky you had the parts."

They came out to Brendan then, past the light and into the darkness, where Brendan could hardly tell them apart. Solid men with spreading stomachs and thick, sturdy legs, they seemed to have forged a friendship over their wrenches and belts and valves. Brendan felt more insubstantial than ever.

"You guys hungry?" Jackson said. "I caught some bass this morning—I was going to throw them on the grill."

"That'd be great," Henry said. He squatted down until his face was level with Brendan's. "Are you awake? Would that be all right?"

"Fine," Brendan said. In his dream he had eaten no food—the yellow millet, the sorghum, the limp potatoes, had not crossed his lips, and he understood this to mean that he would not eat again. But he wanted to keep Henry happy and fed, and it was too late for them to drive any farther.

"About the bill," Henry said to Jackson.

"Sixty-eight. That sound fair?"

"More than fair." Henry stroked the ridged surface around the dial of his heavy watch and then said, "Would you take this instead? We're short of cash, but this is a Rolex, it's worth a lot. It's all we have." He slipped it off his wrist and held it out.

Jackson turned the gold band in the glow from the garage. "It's a good one?"

"The best," Henry said. "It ought to run forever. Or you can sell it, if you want—you'll get some decent cash for it."

Jackson slipped the watch into his shirt pocket. "Fair enough."

A watch for a van, Brendan thought; a bracelet and earrings for plums. He saw the plums float over the wall again, and the faces of the children who'd eaten them, and then all the faces of everyone he'd left behind.

18

THE SAAB WAS AS SPACIOUS AND SMOOTH AS AN OCEAN LINER: dim, private, silent except for the occasional clicks and squawks of the radar detector on the dash. Cool air flowed over Wiloma's legs and lights gleamed behind the steering wheel. Waldo touched a button and music washed over them.

"What is that?" Wiloma asked.

"New CD player," Waldo said. "Pretty sharp, isn't it? I had it put in a few months ago."

"No, I mean the music—what *is* that?"

"Jazz harp. Isn't it something? Sarah turned me on to this guy—he's German, he does things with a harp you'd never believe."

"Really," Wiloma said. Sarah: the sort of woman who could interest her older husband in something as exotic as jazz on a harp. "It makes me feel old."

"The music?"

Wiloma nodded. "You know. Harps used to be for symphonies, or for ladies in long dresses."

Waldo laughed. "I know what you mean. It seemed strange to me at first, but Sarah just thinks it's wonderful."

"She's young," Wiloma said.

"She is," Waldo agreed. "Sometimes I wake up in the middle of the night, thinking about things that were important to me in high school, or when you and I were first married, or when our kids were kids, and I roll over to talk to her and I realize she won't know what I mean. It's hard to explain."

All that you want is made impossible by all that you want, Wiloma wanted to tell him. That was one of the first things her group leader had taught her at the Healing Center: that needs and desires excluded each other, fed each other, led to despair; that want followed want until your life reached a point where the several things you had to have were at war with one another. *Wants are like lions,* her teacher had said. *They will tear you apart.* Brendan, despite his dislike of her church, had admired that phrase when she'd first repeated it to him and claimed it was simply another version of what the Christian mystics had always taught. *Everything we seek has already been given to us,* he'd said. *We only have to learn how to recognize it.*

"This is nice," Waldo said. "Sitting here with you like this, not fighting. It's relaxing."

"Is it?"

"You know me."

And it was true, she thought. She did. They had known each other all through high school, although they hadn't started dating until later, after Da and Gran had died. She knew his family and his disappointments. She knew how he'd fought against taking over his father's building firm, and how hard he'd worked once he'd given in. He hadn't always been the confident, successful man whom Sarah had married, and sometimes she wondered if he'd divorced her just to shed his years of struggle. Once he'd told her, in the midst of a fight, that it was no blessing living with someone who'd known him so long. *You can't forget,* he'd shouted. *You can't forget a single damn thing.*

But she routinely forgot things now, she forgot them on purpose, and if he'd stop trying to pull her back to the past, she would never think about it. But he couldn't seem to let a minute go by without jolting her memory. "Have you been out to Coreopsis?" he asked now, pointing out the streetlights of a new development twinkling just beyond the road. "Recently, I mean."

"No," Wiloma told him. "I don't want to see it." The development slipped behind them, but not before she'd seen cars parked in front of the new homes, lights on in the new kitchens, everything Henry had hoped for Coreopsis and failed to make.

"It'd kill you," Waldo said. "I was out that way a few months ago, looking over a building site for a new client. I drove over to the farm just out of curiosity—Jesus. What a wreck."

You might have tried to save it, Wiloma thought, but she said nothing. Coreopsis Heights was error externalized, a knot of confusion and misplaced desire, and she had tried from the start to detach herself from it. The place was poisoned, she thought. Nothing good could rise from it. Even saying the name out loud was dangerous, but Waldo was too dense to notice.

She looked over at her ex-husband's smooth, pink face. Once, when they were newly married, he and Henry had worked on a project together and had been as close as brothers. But then they'd soured on each other as their tastes developed and their ambitions conflicted, and after the fight they'd had six years ago, they'd almost stopped speaking. They'd trapped her in the middle, each complaining about the other and neither able to see that, although Henry dreamed in broad strokes, a community rising from an empty field where no one had seen one before, and Waldo dreamed a house at a time, this window here, this set of doors, they were otherwise as alike as peas. She was aware, some of the time, that she'd chosen Waldo in part because he so resembled Henry. She'd been aware of that since Brendan had pointed it out.

They complemented each other perfectly but had been driven apart by what linked them: their constant desire to leave their signatures on the land. Me, my, mine, she thought. My house, my idea, my development, my success. Henry had never listened, not once, to Waldo's pleas that he scale down Coreopsis Heights, build smaller houses, lay the place out in steps. When the project began to fail, Waldo had not bent an inch to save it. Henry had gone to Waldo, she knew, when the project began to collapse. Henry had begged for a loan. "I don't have it," Waldo had told her then. "If I could save it, I would—I know how much the place means to you. But I don't have the cash."

She hadn't been able to blame him for that—anyone could see that the project was doomed—but in her heart she blamed him for much else. For not stopping Henry in the first place, for not being the man she'd married. For falling in love with someone young.

But she would not say an unpleasant word to him now; she had vowed, when she'd opened the door of this car, that they wouldn't fight. She looked at herself in the small mirror embedded in the visor and said, "Do you think I should cut my hair?"

"I don't know. It looks okay. You could dye it, maybe."

She winced; her hair was very gray. "That seems so weird."

Waldo touched the transplanted plugs on his head. "Weird? *This* is weird—what do you think of this? Really, I mean."

"It looks good." In the dim light it looked the way it had when he was young. She didn't say how earlier, in the afternoon sun, she'd seen the plugs sticking out of his scalp like tiny trees.

"I didn't mind being bald," Waldo said. "But it bothered Sarah."

Sarah again. "It's hard. With someone so young. I met this

man at a retreat last year, he was nine years younger than me. . . ."

"You've been dating?"

"Not really—he was just a friend. But I felt like something might happen between us, and for a few days I just went crazy. I was supposed to be meditating and leading some group sessions, but every free minute I was standing in front of the mirror, changing my clothes or fussing with my hair or trying different lipstick. All of a sudden I cared about how I looked. I cared a lot. And when he got involved with this twenty-five-year-old girl, I felt ridiculous. Really old."

The girl had been unremarkable, neither beautiful nor smart, but her flesh lay over her bones like butter and she looked the same in the mornings as she did at night. Wiloma had watched them move together with a pain that felt like panic, and at night, when she paced her room, she had known in her bones something that, when she'd been younger, had been pure abstraction: that when she was sixty, eighty, when her body had betrayed her completely and left her only raddled flesh, her heart and her desires would still be adolescent.

You will always want the same things, her group leader had said, back before she'd felt the truth for herself. *You'll just stop being able to get them. The only cure is to break the cycle of wanting.* She had shared that line with Brendan, one of the times he was pressing her to explain what made her church different and better than his. He'd laughed and retorted with something from one of his old saints. *It is a hard matter to forgo that to which we are accustomed,* he'd said. *But it is harder to go against our own will.* It was dark out now. She hoped he was safe. If she believed he was safe, he was.

"Sometimes," Waldo said, "when we're at a party, I'll turn and see Sarah talking to some young guy and I'll get so jealous I'll have to sit down. Sometimes it wears me out."

So why did you marry her? Wiloma thought. Why did you leave me for her? But these were old thoughts, the thoughts that had led her nowhere and almost cost her her children, and she put them out of her mind. On the dashboard the radar detector clucked and muttered and then cycled into its full warning hiss.

Waldo's eyes widened and he pressed his foot gently on the brake. They'd been doing eighty, Wiloma saw. Waldo always drove too fast. Seventy-five, seventy, sixty-five. "Don't look around," Waldo cautioned her. "Act like nothing's happening, like we're just talking. Now move your hand real slowly over here and unclip the detector and slip it under your seat."

She did as she was told, keeping her head and shoulders erect and facing forward. "Shit," Waldo said. "If I get another speeding ticket this year I'm going to lose my license."

She slipped the box behind her feet, and as she did she saw the state trooper tucked under the overpass at the base of the hill. His headlights came on as they passed him, and Waldo stared straight ahead with both hands clenched on the wheel. "Shit, shit, *shit,*" he whispered. She felt a glee that surprised her, and a desire, even more surprising, for him to step on the gas and send them shooting into the night with sirens wailing behind them. When the trooper took off after a small car that sped from behind and then passed them, she felt both relieved and disappointed.

Waldo took his right hand off the wheel and shook it several times. "That was close."

"Pretty close," she agreed. His face looked calm, and she was surprised when he pulled into the next rest stop and insisted on calling St. Benedict's. "In case they've got any news," he said, although she couldn't imagine what would have changed since they'd set off. "And I want them to know we're looking."

She wondered if what he really wanted to do was to catch his breath away from her. He wedged himself into a phone booth, one hand crushed to his free ear to block out the cars roaring by. When he returned, he said, "It's just what you thought."

"They're back?" Brendan was safe, then. Her worries hadn't harmed him. "We were wrong?"

"We were *right*," Waldo said impatiently. "I talked to one of the administrator's assistants, and I told her you thought your uncle was headed for Massachusetts. And she got all excited—she said they'd sent one of the orderlies around Brendan's floor, asking everyone if they'd seen or heard anything, and one of the old guys said he'd overheard Brendan talking to someone in the hall. She said this guy said Brendan said, 'I want to go to Massachusetts. I want to see the reservoir,' but that he hadn't thought much about it because they all talk like that all the time, about the places they want to visit and can't."

"Except this is different," Wiloma said. Although the trip couldn't have been Brendan's idea—he might have said something wistful, thinking nothing would ever come of it, but it would have been Henry who had leapt on the words, stolen the van, engineered the details. Henry had pushed their uncle, Henry was behind this. But the men Brendan had left behind wouldn't know that.

Wiloma could imagine them sitting up in bed as the news spread, wheeling themselves into clusters near windows, laughing and whispering and already turning Brendan's flight into legend. Misinterpreting his departure, the way she'd misinterpreted his arrival in Coreopsis so many years ago. When Gran had told her that Brendan was coming to them, she'd pictured another version of her father. He'd left his Order, Gran had said. He was coming home. For the week between that announcement and his arrival, Wiloma had felt as if her father had risen from the dead. Her uncle was coming to rescue her, she'd thought. But all he'd ever been able to do was listen.

The men in the Home, she knew, would be dreaming just as fruitlessly. Someone, she could hear him already, would be claiming he'd known about the plan all along. Someone else would be claiming to have helped. "I saw him," someone else would say. "I saw him take the keys." They were men who went years without visitors, who never got mail, who were starved for something to break their boredom. She couldn't blame them for seeing in Brendan all their own frustrated hopes, but it was wrong to let them think he was something he was not. *He's not a hero,* she wanted to say sternly to those men. *He didn't choose. He was pushed.* And, she might have added, even if he *had* chosen, he had made the wrong choice. A hero would put himself into her hands and let his Healing take place. *Surrender,* he used to tell her. *In surrender is salvation.* He had been on the verge of surrendering himself to her when Henry had interfered.

Waldo eased them back into the river of eastbound traffic. "I *told* her it meant something."

Wiloma's attention snapped back from her vision of the deluded old men. "You didn't . . . ?" If he'd been shaken before, the phone call had calmed him down. Already he was speeding again.

"I didn't," he said. "She asked me where I thought they were headed, and I said I wasn't sure, it could be a lot of places, we were just going to take a little drive and check some of them out. She wanted me to give her some idea, so she could maybe alert the police, and I said I couldn't but that I'd call her as soon as we had any news."

"They called the police?"

"Just the local ones, so far." Waldo looked at her curiously. "You knew that—you told me that cruiser in Irondequoit called in about the van."

"I forgot," she said faintly. She had also, she suddenly realized, forgotten to call Christine and tell her Brendan's arrival would be delayed. "Don't call them again," she said. "Please? Don't call anyone. There are so many people involved already, I can't keep everything straight . . . we can do this ourselves."

146

"He's your uncle. I'll do whatever you want."

Whatever you want, she thought sourly. Not for me, but in the hopes of getting that land. His words were kind but he avoided her eyes, and already she half-regretted bringing him along. If he'd had the sense to stay married to her, her half of it would have been half his. Automatically, just like that. It would have fallen into his hands. She hoped that thought had crossed his mind; she hoped he realized all that he'd lost.

19

HENRY STRIPPED FILLETS FROM THE SKELETONS OF JACKSON'S fried fish, set the bones and heads aside, and cut the flesh into pieces for his uncle. He stood roasted corn on end and sliced the kernels from the cob. Then he sprinkled salt over everything and set the plate in Brendan's lap before he bent to his own food. From the practiced ease with which Jackson had made it, he realized that Jackson cooked over this fire every day.

"Are you living out here?" Henry asked. "In your garage?" He regretted his question immediately.

"Pretty much." Jackson wiped out the frying pan with a wad of newspaper. "But I used to have a house, just like everyone else. A green ranch on Town Line Road, past the insulator plant."

Brendan, who'd been very quiet since waking from his nap, set down his untouched plate. "What happened?" he asked. "Did you lose it?" His face was so thin that his cheekbones stood out in the fire's glow.

Jackson said, "What happened was—" but before he could start, Henry cleared his throat. The idea that Jackson could be living like this was horrifying; the last thing he wanted to do was to listen to Jackson's story. It was bound to be long and sad, and he had no idea where he and Brendan were going or where they might find a place to stay. "Dinner was great," he told Jackson. "We really appreciate it. But we ought to get going."

Jackson set down the frying pan and strode into the garage. When he returned, he held a pile of old blankets. "Why don't you camp here tonight? You can put these in your van—you ought to be pretty comfortable."

Henry looked at Brendan, sure that he'd want to get on the road again, but Brendan answered for both of them. "That's very kind of you," he said. "We could use a place to stay."

"You're sure?" Henry said. "You won't be very comfortable."

"I'll be fine," Brendan said, and Jackson said, "Stay. I could use the company."

Henry gave up. This was Brendan's trip, Brendan's idea entirely, and if the old man wanted to sit in the damp night air and let the mosquitoes get him, that was fine. He was as tired as he'd ever been. Kitty, Coreopsis Heights, the diner, and then the breakdown—it was too much for one day, more than he could sort out. He longed to rest.

Brendan sat in his wheelchair, his hands flapping against the armrests from time to time. Bongo lay next to him and worried the fish heads that Henry had set aside. Henry lounged in one of the tattered chairs, and when Jackson's three-legged cat slunk by he scooped her up. Jackson had said that her left front leg had been caught in a trap when she was a kitten. The vet had popped the stump from the shoulder joint and closed the wound, which had healed so smoothly she might have been born that way. Henry liked the way his hand passed from her neck to her flank without interruption.

Jackson said, "I've been living here since spring. My wife, she fell in love with a guy who works at the bowling alley. And she threw me out of the house, like our twenty-two years together didn't mean squat. You know what she said?"

"What?" asked Brendan. He was bent forward, listening intently. Henry imagined him sitting like that at St. Benedict's, listening to the stories of the other old men while years and years went by. "What did she say?" Brendan's voice was low and kind.

"She said, 'Jackson, you don't mean nothing to me anymore.' " He pointed at Henry's lap. "Like I was that cat there. Which she didn't want me to fix because she thought it was a waste of money and what good is a three-legged cat? She said, the kids are grown now, and I want something out of this life before I'm too old to enjoy it. She loved this guy, she said.

"I said I didn't care, I loved her anyways. And she said if I really loved her, I'd move out. Leave her alone for a while, she said. Let her figure this out. So I've been sleeping out here these last few months, with just Rosie here for company, and she's been letting this jerk live in our house with her, and I'll tell you, I'll tell you—do you think I'm a fool?"

"Who's to say?" said Henry. The cat squirmed in his lap, settling her head into his armpit and her strange smooth chest against his. He tried to imagine what had kept Jackson from beating his wife, driving her lover off, laying claim to his own house, but when he thought about how he'd let Kitty push him away, he knew. Houses belonged to women—despite all the houses he'd sold to men, and all the ones he'd owned himself, he believed that. Men bought them, but women folded them around their bodies like shells as soon as they moved in. He could see Jackson's wife sealing doors and windows until Jackson had no place to go.

"I'm trying to wait it out," Jackson said. "She'll let me back when she's ready. Do you think she will?"

No, Henry wanted to say. *No more than Kitty ever will.* He knew, listening to Jackson's tale, that his marriage to Kitty was over. She was never going to change back into the girl he'd married. She was never going to forgive him for losing their home.

"You had troubles," Brendan said. "Always?"

Jackson shrugged. "Things were tough. Like they're tough for everyone. Ronnie—that's our oldest—he's been in trouble since junior high. And Barbara got pregnant last year, and there's never been enough money—but what does Rhonda complain about? She doesn't like the way I smell, she says. She doesn't like the way I look. 'Jackson,' she says, 'I want some *romance.*' Like we're still kids. Shit, she's forty-three, you'd thinks she'd know better. This guy she's seeing can't be more than thirty. He doesn't know anything about her and she doesn't care."

"Nobody knows her like you do," Brendan said. "That matters." Henry thought how it *did* matter, but in the wrong way; Kitty hated some of the things he knew about her. That she was cranky in the morning and had frequent bladder infections and cried when she was angry; that the curl in her hair was not natural and that she scratched in bed.

"I tell myself that every day," Jackson said. "But I'm sleeping on a cot here and cooking outside, and I'm lonely all the time."

"We're all lonely," Brendan said. "It's what we do with it that counts."

"You want to see what I do?" Jackson said. "Check this out."

He went into the garage and returned with two gas cans and three empty cans of oil. He made more trips for the five-gallon drums and the hubcaps and the leaf springs. While Henry and Brendan watched, he arranged the metal pieces in a circle at his feet. Then he seized two long sticks and started pounding.

The cans and car parts gave out different notes, something like steel drums, and Jackson pounded out a wandering mel-

ody on them. The notes rose in the cool air and settled like
birds in the branches. Jackson's face was red and heavy-
cheeked; his legs were thick; his hands were enormous. The
sparse, long strands of his hair stuck up from his head like
wires.

"I made that up," Jackson said when he was done. "I
made it up for Rhonda."

"It's something," Brendan said. "Really. I bet she comes
back."

"Maybe. But it's all right out here, in a weird way. Sometimes I almost like it."

Brendan said, "There's a certain quiet that comes, when
you've been alone for a long time," and Jackson said, "I get
these ideas for my cans, when I'm alone for a couple of days,"
and Henry listened to them and wondered what they were
talking about.

When he was alone, the way he'd been for the past six
months in Waldo's awful apartment, the silence drove him
wild. He left the TV on all the time, even when he wasn't
watching; sometimes he turned the radio on as well. He left
his window open through rainstorms, just to hear the pounding water and the occasional noises from the street. He'd
thought about Brendan on those nights, surrounded by other
old men and talking, talking, talking, and sometimes he'd
actually envied him. Old, sick, stuck in a home that wasn't
his, at least Brendan had some company. There had been
nights when Henry had wondered how sick he'd have to be
to enter a place like St. Benedict's himself.

And here Brendan was explaining to Jackson that he'd lived
in a nursing home for years, and no, he didn't always like it,
sometimes the lack of solitude had been very trying; and yes,
he surely was glad to be out for a while, he was grateful to
Henry here. They were going, he said, to visit some family:
"Cousins. Some second cousins of mine, in Massachusetts."

They had, as far as Henry knew, no family left there at all,
but when Jackson looked at him he nodded. "Cousins," he

said, wondering again why Brendan told these half-truths to everyone they met.

"We ought to sleep now," Brendan said. "We have to leave early."

The back of the van was a jumble of odds and ends, but Jackson helped Henry move things around until they'd cleared a space big enough for two men to lie down. Henry set aside the two blankets he'd taken from Kitty's house and then folded Jackson's blankets into a thick pad for the floor. He and Jackson lifted Brendan from his wheelchair and stretched him out on the pad. Bongo leapt in and tried to lie down next to Brendan, but Henry tossed him into the front seat.

"Sleep well," Jackson said. "I'll be around if you need anything."

Henry wedged himself next to Brendan, who lay very still with his hands drawn up on his chest. Over both of them, Henry draped one of Kitty's blankets. The blanket smelled; he drew it over his face and inhaled deeply. It smelled of leaves and dirt and his girls, and he remembered how Lise and Delia used to take it into the backyard and drape it over a tree limb to make a tent. The girls were so angry at him— too angry, he thought, for it to be just a reflection of their mother's fury. It was as if they'd been angry at him for years and had only just figured it out. He couldn't understand what he'd done that was so wrong.

Outside he heard the little pongs and pings of Jackson tapping gently on his homemade drums, and he wondered if Jackson's children were angry as well. A kind man, Jackson—who else would have fed them dinner and let them camp there for free? Who else would have fixed the van in exchange for a watch that might easily have been fake? The watch happened to be real—Henry had bought it back when he had money, and he knew Jackson had gotten the better part of that exchange. But it could have been fake, and he and Brendan could have been murderers, and Jackson would have trusted them just the same.

He eased himself onto his right shoulder, trying not to disturb Brendan. The van was no wider than two coffins laid side to side. Their hips touched and his feet banged into the junk piled by the rear door. Bongo, curled in the front seat, whimpered and twitched. Brendan snored. Henry rolled over again. He could not, he thought, blame Jackson's wife, or not completely; as kind as Jackson was, he was overweight and had bad teeth and blackened hands. His body was worn, wrinkled, used, and maybe Rhonda had only craved newer flesh.

The van was impossibly hot and noisy—his breath, his uncle's, his dog's; snores, creaks, groans. He sat up suddenly and grabbed Kitty's other blanket and slid the side door open. The outside, bugs and dew or not, could not be worse. He found a spot twenty yards from the van, where the ground seemed fairly smooth, and he lay down wrapped in his blanket. The stars above him shone brilliantly and the trees made a black fringe against the horizon. Water was running somewhere, in a creek or a stream nearby. Jackson's drums were silent now, and he thought of Jackson lying on his cot inside that empty, dirty garage, waiting for Rhonda to call him home. He fell asleep thinking of his own young-fleshed mistake, of Anita, who had left him.

He had met her at the bank and she had not, despite what Kitty had said, been stupid at all. She had only been young. She had processed the application for his doomed loan on Coreopsis Heights, and when he'd driven her down to look at the land he'd been able to make her see the finished project through his eyes. She believed him. She believed everything he said. She slipped her hand around his elbow as they paced the hummocked ground.

Anita had beautiful thighs, as smooth and curved as a swan's wing, and she'd lost her job because of him. When Coreopsis Heights had failed and he'd defaulted on his loans, the bank had blamed her for approving them in the first place. She'd stood by him during his long slide, during the months when Kitty had screamed at him nightly and he'd scrambled for a foothold in the mounting heap of bills, but when she lost her job, she dumped him. She didn't tell him face-to-face; she didn't even call. She sent a cool, cruel letter to his house, which Kitty opened. Then Kitty threw him out and he crashed his car.

They were gone now, both of them. He dreamed of a green stretch of land, cut through by a broad river—the land of the blessed, the fairy-tale land that Gran used to tell stories about, which had come to her from her own grandmother in Ireland. Across the ocean and hidden by mist, she said, lay a temperate land of warmth and light. Grapes there grew to the size of apples. Otters stepped from the streams and walked on their hind legs, bearing gifts of fish. The men were brave and the women were lovely; no one ever grew old there and no one ever died. A monk, the one Gran had named Brendan for, had set sail from Ireland with his companions, bobbing and tossing for seven years in a hide-covered curragh until they found the land of promise. They wandered there for forty days, which passed like a single afternoon. Then an angel found them and sent them back home.

Gran had called that place the country of the young. In his dream, Henry stepped out of a leather-skinned boat and set foot on a soft white beach. Deer stood in the grass where the beach merged into the forest. The river was full of salmon and the trees were heavy with fruit. Henry made his way through the woods until he came upon a clearing. In the clearing a fire burned in a ring of stones, and around it stood all the women he had ever loved.

All of them were young. Anita, as she'd looked on the day when Coreopsis Heights was still a dream; Kitty, as she'd looked on the shore of Canandaigua Lake; Lise and Delia; his mother. Even Gran looked as she had in the wedding picture that had hung over the mantel in Coreopsis. He

looked down at himself and saw that he alone had a fifty-
year-old body. He had hair in his nose and his ears and his
eyebrows were growing together. His stomach hung down,
no matter how hard he tried to suck it in. His hands and feet
were callused and freckled and the skin where his thighs met
his groin was creased. In the soft breeze, against the fresh
vegetation, he looked obscene.

He threw himself onto the grass and rolled like a dog, and
when he stood he bristled with green stems. He pranced in
his green coat; he danced and threw his hands in the air;
and when the smooth-fleshed women still ignored him he
jumped into one of the trees and sang like a mad bird. The
stems clothing him had turned into feathers. The women, he
realized, could neither see nor hear him, and he raised his
tattered wings and flew over the water.

He woke when he heard his uncle calling, "Henry?
Henry?"

Feathers? he thought, feeling his clothes with his hands.
Where had that come from? He walked to the van and stuck
his head through the open window.

"What is it? Are you all right?" He couldn't see Brendan's
face at all.

"I have to take a leak," Brendan whispered. "I had a little
cup, I left it on my chair."

The chair stood next to the van, and Henry felt along the
seat until his fingers touched a plastic cup. He passed it
through the window. "Do you need help?"

"No. But you can toss it for me when I'm done." Henry
heard water again, just a trickle this time, and then Brendan
said, "Here." Henry emptied the half-filled cup on the
ground.

"Can you sleep?" he asked his uncle.

"On and off. How about you?"

"I was dreaming," Henry said. "I had such a strange
dream."

"Go back to it," Brendan said. "I'm sorry I woke you."

Henry went back to his blanket, but his dream was gone.

20

THE EVENING HAD PASSED SO SMOOTHLY, AND IT HAD BEEN SO nice to have the house to themselves and not to think about what their families were up to, that Wendy had let time slip and slide and high-step past her without telling Delia what had happened. Sometime after eleven, though, in the living room littered with cartons of grapefruit juice and vodka bottles and pizza boxes, Delia said, "So where'd your mother go, anyway? One of her weird retreats?"

Wendy had almost forgotten how strange her story was. Casually, almost flippantly, she explained about Grunkie's disappearance and her mother's reaction to it, and her father's reaction to her mother's reaction, and her mother's suspicions that Henry had actually stolen Grunkie away. Wendy's embroidered bag leaned against her chair with the rag dolls showing at the top, and as she spoke she took the dolls from the bag and manipulated them like puppets. The story, backed by the dolls' gestures, seemed almost funny. She said, he said, I said; she said he said; I said to her;

rumors, guesses, speculations. She was not prepared for Delia's response.

"My father did *what?*" she said, and it took Wendy a minute to realize that Delia might see the story from a different
perspective, evidence of one more link in the endless chain
of her father's recent fuck-ups. She forgot, sometimes, that
Delia took her father's escapades so hard. She'd had less than
a year to get used to them, and she felt guilty about the way
he'd ended up. Lise and Kitty had shed Henry like snakes,
but Delia still seemed tied to him by a tag of obligation or
love, like the string of flesh left behind by a pulled tooth.

"This whole thing's probably in my mother's head,"
Wendy said soothingly. "You know how she gets. All anyone
really knows is that your father and Grunkie left St. Benedict's together in this van they borrowed. Mom and Dad both
think they went to Massachusetts, so that's where they've
gone to look for them."

Delia bent over until her head met her knees. "Asshole.
Asshole, asshole, asshole."

"Your father?" Roy said. He rested his hand on the back
of Delia's neck.

"Of course my father." She sighed and lifted her head and
stretched her arms behind her back. "He's such a jerk—after
all he's done to us, after all he's done to his family, you'd
think he'd give it a rest. But no—he has to take a helpless
old man from a nursing home, fuck up everyone's lives
again. . . ."

"We don't *know* that," Wendy said. "We don't know what
happened at all. I'm only telling you what my mother said."

Win, who had finally agreed to stay home, had been playing with the Nintendo paraphernalia Waldo had loaned him.
The television bleeped and flickered as a helicopter exploded
again and again and was miraculously resurrected. Now he
set down the controls and drifted toward Delia. "What's
going on?" he asked. "What's the problem?"

"The problem," Delia said, "the problem is . . ." Without

warning, and with considerable grace, she hurled her glass of grapefruit juice and vodka into the fireplace. "I'm so sick of this family," Delia said more calmly. "I'm so sick of my father I could puke. This is all his fault, I know it is—I don't even have to know what's going on to know he did it. He's like a bulldozer without a driver out there, crashing through the world and wrecking up everything. He's such a child."

With her flushed face and her curly hair, Delia looked like a child herself. Win bent over the fireplace and began picking up the shards of glass. "What's the big deal?" he said. "Your father, my mother—they're both crazy. It's not like this is news. What's the point of getting all upset?"

"You're sixteen," Delia said scornfully. "What do you know?"

"More than you do. I know there isn't any point in worrying about whatever they're doing. They're all out there on the road somewhere, buzzing around each other, and you watch, whatever's going on, they'll all be back tomorrow acting like nothing ever happened. And that's because probably nothing *is* happening. You can't take them seriously."

Delia rose unsteadily and headed for the kitchen. "I have to call Lise," she said, as if Lise had ever been any help to her. She shook off Wendy's hand when Wendy reached out to stop her. "Don't touch me. I can't believe you didn't tell me this was going on."

"I *did* tell you," Wendy said. "I just did."

"*Now.* After letting me sit here all night, thinking everything was fine." Delia vanished into the kitchen and Roy touched Wendy's forearm gently.

"It's not your fault," he said. "She always overreacts when she hears anything about her father. She can't stand to side with him, but she still feels sorry for him and she gets herself all tangled up."

When Delia returned from the kitchen she looked grimly satisfied. "You won't believe this," she announced. "Lise is over at Mom's helping her pack up, and when I told her

159

what was going on, she said that Dad and Grunkie had been there around lunchtime, in a van no less, and that Dad was in this really strange mood and he and Mom had one of their fights. Lise said she heard Dad tell Mom that he was bringing Grunkie over here for dinner."

She said she heard him tell her, Wendy thought. "Not for dinner," she admitted. "To stay."

"What?" Delia said. "What else aren't you telling me?"

Win frowned across the room at Wendy, but Wendy kept on talking. Somehow, even without the dolls in her hands, her words didn't seem to matter anymore. All the words that had sprung from everyone's lips all day had fused and mutated and taken on a life of their own, which seemed bound to sprout strangely no matter what she did. She said, "Grunkie was supposed to stay here. Until—you know."

"Until he dies," Win said firmly. He came and stood next to Wendy and picked up the dolls she'd set against the pizza boxes. "Where did you get these?" he asked Wendy quietly. "Did you take them?"

"I borrowed them."

"I don't get it," Delia said, while Win scanned Wendy's guilty face. "Why would Grunkie come here?"

"Because," Wendy said. "Mom wanted—he was due for some chemotherapy, and Mom said it wasn't going to do any good, and she wanted him to come stay here so someone from her stupid church could try some sort of diet on him." She rose and beckoned to Delia and Roy and then led them into the spare room her mother had readied for Grunkie.

"Look at this," she said. She showed them the Manual, the bookcase filled with Church literature, and the cross-stitched sampler bearing the Church motto. *Nothing exists external to our minds,* she read for the second time that day. *Things are thoughts. The world is made up of our ideas.* She made a mental note to add another item to the list in her closet: *I will remember that the world is real.* Ideas had gotten them nowhere, she thought. Ideas had brought her mother to this.

"He was supposed to come tomorrow," she said. "Mom was going to pick him up. And then somehow she was going to take care of him. Except she can't even take care of herself half the time."

Delia laughed bitterly. "Look at this crap."

Wendy drew a deep breath. She and Win used to try to hide their mother's strangeness from Delia and Lise, but Henry's crash had offered them a peculiar relief—since Delia had started confiding in them, they'd started confiding back. Sometimes, caught in a long exchange of "my mother said" and "my father did," they had actually laughed. She had nothing to lose by saying what came next. "Mom said Grunkie must have told Uncle Henry about the neuro-nutritionist who's supposed to come."

"The what?" Delia asked.

"This nurse, this lady from the Church who's supposed to help him. Grunkie wasn't all that thrilled about the idea, I guess. And Mom said Grunkie must have told your father, and your father maybe took him away so he wouldn't have to come here. You know how he hates Mom's Church stuff. He thinks it's crazy."

"It is," Delia said. "You told me so yourself."

"Your father isn't?"

They stared at each other until the doorbell rang.

"That's probably Lise," Delia said. "I told her to come over."

Wendy groaned. "Now? You know she'll just make things worse." Lise knew everyone's weak spots and hit them unerringly, and Wendy had always wondered if Lise noticed the way her words drove everyone away. The way she had of acting forty instead of twenty-three, as if she were decades older than the rest of them—Wendy felt a stiffness creeping up on her already, an echo of Lise's rigid posture. Delia had, she knew, long since stopped telling Lise about anything important, and as they moved to the door she whispered to Delia, "Did you make up something?"

"About what?"

"Why you're home. What you're doing here. Roy?"

"Shit. I forgot all about that. Tell her I'm visiting you, okay?"

"Okay. But she's going to remember Roy."

Delia rolled her eyes and then pulled Roy to her and whispered something to him. Roy laughed. Delia said to Wendy, "Tell her Roy's with you now. That you two hooked up after I left."

She gave Wendy the same conspiratorial grin they'd shared as children, whenever they'd banded together to protect themselves from Lise's prying. Before Wendy could say anything, Roy left Delia's side and moved to hers. "My darling," he said in a joking voice. "My own true love."

Her whole arm grew warm as he took her hand and held it. "My prince," she said, trying to keep her voice as light as his.

Win, who had been watching all this, said, "Are we ready?" His voice was sarcastic. "Everyone got everything sorted out?"

Wendy and Roy and Delia nodded, and Win threw open the door. A woman stood there, not Lise, a woman older than Wiloma with short white hair and very white skin and a face so creased and lined and scored that it resembled a cotton shirt someone had washed and then forgotten to iron. Her gauzy printed skirt sagged almost to her ankles and was topped by a blue blouse. A large wicker basket was strapped to her back.

"Hello?" Wendy said. "Can I help you?"

"You must be Wendy," the woman said. Wendy felt a prickle of fear. "Is your mother here?"

Win pushed himself in front of Wendy. "Who are you?" he asked. "What do you want?"

"I'm Christine. From the Healing Center. Your mother asked me to come."

"Tomorrow," Wendy protested as Christine walked past

them and into the living room. "You're supposed to be here tomorrow."

"I always come the night before, to make sure the treatment area is properly arranged."

"Who the hell do you think you are?" Win asked. "Barging in here like this."

"I come where I'm called," Christine said.

Delia laughed. "This is a joke, right?"

Christine gazed at the filthy living room and the dolls on the table and the spray of juice on the fireplace. "Nice," she said. "Does your mother know about this?"

"Our mother's away for the evening," said Win.

"Why?" asked Christine. She wandered toward the kitchen before Wendy could answer, with her hands out before her like a blind woman's. She touched the walls and the doorframes and the chairs and the drapes, as if she were trying to read them with her hands. As Wendy and Win and Roy and Delia followed her, she touched the stove, the sink, the dishwasher, and the refrigerator. Then she turned to Wendy expectantly. "On the counter," Wendy blurted. "Under the phone." She couldn't understand what had made her speak.

Christine picked up the note Wendy had placed there earlier and read it. "But this is serious. Explain."

Wendy told her the same story she'd told her father and then Win and then Delia, aware that it sounded worse with each repetition and afraid that she'd twisted, somehow, the already twisted tale her mother had told her. He said, she said, we said, she thought. They said, you said, I said. I said. She closed her eyes and felt the world chipped into bits around her, made up of the same small squares that formed the creatures and obstacles of Win's video games. Nothing smooth and blended, everything sharp-edged and discrete, every word and act and person separate from every other, and the illusion that they formed a whole just that, just an illusion, visible only from a distance that blurred everything. Her voice trailed off and she opened her eyes to find Christine staring at her. "I mean," she said faintly, "I mean that's what my mother thinks. I don't know what my father thinks. I don't know why he went with her."

"Your mother has good instincts," Christine said. "Her hypothesis may be correct. Your great-uncle's been a little resistant to the idea of being Healed. And if your uncle feels the same way . . ."

"He's my *father*," Delia said impatiently.

Christine turned toward Delia, her gray eyes shining like lamps. "Your father?" Wendy noticed that her eyebrows were almost invisible. "You're the niece?"

"Wiloma's niece," Delia snapped. "Henry's daughter. Grunkie's grandniece. And my father feels the same way Grunkie does. He thinks you're all crazy."

Christine nodded gravely. "That would be consistent. Your father is the one who lost the farm in Coreopsis?"

"That's him," Delia said, while Wendy wondered what else this woman knew. "The one who loses everything."

Christine moved to the stove and started heating a kettle of water. "But he doesn't just lose things," she said. "Does he? He takes things all the time, to make up for everything he's lost. Other people's land, other people's love . . ."

Delia's face turned a strange color, and Wendy felt her own face flush as she thought of the dolls in the living room. It was sickening, what this woman knew. Her mother must have told her everything.

Christine had kept her basket on her back, but now she leaned against the counter and slipped her arms from the straps. Quietly, she unloaded a bundle of branches with waxy leaves and shiny white berries, and then an assortment of small paper sacks that were folded, stapled, and labeled. She said to Wendy, "Where are the cups?"

Wendy gestured toward the cabinet over the sink, and when Christine reached in for the mugs, Wendy's arm stole out and plucked a branch from the bundle and slipped it into her pocket. Win and Roy and Delia were all watching her but she couldn't stop herself. She had to see if this woman knew everything. Christine looked back over her shoulder and said, "Are you very drunk?"

Wendy, suddenly speechless, turned to Win. "No," he said. "We haven't been drinking."

"Not you two, the others."

"What business is it of yours?" Roy asked.

"None," Christine said. If she'd seen the branch disappear, she apparently wasn't going to mention it. Wendy pulled her shirt over her pocket. "But I have some tea here, it's sassafras. It'll clear your heads."

She measured out something brown and dusty from one of the sacks and then poured water into the teapot that stood near the toaster. Wendy watched her helplessly, wondering if there was a way to push her out into the night, and then she followed her to the table and sat down. The four of them sipped at their tea as if Christine had cast a spell on them. Her mouth was too small, Wendy decided. Or maybe it was her eyes that were too big, or the way her eyebrows vanished unless the light hit them just right. Whatever the reason, her eyes seemed to take up half her face.

"The question," Christine said, "the question *is* . . . ," but before she could finish Lise walked in and Delia burst into tears. Roy, as if Lise were a gust of wind, leaned away from Delia and toward Wendy. Lise had shoes on, Wendy saw. Not sneakers or flip-flops, but shiny hard shoes with pointed toes. And stockings. And she carried a purse. She had cut her hair and she looked like Henry in drag. She squared her bony shoulders and said, "Does someone want to tell me what's going on?"

"You would be . . . ?" Christine asked.

"Lise. Delia's sister. Who are you?" But before Christine could answer, Delia rose and took Lise's arm and led her out of the room. Wendy could hear Delia's voice behind the wall, rising, falling, crying—Delia, she realized, was drunker than she looked. Roy covered Wendy's hand with his. "Let her get it out," he whispered. "I usually just let her cry for a while."

Win slapped his palms against the table. "I don't suppose," he said to Christine, "there's any chance you'd pack up your stuff and get out of here."

"I have to go where I'm called. That's my job. I'm sorry you feel I'm infringing on your space."

Win rolled his eyes at Wendy. Roy said, "This seems like sort of a family thing. Maybe I ought to get going."

"Stay," Wendy said. "Please." She was so tired that she wanted to rest her head on the table and sleep, but she knew something dreadful would happen if she closed her eyes in Christine's presence. She'd go to sleep as one person, wake up as another; she'd wake up believing everything her mother believed she believed. She'd wake up on Christine's side, sure the world could be fixed by faith in a simple set of rules. Christine had power; Wendy could feel it flowing across the table from those clear eyes. Something in her was so calm and strong, or so calmly mad, that Wendy could almost imagine what had lured her mother into the Church.

Christine leaned over and fixed her gaze on Wendy. "Your great-uncle's Spirit is getting ready to transit. If I don't help him soon, he's going to be lost."

Win snorted into his tea. "Lost where?" he said. "Mom told us you were going to cure Grunkie. Keep him alive."

Christine kept her eyes fixed on Wendy. "Your mother said I was going to *Heal* him. You weren't paying attention to her words."

"You can't cure him?" Wendy said.

"Maybe not his body. He's let this disease get a grip on him, and it's gone a long way—he believes in it and believes it's going to kill him, and as long as he does, it will. But I can Heal his Spirit—I can teach him how to think correctly and give him certain herbs and foods that will free his Spirit from his disease. I can make sure his Spirit finds the Light."

Roy tipped himself back in his chair. "I don't get it. Are you some kind of priest?"

"I'm a certified spiritual neuro-nutritionist," Christine said quietly. "From the Church of the New Reason."

Roy shook his head, but he was polite and Wendy was grateful for that. What must we look like? she wondered. This house, this woman, this family—to an outsider, we must all look nuts. There was a reason she never brought friends home, a reason she never dated, and this was it, right here, sitting across the table. Their lives sometimes sailed along normally for months, but when she least expected it, when she was most lured into thinking they lived like everyone else, things like this came out of nowhere. A Christine appeared, or a convoy of cars loaded with people prepared for a group meditation, or two men in dark suits rang the doorbell and wouldn't leave.

Lise led Delia back into the kitchen just then, and this time she looked sharply at Roy. "Don't I know you?"

Roy draped his arm over the back of Wendy's chair. "I used to go out with your sister. Till she went away to school. Then I met Wendy." Wendy reached her hand back for Roy's.

"You," Lise said. "I remember you. You had that ugly dog." Roy flinched and Lise addressed herself to Wendy. "Delia told me what's been going on. It's just outrageous. Grunkie ought to be in a hospital, or at least back at St. Benedict's. The *idea* of bringing him here—I don't know what Dad's up to, and it figures he'd mess up whatever it is, but I can certainly sympathize with his wanting to keep Grunkie out of this."

Christine looked at Lise. Her eyes, Wendy saw, were not gray but almost violet. "You aren't very happy," Christine said. "Are you."

Win laughed out loud at that and even Delia smiled. The tip of Lise's nose looked white and pinched. "I don't know who you think you are," Lise said, "but if you think you have any right—"

"Have a seat," Christine said, and Lise frowned but sat down. Delia sat, too, and then Christine said, "Now listen. We have a situation here. You two"—she pointed at Delia and Lise—"are worried about your father." Lise opened her mouth, but Christine silenced her with an upraised hand. "You're angry. Disgusted. But also worried. And you two"— she looked at Wendy and Win—"are worried about your mother. And you're all worried about your great-uncle and I am, too. And the question is—what are you going to do?"

She glanced over at Roy, who was staring out the window. "I'm not ignoring you. You're worried about the girls. You're part of this."

Roy drew his eyes back from the window. "That's right," he said. "I am."

Then Win looked at Wendy and Delia and said, "We're not part of *anything*. Don't you get it? If we let ourselves get caught up in this, then we're acting just like them—we have to stay out of this. Just stand by."

Christine said, "Yes? Like you did when your mother was sick? Did you find that helpful?"

Win paled beneath his tan and Wendy caught her breath. That was cruel, she thought. We were children then. We did the best we could.

"Why don't *you* do something?" Lise said. "If you're so smart."

"Because I am not allowed to intervene," Christine said. "Except in matters of the Spirit. I can listen. I can counsel. I can heal. Nothing more. And anyway, my concern isn't with your parents, except as their actions affect your great-uncle. My concern is with him."

For a minute they all sat silently. Roy rubbed his thumb along the back of Wendy's chair, causing a tiny vibration that Wendy felt in her flesh. Lise crossed her legs and plucked at her stockings. Delia pouted. Win rose, opened the refrigerator, and started pawing through the white sacks Christine had deposited there. "Lily buds," he said, reading the labels.

"Poppy seeds. Horseradish root. Cattail tubers. What do you do with this stuff?"

"Same thing I do with the mistletoe," Christine said, laying a hand on the bundle that was now missing a branch. "Release the Spirit from the flesh. Connect it to the great Spirit that animates the earth."

"We could call the police," Lise said, her sharp face brightening. "Have you arrested for practicing medicine without a license."

"We're an official, tax-exempt church," Christine said. "And I'm an official Church representative, and the Healing is an official Church ceremony. We're completely legitimate—why can't you accept that I'm here to help?"

Wendy fingered her stolen twig. The leaves felt smooth and soft and gently sticky; the berries were hard and cool. Her uncle's salvation, if Christine was to be believed, was lying right here in her hand. She thought of all the people who'd tried to rescue her when her mother had been sick, teachers and neighbors and friends' parents who'd held out their hands and tried to help. But all along she'd known that the salvations being offered were not her salvation, that whatever she needed was beyond their ability to give. Christine couldn't help them, and her twigs and powders couldn't help Grunkie. But perhaps there was something she and Win and her cousins could do themselves.

An idea had been forming in her mind while Lise and Christine spoke, and in the pause that followed, it rose to Wendy's lips and escaped like a bubble. "We ought to go after them."

"You could do that," Christine said. "If you chose. You're old enough to know your own mind."

The others turned to look at Wendy, and Wendy focused on them and tuned out Christine. "Mom and Dad can't do anything together," she said. "You know how they trip each other up. Even if they find Grunkie and Uncle Henry, Mom

169

will mess up anything Dad figures out, and Dad won't be able to get Mom to agree to do anything."

Delia, after a guilty look at Lise, chimed in, "And our father's out of his mind. Honest to God—he's dangerous. I don't know what he's doing, but I know he can't take care of Grunkie the way Grunkie needs. I'm not saying we should bring Grunkie back here—but at least if we could find them, we could maybe keep Dad from getting arrested. Or worse— what if he smacks up the van the way he smacked up his car?"

"Except," Win said dryly, "except that you don't know where any of them are."

"But we do," Wendy said. "You saw those maps Dad showed us—he was all excited about that land."

"What land?" Lise asked.

"This land in Massachusetts, where Grunkie grew up. He told your father and my mother he was leaving each of them half of it, and your father got all excited about it, or at least that's what my mother says, and then my father got all excited, too—he showed us these maps of the reservoir the land's on, or under or near or something, and then . . ."

Rumors, lies, and speculations, she thought as her voice trailed away. She knew those; they were what fueled half her waking hours. She told herself she was not falling under their spell but combating them actively. If she found her family and herded them home she'd be doing something real, which might reverse the events her mother's phone call had set in motion. She might be able to unwind the day and set them all back to the place where they'd been before.

"But we don't have the maps," Win said.

"But I remember," Wendy said. "Sort of. Don't you? All we have to do is head for the reservoir. We could find it on a road map, and once we were there we could figure out the rest."

"You're out of your mind," Win said.

"Completely," Lise agreed.

But Christine was smiling at her broadly. "What an intelligent young woman you are," she said, and Wendy's skin prickled in warning. "You'd be doing your mother a favor if you could help her out, keep your father from interfering— and you'd be helping your great-uncle, too. I need to see him very soon."

"This is *my* idea," Wendy said. "We're not going because of you." She turned to Delia. "Would you come with me?"

"I guess." Delia looked at her sister nervously. "You can't go by yourself. Maybe Roy . . ."

"I'll drive," Roy said. "If you have to go, we'll take my car. You've had too much to drink."

"If you think you're taking off at this hour with these two girls . . . ," Lise said.

"You can come," Roy said mildly. "If you want."

"I'm not staying here alone," Win said. He tilted his head toward Christine. "Not with her."

"I'll stay here," Christine said. "Keep an eye on things."

She smiled at Wendy again, but Wendy ignored her. This wasn't Christine's idea, it had nothing to do with her. They weren't going after Grunkie just to bring him back to Christine. They were going, she thought, because their parents were children; because they were confused and lost and destructive and incapable of caring for themselves. They were so busy chasing after a past they couldn't recover that they couldn't see what was happening right in front of their eyes. Somewhere, she knew, her mother was sitting next to her father and pretending they were still married—wishing, dreaming. Undoing everything she'd spent four years working through. Somewhere her uncle Henry was trying to fix his life by tunneling back to the years before he'd wrecked it.

They'd always been that way—she and Win had known that for years, and now Lise and Delia knew it too. Their parents weren't like other parents because they had no parents of their own. Sometimes, when she and Win had been living with their father, she had tried to imagine growing up

171

without her parents, in the care of two people as old as Grunkie. Sometimes she tried to imagine the moment her mother had once described, when strangers had come for her and Henry and said, "Come with us. Your parents have been in an accident." Then, for brief stretches, she'd been able to understand her mother's quirks.

Their parents needed looking after, and watching over, and she and Win and Lise and Delia were going to rescue them and bring them home. This time it wouldn't turn out the way it had when she and Win were children. They were adults now, capable and smart. They could fix whatever it was that had gone wrong, and when they were done they could put the past behind them and move on.

"Let's go," she said. "If we're going. They're hours ahead of us." She went into the living room and grabbed her flip-flops, a light jacket, and the big embroidered bag. The dolls looked forlorn, propped against the pizza boxes, and at the last minute she took them with her as well.

21

SOMEONE HAD WANTED THE RESTAURANT TO LOOK OLD. THE outside was clothed in the same white concrete as the sporting goods store and the discount outlet, but inside someone had paneled the walls with barn boards and installed ceiling fans and a long, scarred wooden bar with brass footrails. The tables were round and sturdy and the chairs were soft; the pink glass of the sconces cast a kind light on the middle-aged crowd. Wiloma had had two margaritas already, although she hadn't had more than a glass of wine in years. And after the long, dark drive, and the excitement of finding the park at the reservoir's southern tip, and then the disappointment of discovering that the Visitors' Center was closed until ten on Sunday morning, the drinks had hit her like a hammer.

She and Waldo had arrived too late for a real dinner; their waitress, no older than Wendy, had offered them a snack menu composed almost entirely of batter-fried foods. Fried onion rings, fried zucchini, fried mushrooms and mozzarella sticks—the potato skins had seemed like the safest bet, but the orange cheese stuck to her teeth like gum and left a waxy film on her tongue. She looked across the table to Waldo and he said, "Another?" Before she could stop him, he'd ordered a new round of drinks.

He was at home here, Wiloma saw, at ease with the waitresses, familiar with the crowd and the food. She wondered if Sarah often brought him to places like this. He touched her hand lightly and said, "Those skins okay? I'm sorry we couldn't get something more substantial."

"They're fine. It's nice here." And it was pleasant enough, especially now that the drinks had made her so relaxed. Her feet and fingers tingled. Her face felt warm. And Waldo had been kind all night, even before they'd finally found this place. At the park, when they'd driven up the narrow road and found the gates closed in front of the Visitors' Center, with the Ronan Dam shining huge and dim in the moonlight just beyond the building, he had patted her shoulder while she wept.

The sight of the dam had broken through the discipline of her detoxification and made her remember all the Sunday mornings her father had taken her and Henry and her mother there. It had made her remember him—how he'd cried when he'd first seen her and nearly crushed her in his arms. She had been almost four when he came home from the war, and she'd never heard his voice before or seen more than a picture of him. He'd been a stranger, thin and pale and hoarse, his skin splotched and scarred. He slept beside her mother, in the warm hollow that had always been hers, and she had been moved to a cot in Henry's room. At first he'd hardly talked at all. But slowly, as they got used to each other, he'd begun to take them on walks around the edges of the reservoir. They'd explored the peninsula that stretched around their home; he'd pointed out the roads that ended in water, the cellar holes, the crumbling stone walls. Later, after he bought a car, they'd driven to the north tip and the narrow western finger, and then finally to the base where the dam rose up. That had become the place they'd visited most often. For three years, until the accident, that had been the place where she'd begun to know the stranger who was her father.

There had been no park then, no paved lots or neat signs or picnic tables: only the one road to the dam, which was closed to the public, and a handful of trails winding through woods and weeds. The trail Wiloma's father always took them on led to a knoll quite close to the dam. They had sat there on an old blanket and gazed at the long, low mass holding back the water.

"I watched them build that," her father used to say. "It's just dirt inside the facings: packed dirt. That's all that's holding the water in." He'd pointed to the islands dotting the water and said, "Mt. Washburn. Mt. Doubleday. Those used to be hills—we used to climb them." Then he'd launched into stories about the drowned towns. Winsor, Stillwater, Pomeroy, Nipmuck; where he used to live. The tiny branch of the railroad that had run north and south through the valley, following the Paradise River and stopping every few miles. On and on he'd gone, using words she couldn't understand, describing sights she couldn't imagine—she'd been five, and then six and then seven, and it was all she could do to get used to his presence.

She'd loved the water, which sparkled and danced and was full of fish and harbored long-legged herons and ospreys, but she thought of the dam as a monster. Men were buried in it, her father said. Men who'd died working on it. There were fish who'd been sucked up by the huge hydraulic pumps and laid down in the silt, snails and weeds and clams and tools and lost gloves and toads. After he showed her the cemetery, just beyond the dam, where the dead people from the lost towns had been reburied, she had nightmares in which she saw the dam as a dragon, devouring everything and then wedging itself across the river's mouth.

She'd forgotten all that until she saw the dam again. In the moonlight, the dam had looked clean and pale and benign, but she had bent over the dash of Waldo's car and cried.

"What is it?" Waldo had asked. "Is this where your house used to be?"

"No," she'd managed to tell him. "Not here—it's miles north of here, this is only the dam. This is just where I thought we'd start looking."

"Do you think your uncle's here?"

"No. Maybe. I don't know—he could be anywhere."

"We'll find him in the morning." Waldo had been sweet and soothing; he'd given her his handkerchief and then had taken charge of finding them places to eat and stay. A little motel lay just down the road from a restaurant he liked the looks of, and he'd driven up to it and checked out the rooms and taken two in the back, where it was quiet. She hadn't had to do anything. He hadn't asked her what she wanted or what she thought; he had taken the rooms, brought back the keys, driven them to the restaurant and steered her in, ordered their drinks. He had listened patiently to her choked tales of childhood. Now he sat tipped back in his chair a bit, with his legs crossed and his shirt collar open and his jacket unbuttoned. His left hand, resting on the arm on his chair, tapped in time to the music playing in the background.

"How are you doing?" he asked. "Feeling better?"

"Much." She had been so calm when they started their trip, and the trip had been so pleasant and civilized, that the upswelling of emotion she'd felt at the dam had caught her by surprise. She hadn't cried like that in years, and certainly not in front of Waldo. But she felt calmer now, numbed by the noise and the alcohol.

The music pulsing through the restaurant had gentled and slowed, and she saw that some people had risen and were dancing in a small cleared area near the bar. Waldo said, "Would you like to?" and she said, "What?"

"Dance." He gestured at the spinning couples. "We used to be pretty good."

"I don't know. I haven't danced in years."

He rose and took her hand and helped her up. "Come on. We'll dance a little and then we'll call it a day. Things will sort themselves out in the morning."

Her legs were floating, disjointed. He held up his left hand and she folded her right hand into it and placed her other on his shoulder, against his jacket. His right palm pressed firmly between her shoulder blades, steering her among the other couples. Her feet followed his as if they had eyes, remembering the hundreds of times they'd danced together. Weddings, parties, anniversaries—they had always danced well together, or at least they had whenever they weren't fighting. He led firmly, without hesitation, and when she wasn't angry at him she had always loved letting her body relax and follow his.

He pulled her a little closer and she rested her cheek on his shoulder. His neck was still as heavy and muscular as it had been when they'd first met, and the same smell still rose from the skin pressed next to her nose—a mixture of soap (Dial soap, which she'd long since banished from her house after being haunted by visions of Waldo every time she stepped in the bathroom) and after-shave and starch from his shirt collar and the underlying tang that was purely him. When she moved her cheek up she found that his skin was scratchy; his beard was heavy and he'd always needed another shave in the evenings, before they went out. He said, with his lips right next to hers, "You feel exactly the same." She said, "You smell the same. It's so strange."

They danced for half an hour, drawing closer until they were pressed together like teenagers at a prom, and when Waldo finally said, "Shall we go back?" she could answer him only in a whisper.

Outside, in the parking lot, she stumbled over the curb and Waldo wrapped his arm around her shoulders. "Are you all right?" he asked.

"Tired," she murmured. "A little drunk. I hardly ever drink anymore." They drove to the motel in silence and walked around to the back, to the two rooms Waldo had taken side by side. "Well," he said as they stood before her door. "Who would've expected this to be so nice?"

He bent down—this man who had fathered her children, beside whom she'd slept for fifteen years—and he kissed her. He might have meant no more than a gentle, friendly kiss, good night, sleep tight; he might have meant no more than to be kind and reassuring; but her mind was lost at the dam, at the bottom of that pool of water or in the depths of the glasses she'd drained, and she kissed him back without thinking, the way she had when his kisses had been a question before they got into bed at night. She kissed him back yes and touched his neck, and he ran his hand down her back and over her hips, and they stood in the lighted doorway necking like kids.

She forgot about Sarah and Courteney. She forgot her dislike of him, and all her suspicions—that he had driven her here, that he was being so kind, only because he wanted a crack at the land that Brendan had promised her. She heard herself say, in a husky voice, "This is crazy, standing out here like this." She heard him answer, "Let's go inside." She watched his free hand fumble with the key in the oversize lock, but it was only when they moved inside her darkened room and he held the side of her head in his hand that she realized what she was doing. If they fell into bed, into their old, practiced embrace, she would never be able to let him go again.

She drew back from him. She tried to smile, although she knew he couldn't see her in the dark. She said, "You're sweet, taking care of me like this—really. I appreciate it. But maybe we should get some sleep." Her tongue was thick in her mouth.

She heard Waldo take a deep breath and then laugh. "Sorry," he said. "All that dancing—I got carried away. I don't know what I was thinking."

You were thinking of us, she wanted to say. The way we

used to be, all the time we spent together—how could you give it all up? She said, "We're both exhausted. Will you wake me early?"

"Seven? We'll have some breakfast and then we'll take a look at the maps and start wherever you want." He touched her hair and then he left.

Wiloma undressed in the dark and then lay down carefully on the bed. When she closed her eyes the room began to spin. She sat up, her spine pressed against the headboard, and she turned on the reading lamp. Her body felt prickly, warm, oversensitive; next door, through the thin wall, she could hear Waldo moving around. He brushed his teeth. He dropped his shoes on the floor with a thump. She tried not to remember the slow, deliberate way he used to undress in their bedroom. She tried to tell herself she was glad she'd sent him away.

She did some breathing exercises and then meditated for ten minutes. Body is a reflection of Spirit, she reminded herself. The body cannot desire what the Spirit does not want. Her Spirit did not desire Waldo, not at all; she and Waldo were totally unsuited. And the yearning she felt in her skin and bones was false, an artifact, a creation of the alcohol that had poisoned her system and of her exhaustion and fear. It was insignificant, nothing, and she was glad she'd had the sense to send him away.

She was glad, and yet she could not sleep. She picked up the phone, thinking that she might, despite the lateness of the hour, check in with Wendy and make sure she and Win were all right, but when she dialed her number, a voice she couldn't place right away answered, "White residence."

"Hello?" The voice clicked in her brain. "Christine? Is that you?"

"Wiloma," Christine said.

Wiloma held the phone away from her and stared at it. Christine—what was she doing there? "I thought you were

179

coming tomorrow. I'm sorry, I meant to call you earlier. There's been a little problem with my uncle."

"I heard. Wendy told me all about his disappearance. But I know you'll find him—you know how important it is that I start work with him immediately."

"I know," Wiloma said. "We haven't found any trace of him yet, but I think I know where he's headed—with some luck I'll find him tomorrow morning. I'll have him home with you by dinnertime."

"Your husband's with you?"

"Ex-husband."

"Whatever. Don't let him distract you—remember that he does not have the best interests of this Healing at heart."

With her words, Wiloma suddenly saw the evening's events in a different light. Christine was right, she thought—Waldo had not come on this trip to help Brendan, nor had he held her out of desire or love. He wanted something, several somethings, and none of them were worthy. She would have to guard herself against confusion. He was sleeping already, in the room next to her; she thought she could hear his gentle snores. He was sleeping, and dreaming of Sarah and Courteney, and plotting the houses he hoped to convince her to let him build on Brendan's land, and she'd been a fool to let his warm hands and the bewildering fragrance of his neck seduce her. She was here to find her uncle; nothing more.

"I'm all set up here," Christine said. "We're ready to go. But you have to bring your uncle to me soon. We don't have much time."

"Tomorrow," Wiloma said, and she thought of her children. They couldn't have been pleased to have Christine arrive unannounced. She hoped they had been polite. "May I talk to Wendy?" She wanted to hear her daughter's voice, wanted to tell her what had happened—not about the restaurant, not in detail; not about Waldo's warm hands or the dancing or the moment at the door, but just something, anything: "We had a pleasant evening," she might say. "Your father and I."

Christine said nothing. "Hello?" Wiloma said. "Are you there?"

"I'm here."

"Would you put Wendy on?"

"It's terribly late," Christine said after a brief hesitation. "The children are fine, but it's so late—maybe it would be better to wait until tomorrow to talk to them."

Wiloma looked at her watch. It was late, it was quarter past one; it wouldn't be fair to wake Wendy just for the comfort of hearing her voice. And Wendy and Win were safe, she knew, in Christine's care—she hadn't felt entirely comfortable leaving them alone, and Christine's presence in the house reassured her. "It's all right. I'll talk to them tomorrow."

"That would be best."

"They're all right? They must have been surprised to see you."

"They're fine. They were a little startled, but you prepared them well. They're nice children."

"They are," Wiloma said.

"How about you? Are you all right? You sound a little displaced. Disoriented."

"I'm fine," Wiloma said. She felt a sudden yearning to confide in Christine, but she pushed it aside; Christine had enough to do, she had to focus on Brendan. "I'll see you tomorrow."

"Tomorrow," Christine said.

Wiloma hung up and slept for a while, but her dreams were haunted by visions of Brendan, shrunken and writhing in pain, trying to die and unable to free his Spirit from his body. She woke drenched in a clammy sweat. I have to find him, she thought. I can't let him die like Da. Then she lay in the darkness, unable to keep herself from reliving her grandfather's last days.

She'd been alone in the house with him, in Coreopsis:

1961, six weeks after her nineteenth birthday. Gran had died that March of a heart attack, and Brendan had left for St. Benedict's; Henry had married Kitty and fled with her to Irondequoit. Her neighbors had been busy baling hay and her friends were working or off to college or newly married or pregnant or both; and she'd been trapped alone with Da in a house that smelled of death.

The house had smelled of other things as well. It smelled of a refrigerator seldom cleaned, of food left out on countertops, of the damp spot below the sink where water dripped from a leaky pipe. It smelled of the mice that had drowned in the basement—that July had been wet, there'd been puddles down there—and of cat: Mimi had been fifteen, and sometimes she went on the furniture. It smelled of Da, who had lain in his bed all summer, wasted and incontinent, while the cancer that had first appeared as a lump in his armpit ate him away.

She had dreaded Da's death and feared that he would never die. Weeks went by when she spoke only to him, and to the doctor who came once a day to give him morphine. Henry had been so caught up with his new wife, his new life, that he hardly ever called, and when he did she could feel him straining not to hear her need for help. He was very busy, he said. He was starting his first development and finishing his first house. He was in love, he said; he could not leave Kitty even for a day; did she need any money? He sent handsome checks she didn't need, and when she said she was frightened, he offered to hire a nurse.

But Da slept most of the time, and he didn't want a stranger in the house. When he woke his dreams spilled over into his conversations, and he spoke of the flock of birds he saw on the walls, of a lake where he'd once fished, of dirt, water, moss, rocks, clouds. He fell inward, behind his eyes, and he talked to Gran and to Wiloma's dead father, and to Brendan, who was gone. There were bees, he said, in the ice that formed on their pond, and sometimes he moved his swollen hands on the sheets and said, "A reservoir?" in a voice still fresh with disbelief.

He floated through his past like a leaf on the river, and while he dipped and swam Wiloma sat beside him and read. She sat next to the bed on which she'd arranged his limbs—he'd been big, but now he was nothing but bones and knobs so dense it took two hands to lift them. She read to fend off the urge to flee and to keep at bay the scenes she saw: her own life, about to open up to her. The city where she might live, the children she might someday have—she saw the house locked, empty, gone, and the life she'd lived there finally done.

On the night before Da died, when he said, "I want to go. I'm ready," and then closed his eyes and waited, she saw the stone walls of their house tumbled and covered with grass. Da said, "Help me," and she thought of placing a pillow over his face, releasing them both. She picked up the pillow and held it and then knew she couldn't; he was in pain but he was still alive. She rubbed the brittle bones of his hands instead. Then she reached for the book on his table, which had lain there all along but which she'd never touched before. Words, she remembered thinking. Distraction. The book had been written by a British scientist and published in 1872, twenty years before Da was born: *The Forms of Water in Clouds & Rivers, Ice & Glaciers*, faded gilt words on a faded red spine.

That night, while Da lay struggling to shed his body, she read the first few pages and learned again that water might be a gas or a liquid or a solid; clouds or steam or rain or breath, rivers or ice or snow. She had that book still, in a cedar chest in the attic. The title and long passages were still burned into her brain. *You may notice in a ballroom*, she read— oh, she remembered this, she remembered the words exactly—*that as long as the door and windows are kept closed and the room remains hot, the air remains clear; but when the door or windows are opened a dimness is visible, caused by the precipita-*

tion to fog of the aqueous vapor of the lungs. If the weather be intensely cold the entrance of fresh air may even cause snow to fall.

In the margin, surprising her, were words in Da's spidery hand. *I have not seen this,* he'd written. *But perhaps it snows more heavily over the reservoir than elsewhere? All the breath in all those drowned houses . . .*

He meant the Stillwater, Wiloma knew—the very place she'd seen tonight for the first time since childhood. An easy seven-hour drive, which she'd never made; the place Da had ranted and raved about and that her father had brooded over. Da had told his stories again and again while she and Henry sat trapped at the dining room table in Coreopsis, and the stories had been different from, but related to, the ones their father had told them on Sunday mornings. Six villages lay in that valley, Da had said; and he had been born there and Gran had come as a little girl, from Ireland; and he and Gran had married and had two boys and one had gone to China; and he couldn't leave his farm to Wiloma's father because it lay under the water; and the land was taken and leveled and burned. Of course she'd never made the drive, she'd always known what she'd find here. Graves, ashes, ruins, bones. Being back here was like losing her parents all over again.

In the weeks before Da's death, he had hardly ever recognized her. She'd been grateful for that—she did not want him, did not want anyone, to know the ways in which she touched him. For weeks she had rolled his body from side to side each day and changed the sheets beneath him. She'd washed and powdered and bandaged the sores on his shoulders and elbows and back; she'd passed a damp cloth over his nipples and crotch and the deep hollows above his collarbones. She'd taken his pulse, she'd taken his temperature, she'd cleaned his mouth and ears. But Da had slept through all that, or drifted in some state that was like sleep, only wilder, and she'd told herself he didn't know whose hands touched him.

On the night before his death, she read and dozed and

tended to him and read. The sun rose and the cicadas began their August drone. From time to time she touched his head or raised him slightly or lowered him, trying to ease his labored breaths. In his dreamy state that wasn't sleep he could follow her instructions: *Lean forward, Da. Can you swallow this?* The doctor had left pills for her to place under Da's tongue, but sometimes the wedge-shaped hollow there was so dry that the pills wouldn't dissolve. She lifted his tongue like a piece of cloth and dripped water onto the tablets, rain from her fingertips.

Swallow, Da, she remembered saying. *Can you swallow?* He lay somewhere between sleep and death, already far away, and when she could pull her eyes away from him, she read. She skipped around in his book and read the bits he'd underlined, trying to find what had comforted him.

What is the structure of the ice over which we skate in winter? she read. *Quite as wonderful as the flowers of the snow. I have seen in water slowly freezing six-rayed ice stars formed, floating freely on the surface. Lake ice is built of such forms wonderfully interlaced.*

Da and Gran had brought her and Henry to Coreopsis in the winter, when the reservoir was frozen; she and Henry had come because they had no place else to go and stayed because they were children. A stream ran through their new place and fed the onions and corn and squash; rain fell and became confused with the rain that had fallen the night of the dance and the steam that rose from the cows in winter and the snow that fell and would not stop. *The old pond,* Da had written in his book, near the drawing of an ice flower. *I pulled Brendan out the day he went through the ice.*

He and Gran had saved her and Henry just as surely, Wiloma thought, but they hadn't been able to see it then. Exhausted, broken-tongued, they'd clung together at school, where their new classmates had treated them as if their misfortunes were contagious. But the farm had been so silent it had frozen them silent, too, and Da, so old even then, hadn't been able to find the words to make them talk.

Da breathed through his open mouth, the three teeth that had anchored his bottom plate standing dry and yellow, like stumps. "Tonight, maybe," the doctor had whispered, when he'd visited at noon. He'd moved his stethoscope over Da's back and said, "His lungs are filling. It won't be long." When he left, she'd moistened a cotton swab and rubbed it over Da's lips and gums. He'd moved his tongue; he'd swallowed.

You cannot study a snowflake profoundly without being led back by it step by step to the contribution of the sun, she read. *It is thus throughout nature. All its parts are interdependent and the study of any one part completely would really involve the study of all.* The words were engraved on her brain still—all the words she'd read those last two days. She had never been able to forget either them or the way Da had looked.

At ten, that last night, he opened his eyes after rolling in pain for hours. He said, "Eileen! Watch out, you'll tear your dress"—he'd been talking to Gran, Wiloma remembered, as if Gran were there in the room with them—but then he said, quite lucidly, "Wiloma. Am I going someplace after this? Will I know you're all right? Will I see you?"

This, when after Gran's sudden death he'd begged to follow her. All his bark had vanished, all the flinty reserve that had made her hide her heart from him, and she looked into his cloudy eyes and lied. Or said what felt to her like a lie: "Yes," she said.

"How do you know?"

"I just know," she said, thinking of the times, all through high school, when she'd dreamed of leaving Coreopsis. A hundred times she'd imagined taking her diploma, leaving the stage, setting aside her cap and gown, and picking up her suitcase. Taking a bus to anywhere, leaving that life for another. She tried to offer Da a similar version of comfort—not the one she would offer now that she had the Church, but the best she could manage then. "You have to have faith," she said.

He shuddered and she knew what was troubling him: he'd been raised a Catholic but had scorned his church since the reservoir had drowned it.

"Not what the priests told you," she said. "Just faith. That there's something else, another place."

"What does it look like?"

And she tried—she'd been so young then, so ignorant, it had been the best she could do—to invent something pleasing. "There's a valley," she said, and as she spoke she saw it clearly in her mind. Gran had told her and Henry a story when they'd first come to Coreopsis. A boat, a journey, a secret place. Talking animals. The land of the blessed, Gran had said. The country of the young. Henry had sat on the chair beside them, rocking, waiting, and she had curled around Gran's legs, listening to her tales.

"There's a tree," she told her grandfather. "In the valley." His lids were transparent and the veins in them branched like coral. She told him about the fields and flowers and streams, the animals grazing, the flocks of birds. How the sun shone all day, how it was never too hot or too cold; how at night it rained just enough for the plants and how fruit hung from the branches.

"Are there people?" he asked.

"Lots," she said. "No one ever grows old there. No one ever dies." He grasped her thumb with his finger and held on. "Gran is there," she continued. "And my parents, and yours. It will feel like you've come home."

The words seemed to comfort him, and he fell back to sleep before she could say anything else. The stars moved; his fever rose. When she went to take his pulse, his arm felt cool and waxy, and she couldn't find the flutter she'd counted with her fingers for so long. She brushed her hair from her ear and pressed her head to his chest—there was his heart, beating still, but muffled and much too fast.

He coughed from time to time, wet gasps that cleared nothing. She understood that he would not wake again. She wished—she had wished then, and she wished it even more strongly now, had felt it more and more every year—that she'd held his hands and stretched the truth and said, "We were happy here. We loved our lives. We hardly missed our parents once we had you." He had given them what he could, everything he had. Mimi jumped on his bed and crept among the pillows wedged beneath elbows, hips, and knees; pillows meant to take the place of flesh and keep bone from metal, bone from bone. Da's head fell sideways, his neck so stiff she couldn't move it back.

In her book, Da's book, Da had marked the last page, where the author had bidden his readers farewell. *Here, my friend, our labors close,* she remembered reading. She read out loud; she slipped a hand between Da's cheek and the pillow it was pressed against. She read slowly, her lips at Da's ear. *It has been a true pleasure to have you at my side for so long. In the sweat of our brows we have often reached the heights where our work lay, but you have been steadfast and industrious throughout. Here and there I have stretched an arm and helped you to a ledge, but the work of climbing has been almost exclusively your own.*

Parents and children, Da had written on that page. Or maybe it was *parents are children*—his handwriting was so bad it was hard for her to be sure. He drew one last breath after she read those words, and then he was silent. She looked up from her book. Silence. His hands and feet were cold and his skin no longer felt like skin. She laid her head on his chest again and heard only her own blood, rushing in her ears. Air filled his open mouth—air, not breath—and when she pushed his lower jaw gently up, his mouth would not stay shut. She closed his eyes with her right hand and bathed him one last time. His left hand was bent in the shape that had held her thumb, and she unfolded it and dressed him and settled the blanket around his feet.

THE FORMS OF WATER

Mimi jumped up on his chest, she remembered, and his right eye floated open, but there was nothing left, it wasn't him, it was flesh, stone, clouds. The wind blew through the open window and caught his spirit, which spiraled up like a moth and took part of her with it. Ice to water, water to vapor, vapor to snow and rain. *Here then we part,* she read over his shell: the last words in the red-bound book. *And should we not meet again, the memory of these days will still unite us.*

He was gone before she could say all she'd meant to, gone years before she'd had any knowledge of the Church or of how she might have eased his Spirit's passage. She would not, if he were dying now, have told him a fairy tale about a valley or read to him from a red book that was full of pretty words but had no substance. She would have read to him from her Manual. She would have said what she still had a chance to say to Brendan, the words Christine would recite with her as a part of the Healing: *Our bodies, consisting of flesh and bone, are made of the dust of the earth and have no significance. Without the light of the Spirit they are corrupt and mortal. Every creature is created Spirit and shall return to Spirit, swallowed up like a drop in the ocean.* She would have said to Da— she would say to Brendan, she would not let him die as Da had, comforted clumsily by an ignorant girl—*Paradise is not a place but a state of mind, in which all manifestations of Spirit are immortal and in harmony. We are as angels there, pure shafts of ethereal light.*

But in order to say that, she had to circumvent Henry. Henry, with his transparent excuses, had left her all alone when she'd most needed him. Now, when Brendan most needed her, he had stolen Brendan away. In the darkness of her motel room, she thought of Henry as he'd been when they'd first arrived in Coreopsis. A little boy, but still older and wiser than her, he had whispered *no* as they hid in their rooms and puzzled over Da's outbursts.

"Does Da hate us?" she remembered asking Henry then.

"No," he'd said. "Da misses Dad. We remind him of him."
Henry had understood that, but he didn't seem to understand anything anymore, and she was, she realized now, afraid of him. Afraid the way she'd fear a cobra or a Martian: afraid they no longer shared any common speech or understanding. She would charm him, she thought. Lie to him if she had to; fight him if it came to that. But she would not let her uncle die alone.

22

Two Hours into their trip, Lise told Roy he had to let her drive. It was only fair, she said, that they split the drive into equal segments. It was only reasonable.

"Sit up here with me," Lise told Delia next, after they'd all finished stretching their legs by the side of the road. "Keep me company." Win claimed the passenger-side window in the back, and so Roy ended up in the middle, wedged between Wendy and Win. When Wendy whispered, "Why did you let Lise do that?" Roy whispered back, "What's the point of fighting? She'll only take it out on Delia."

Which was true, Wendy thought; when Lise was crossed she always turned on Delia. But she wondered how Roy had figured this out. Then she wondered if any man would ever know something like that about her.

As soon as Lise started driving, she looked over her shoulder at Roy and said, "Why do you keep this car? It's a piece of shit. The steering's so loose I feel like I'm floating. The brakes are soft."

"It's an old car," Roy said patiently, but Lise couldn't leave it at that; every rattle and wheeze upset her. "Is that one of the tires?" Lise said. "Is something loose in the trunk? Do you think that tapping means anything?"

"I don't know," Roy said finally. "Do you think it's going to blow?"

Delia laughed loudly and Wendy snickered despite herself. Delia had brought along a bottle of vodka, which she sipped from now and again despite Lise's objections. When Delia passed the bottle back to Roy, Roy took a long hit and then held it out to Wendy, who shook her head. "I better not," she said, not wanting to tell him that she never drank anymore. "I'll drive after Lise."

"Suit yourself," Roy said. He drank some more and then passed the bottle back to Delia, who turned up the radio and started singing along with the tunes that filled the car. Roy sang, too, and eventually Wendy joined in. For a while, then, except for Lise's brittle silence and the fact that Win had somehow fallen asleep against the window with his own radio plugged into his ears, Wendy found the journey almost festive. They might have been driving to the mountains or the ocean, she thought. Driving all night like any other group intent on landing someplace wonderful by morning. No one said a word about what they were really doing, and the music almost muffled her fears.

Christine's words echoed in Wendy's head in the gaps between the songs. *Your great-uncle's Spirit is getting ready to transit,* she'd said. *I can make sure his Spirit finds the Light.* But there was no light, Wendy thought, as she tapped out a rhythm on her thigh. There was no way out of this. The best she could hope for was that she found her family before her mother flipped out completely, before her uncle did something stupid, before Grunkie got hurt. All she could do on this trip was hope to restore everyone to the state they'd been in before Grunkie vanished in that van. Only this morning, she'd dreaded and despised that state. Now it seemed almost desirable.

She pushed away Christine and Grunkie, her parents and her uncle. The car was moving, the music was blaring. She was young and Roy was sitting next to her. She thought of the way he'd looked the afternoon he'd opened his door clad only in his shorts. She thought of him and Delia intertwined on his mattress on the floor; she thought of how she belonged in the front seat with Lise—crabby, frustrated Lise—and Delia belonged back here with Roy. Then she thought how nothing, not even her fears, could move her from this seat just now. Her body felt very peculiar, as if her bones had expanded and were stretching her skin into a thin, taut film. Roy's hip was touching hers, and although she had only Lise to thank for this she relished the gentle contact.

Lise refused to give up the wheel when they stopped at one of the Thruway plazas for gas. Delia said she was hungry but too tired to move. Roy said he needed to take a leak and so Wendy had to move after all; once she'd stepped out to let Roy by, she decided to go inside and find something to eat. She bought a bag of chips from the vending machine in the lobby, as well as a bag of M&M's and another of pretzels. Then she went into the gift shop next door, and as smoothly as if she were still fifteen and used to doing this every day, she lifted two road maps, a white plastic mug that said I ♥ THE ADIRONDACKS, a T-shirt printed with a picture of a moose, and a toy log cabin. One by one she slipped these things into her bag, although she wanted none of them. In her mind she could still hear Christine's acid comments about the things her uncle Henry had stolen, but his actions didn't seem related to her in any way.

The woman at the counter had thin, dry hair, scraped back into a wispy tail and splotched with white roots. Her arms were bare and enormous. She'd looked at Wendy when Wendy walked in, but after a brief glance she'd turned back to her magazine and Wendy had realized that she was invisible. Her clothes concealed her, and her well-cut hair and her straight teeth. She looked down at her neat jeans and her blue-and-white shirt, both of which Sarah had bought for her: her jeans were unfaded and her shirt had extra buttons on the sleeve plackets and crisp pleats at the yoke. It had never occurred to her before that this cleaned-up version of herself, which her father and Sarah had manufactured, might serve as a perfect disguise.

The woman never looked at Wendy, nor did she check the mirrors hanging overhead. Wendy stuck out her tongue. The woman didn't notice. Wendy took a Yankees sweatshirt off a pile, held it out, refolded it, and then laid it quite deliberately in her bag, on top of the rest of her loot. The woman said nothing. She looked up when Wendy walked out the door, but her face was blank and no sirens rang. Wendy realized she could have walked off with anything there. No one looked at her in the lobby either, and in the bathroom women walked past her as if she weren't there. She looked like anyone else, she realized. Like any other middle-class girl, as safe and unthreatening as soap.

When she got back in the car she shoved the bag between her feet, and the next time Delia passed the bottle she took a modest drink. How could anything happen to a girl who looked like her? The vodka tasted like nothing but seemed to relieve the tenseness in her skin. She drank some more. Lise drove just at the speed limit through the quiet night, and Wendy laughed at the steady stream of jokes Delia and Roy exchanged. Delia was funny, she saw. Roy was funnier. Win was asleep and Wendy felt a surge of affection for him and reached behind Roy to touch Win's shoulder. Her hand brushed Roy's neck on its way back. Delia told a long joke about two old women and a vase of flowers, and then she yawned and stretched and leaned her head into the window and said, "I'm going to catch a few Zs, okay? So I'll be fresh to drive." And although Lise protested that Delia was much too drunk to drive even after a nap, Delia just said, "We'll see," and then closed her eyes.

"Are you all right?" Roy asked Lise. "Don't you feel sleepy?"

"Not at all." Lise seemed to have no intention of ever relinquishing the wheel. "I can drive all night."

"We'll take shifts," Roy said firmly. "Just like you said. But if you don't need the company now, I guess I'll try and catch a snooze, too. Let Wendy drive when you're tired."

"I can drive," Wendy said, but everyone ignored her. "I could drive right now."

She sat very still as Roy slumped down in the seat, angled his legs away from hers, and leaned his head and shoulders back. His left shoulder was just touching her right arm. His left hip was resting against her right thigh. After a few minutes, as his breathing slowed, his head slumped over until it rested on her shoulder. A few minutes later, when she was sure he was asleep, she let her head tilt until her cheek rested on his hair. Of course Delia wanted him, everyone wanted him. His hair was surprisingly soft.

She moved slowly, imitating the sleepy movements Win made on the other side of Roy from time to time. She drew up her legs and then stretched them out next to Roy's. Her whole right leg now lay against his left one, which was warm and solid and so delightful that she sighed, just as Delia sighed in the front seat, and let her left arm cross her body and rest against Roy's hip. If Lise looked in the mirror, she thought, she would see only a row of tilted bodies collapsed and crushed against each other and as innocent as a tangle of puppies. Lise had turned down the radio, but the music still drowned out the soft breathing of Roy and Delia and Win and hid the sound of Wendy's, which had quickened.

She still felt invisible. She was just Delia's cousin, playing Delia's game: pretending to be with Roy for Lise's benefit. Everyone was asleep but Lise, and Lise thought she and Roy belonged together, and she let her hand stroke Roy's thigh and her cheek rub gently against his hair, knowing this was stealing more surely than what she'd done in the store. But nothing she wanted came to her when she behaved herself, she thought. She'd bent her life into a shape it wasn't meant to have for her mother's benefit, and here her mother was chasing a paranoid notion over the hills.

Roy turned to her. He was still asleep, or mostly asleep, but he rolled into Wendy's hand and drew his legs up next to hers. He slipped an arm around her and drew her against him, so that her cheek slipped down next to his and their mouths were almost touching. His touch filled her with gratitude. She had thought she might never have this, not even after she escaped from her family. She tried not to move.

She was Delia's size and shape, and she thought that Roy, in his sleep, must be moving against her the way he moved against Delia on the mattress they shared. The car was very dark. He pushed himself gently against her hand and she let her palm press into him. His head turned, searching for her mouth, and at first she kept her lips taut and closed, so that everything might still seem to be his mistake, his desire; so that she might still plead sleepy innocence if he woke. Then he let the arm around her shoulders drop down until his hand was on her breast, and she opened her mouth until she was kissing him back, and his hand was sliding down and under the edge of her shirt and back up against her skin, and his tongue was in her mouth and then on her neck, and he was pressing and pressing against her hand until he lowered his own and unzipped his fly and moved her hand inside.

His eyes were closed, but he could not possibly still be asleep. And yet his eyes were closed, and his face looked trusting and pleased, and nothing about him indicated that he felt anything like the fear and exultation rushing through her. The sprig of mistletoe in her pocket pricked her thigh, and she thought of the powers Christine had ascribed to her twigs and seeds. *Release the Spirit from the flesh*, she remembered Christine saying. As if anyone would want to separate the two. Her spirit was *in* her flesh; her body felt completely beyond her control. Roy ran his mouth down her neck and her collarbones and she gave up then, if she had not already given up minutes before.

She wasn't sure how long they lay like that, groping, rubbing, and she couldn't be sure whether Roy opened his eyes when he came in her hand or the minute after, when he muttered and untangled his legs from hers and then yawned and looked up and smiled drowsily. He blinked; he focused his eyes. He whispered, "Wendy. I'm sorry, I fell asleep. I didn't mean to get all mashed up against you. I was having a dream."

"Some dream," she said.

He moved quickly away from her and she smiled at him. He looked over the seat at Delia, who was still sleeping, and at Lise, whose eyes were fixed on the road. Then he looked back at Wendy and made the strangest face, half sheepish grin and half rueful grimace. She kept on smiling. Her family was so far away that they might as well be on another planet. She stretched herself and smiled and smiled until Roy leaned back to zip his fly and she caught sight of Win's eyes, which were open.

23

FROM THE "LETTERS TO THE EDITOR" OF THE *PARADISE VALLEY Daily Transcript:*

October 14, 1933
Dear Sirs:

I write in support of Mr. William Kessler's recent proposal that valley residents join in sending letters to the Governor, deploring the placement of graves in the newly dedicated Paradise Valley Memorial Cemetery. " 'The woof of time is every instant broken and the track of generations effaced,' " he said, quoting de Tocqueville. " 'Those who went before are soon forgotten; of those who will come after, no one has any idea.' "

And truly the Commission's astonishing oversight is deplorable. Bad enough that some 6,000 of our ancestors' graves must be disturbed, and their remains removed to this new and sterile ground south of the dam site. But that the new graves should be jumbled together so grotesquely, without re-

gard for their placement in the original cemeteries or even for the towns where they once lay—one feels they might as well have been bulldozed into a common pit. Families and neighbors have been separated; old enemies placed bone by bone. And meanwhile the Commission insults the dignity of the living just as surely every day.

Was it truly necessary for our own Cecil Blake, now approaching his 80th year, to be forcibly removed from his hermit's shack in Nipmuck and sent to an institution simply because no one wanted to be responsible for him now that so many of his neighbors have left? Did the railroad have to stop Sunday service on our branch line and reduce service the rest of the week to one train per day? Must the Commission rent out the homes it has already purchased—homes that once belonged to our neighbors—to tourists, so they can live cheaply while gawking at our demise?

One insult follows another; it is almost too much to bear. The first noises of construction are in the air, and the time approaches when all of us must leave. But let us not leave quietly; let us not allow these insults to pass unremarked. Send letters, as Mr. Kessler urges, to our governor and to our representatives in Boston. We cannot leave our homes to our children, but we can leave behind an accurate record of what has happened here.

Frank B. Auberon, Sr.
Pomeroy

Part IV

The World
Is Made Up
of Our
Ideas

24

BONGO, WHINING TO GET OUT OF THE VAN, WOKE BRENDAN well before dawn; Brendan, waking flat on his back in a dark, airless space, felt a jolt of panic that kept him from sleeping again, even after he realized where he was. He listened to his galloping heart for a minute and then he called Henry's name twice. Bongo barked, and Henry opened the door of the van and crawled in.

"Don't you want to sleep some more?" Henry yawned.

"No," Brendan said. The people who might be looking for them had likely gone to bed late and would sleep for hours. This was the time to travel—through the hours of the night watch, during the time when he used to wake silently, gather with the others in the choir stall, chant the psalms of matins, and then watch until dawn arrived. During his first years at the abbey, he'd managed to wake his body each night but his heart had been dull and heavy and his hours of meditation had only been waking sleep. Over time he'd gained a certain alertness, and by the end of his fifth year he'd come to cherish those hours beyond all others. Sometimes, in the utter quiet, he'd thought he heard the earth spinning on its axis. Even now he often woke in his bed at St. Benedict's at two or three in the morning and rested silently until dawn, unable to pray but still able to watch and wait.

Today he wanted to spend those hours driving. He sat up cautiously—his neck felt frail and thin inside his brace, and his intestines felt as painful and twisted as his toes. "We'll miss all the traffic," he told Henry. "The road will be clear, we'll get to watch the sunrise. We'll be at the reservoir in time for breakfast, and then we'll have the whole day. Doesn't that sound good?"

Henry yawned so widely his jaw cracked. "If it's what you want. I can drive if I get some coffee in me." He clipped Bongo to a leash and stepped outside the van with him. In the silence Brendan heard the hiss and splatter as they relieved themselves. "Do you have to go?" Henry asked. "Do you need your cup?"

"No. I can't."

"I'll just say good-bye to Jackson, then."

"Let him sleep," Brendan said, thinking how Jackson was just beginning his long journey into solitude. "It's all he has."

Henry put on a clean shirt he took from the box at the back of the van, and then he dug out some things from Brendan's plastic bag and changed Brendan's shirt and socks for him. The attendants at St. Benedict's had known how to roll the old socks off and the new ones on, but Henry was astonishingly clumsy. "Didn't you ever dress Lise and Delia?" Brendan asked.

"They didn't have feet like this."

In the dim light from the overhead bulb, Brendan contemplated his twisted toes, which looked like the neat, crushed packets of bones spit up by owls. Henry dabbed at Brendan's face and hands, and then his own, with a T-shirt moistened with water from the jug he carried for Bongo. Then he slid Brendan off Jackson's blankets and folded them into a pile on the ground. He lifted Brendan's chair into the van and, after a good deal of struggling, managed to get Brendan back into his chair and the chair locked back into place. The garage was still dark and there was no sound from Jackson. Henry scribbled a note of thanks on the back of an envelope and wedged it into one of the lawn chairs.

Finally, after Henry gathered up Kitty's blankets and refolded them in back, and after he settled Bongo and found his Red Wings cap and asked Brendan what time it was and then cursed when he discovered that Brendan didn't have a watch and that his own was tucked into Jackson's pocket, he started the van and they eased their way down the rough dirt road. It had been dusk when they arrived and was very dark now. After a minute Henry said, "Hell. I don't have any idea where we're going."

"Just follow your nose," Brendan said. They banged and rattled through the woods until they came out on a small paved road, which led in turn to a larger road. There, after a few miles, they found an all-night convenience store with a gas pump. Henry bought some gas and some coffee, grumbling about how little money they had left. The sleepy woman who waited on them gave them directions back to their original route.

"Are you awake enough to drive?" Brendan asked. Henry sucked at his coffee as if it were air. Brendan sipped at his— it was fresh and it tasted fine.

"Sure," Henry said. "I'll just get something going on the radio here, some chatter to keep us entertained. Then we'll cruise."

Brendan had envisioned himself slipping silently through the liquid darkness, alert for the gentle graying that would mark the sun's arrival, but the talk show Henry settled on was not, after the first shock, so unpleasant after all. It ran from two A.M. until six each day, and as Brendan listened to the various callers, men and women, rational or deranged, opinionated or gentle-voiced or full of rage and confusion, he was touched to think of all these souls looking for answers during the same dark hours in which he and his companions had searched their hearts. Alone in their rooms, connected by telephones and a web of radio waves, they pondered questions and looked for answers in common. Is abortion wrong? the show's host asked. A flurry of answers followed. Should we educate our children at home? If a burglar enters your home at night, and you shoot him and he has no weapon, is it murder? Some of the talk was foolish, some of it not. Some callers broke into the subject at hand and said, "I want to tell you a story—something that happened to me, that may interest your audience," and then related the most astonishing tales. Their voices were broken by time and pain; they gave no names. In place of a church, a priest, a confessional, they had the anonymous absolution of strangers.

"This goes on every night?" Brendan asked.

"Every night, all night. There's one on almost every station."

"No kidding."

While Brendan listened, the dark road fell away before their headlights. They passed through Nelliston and Fonda and Amsterdam, East Glenville and Scotia and Niskayuna, and the road was so empty that each new set of headlights startled him. The headlights paled, the sky began to lighten, the Mohawk River appeared beneath a cloak of mist. They crossed the Hudson at Watervliet, just south of where the Mohawk poured in and around the time that a band of gold appeared on the horizon. They saw flocks of birds in Cropseyville and a few more cars and the first movements in diners and houses, and then the show was over and the news came on and then the weather.

"A gorgeous day," the announcer said. "Clear, bright, highs in the upper seventies." And then it was day.

The night watch had been painful for Brendan in China— arid, often despairing. His troubles had stuck in his mind like a swarm of bees, and when he sat in silent prayer the bees rose and buzzed between his ears. The sun had streamed into the cold stone church during lauds and illuminated the faces of his Chinese brethren: of Brother Anthony, who had been poisoned, and Brother Seraphim, whose head had been smashed by rocks; of Brothers Camillus and Anselm, who had died of dysentery during the march; of Brother Norbert, who had broken both legs falling off the narrow mountain trail. They were all gone, as were his companions at Our Lady of the Valley, and yet it was day, and he was alive, and he was out on the road and the sky was soft and golden. Behind Henry's back, he made the hand signs for the names of all the brothers he could remember.

They dropped south through the Berkshire Hills and then drove east on roads that grew smaller and smaller. As they began to head north again, Brendan recognized several small towns he'd visited as a boy. They turned left, right, left again, past new houses, new schools, new shopping centers; old churches and cemeteries; women jogging with dogs who set Bongo barking; small boys tossing balls. They came to a road running, narrow and twisted and pale, like a nerve beside a river. Then, almost without warning, they turned at a stop sign and came upon a shady square that looked much as it had fifty years ago.

"Stop," Brendan said, his voice shaking with excitement. "Stop here."

"Is this it?"

"Almost. We're so close I can smell it. The dam is right here in this town—this is the last one in the valley, the only one that was left. I can't believe we got this far."

Henry shook his head and rubbed his eyes. "I can't either. There's a coffee shop over there—how about I pull up and get us a little breakfast?"

"Get whatever you want. I'll wait here with Bongo."

Henry parked in one of the diagonal spaces fringing the square, under a horse chestnut covered with waxy blossoms.

He lowered himself stiffly to the ground. "I'll be back in five minutes. You'll be all right?"

"Fine." And although Brendan was as numb as a block of wood, although his eyes ached and his head throbbed and his hands were freezing, he still felt wonderful. Of course the names on the storefronts differed from those he remembered, and the big white houses surrounding the square had been cut into apartments or torn down or repainted, and of course the feed store was gone and so was the five-and-dime, but the post office was still in place and so were the Masonic Hall and the Congregational church. The square itself, with its center fountain and the wooden benches and the huge old oaks and sycamores, looked almost exactly as he'd remembered it, a cousin to the square in his vanished village.

On one of the benches near the sidewalk in front of the van, an old man was feeding pigeons. He had a big plastic sack on his lap, full of stale bread, and as Brendan watched he cast a handful of crusts around his feet. The birds, white and gray and tan and mottled, pecked at the crusts and at each other. The man threw some crusts away from the main clump of birds, toward two pigeons too shy or too young to fend for themselves, and when the other birds rushed in that direction he threw more crusts, distracting them, so that the two outsiders could eat. Then he took a bite from his own breakfast, a doughnut folded in white waxed paper.

His appetite, and his obvious enjoyment, made Brendan think back to the days when he could still eat happily. At his place in the refectory at Our Lady of the Valley, he had had a water jug, a spoon, a fork, a knife, a heavy mug, an enameled plate, and a large napkin draped over his mug. He'd eaten in silence, like the others, signing with his hands for bread or salt and listening to the low voice of the reader while he savored each mouthful. When he was done, he'd rinsed his utensils in his mug and dried them with his napkin, emptied the water from his mug into his soup bowl and dried the mug, and then draped his napkin over the mug, as it had been in the beginning. He'd given thanks for the food he'd eaten, but he'd never thought to give thanks for the desire or the ability to eat it.

Hunger had left him long ago, and now even the ability to force down food was gone, but he watched the old man and his pigeons with pleasure. The man finished his meal and scattered the rest of his crumbs. Then, to Brendan's astonishment, he rose and made his way slowly to the van. The bench was no more than twenty feet away, but it hadn't occurred to Brendan that, sitting with his face pressed to the window, he was as visible to the man as the man was to him.

The man wore a short-sleeved white shirt, open at the neck, and faded pants belted high on his stomach. His face was blotched with liver spots and his eyes were pale and watery. Although he looked to be about Brendan's age, his white hair was still very thick and rose in a neat brush cut. Brendan raised a shaky hand to his own wispy strands and Bongo barked as the man tapped on the window. Brendan needed both hands to roll the window down.

"Morning," the man said brightly. "Fine day, isn't it?"

In his voice, Brendan heard the loneliness and eagerness for talk that had made him wheel his own chair out to the stoplight near St. Benedict's. He wondered if this man sat on the bench each morning, snagging passersby. "It is," he agreed.

"Couldn't help but notice your van. You new in town?"

"Just passing through." Brendan found it odd to be on the receiving end of one of these conversational ambushes. Imagine, he thought. A man so lonely he wants to talk to me. He made an effort to be friendly. "I used to live around here," he said. "A long time ago."

"Did you." The man leaned toward the van, craning his neck for a better look at Brendan's face. "Would you be having family here still?"

"They're all gone," Brendan said. "We were from Pomeroy—one of the villages that's under the reservoir now."

The man's face brightened. "Hell, my family lived in Nip-muck—what's your name?"

"Brendan Auberon." Nipmuck had been the second village down from Pomeroy, just south of Stillwater and Stillwater Falls. He had once climbed two-thirds of the way up a horse chestnut in front of the church and seen the entire valley spread out below him. Had they cut down that tree? "My parents were Frank and Eileen Auberon," he continued. "They had a place out Williamson Road, near the abbey."

"Brendan? You're Brendan? Don't you remember me?"

Brendan couldn't find a trace in this man of anyone he'd ever known. "Marcus O'Brian," the man said. Brendan searched his memory.

"Your brother was the one I really knew," Marcus explained. "Frankie and I were altar boys together, and I used to come out to your folks' place sometimes. Frankie and I went into the service the same month. But that was later, after you took off."

"Marcus," Brendan said. A hazy memory surfaced—a small, wiry, red-haired boy who had tagged after him, along with Frank junior, during some of his rambles through the woods. Marcus and his family had walked to the Catholic church in Pomeroy each Sunday, and after Mass, Frank junior had often brought Marcus home.

"Your folks had the summer camp," Brendan said. "Camp Nichewaug, where all the rich kids from Boston came." Was the camp gone? The tidy white bungalows, the warm wooden docks with the splintery ramps, the canoes lined upside down on the racks?

"That's right. Of course that's gone now." Marcus rocked on his heels. "Do you have a few minutes? Why don't you come out and sit with me for a while?"

"I can't." Brendan realized that Marcus could see only his head and shoulders through the window. "But why don't you come in?"

Marcus fumbled with the van door, and then his face fell

as he saw Brendan's wheelchair. "Ah," he said. "I'm sorry.
I didn't know. You've been in that long?"

He climbed into the van and sat down in the passenger
seat. "Long enough," Brendan said.

"The war? No, of course not. You went into the monastery,
I remember. After high school. And then when they tore it
down, they sent you all away. I heard some of the brothers
went to Tennessee."

"Not me. I went to China—I was there during the Japanese
occupation. That's when this happened." Brendan pointed to
his legs. "Just arthritis. But it got a little out of hand."

"China? You monks get around."

Brendan made a face. "I left the Order thirty years ago."

"No," Marcus said. "You didn't."

"I did."

Marcus leaned forward and rested his hands on his knees.
"Was it women?" he whispered.

Brendan laughed. Marcus and Frank junior, he remembered, had once been caught getting drunk on sacramental
wine. "No," he said. "Not women. It was a lot of things—I
was just worn out. It stopped making sense to me."

"I can see that. Never made sense to me in the first place.
All those lists and rules—I was sick of it by the time we were
out of school. Remember Father Quinn?"

"Who could forget him?" Brendan said, but then he turned
the conversation. When he'd dreamed of this trip, he'd never
thought he might see anyone he knew. For years he'd
thought of himself as the valley's last survivor, although there
was no reason why this should be so—he was only eighty
and plenty of people lived longer than that. There were plenty
more, a few years younger than him, who might still remember the valley and yet be only in their seventies. But as glad
as he was to see another survivor, he found that he didn't
want to call back his childhood. Or not yet, at any rate, and
not here: just thinking of his old home, with the woods
stretched all around him and Frank junior still alive and mak-

ing mischief with Marcus, was enough to make his heart stutter. He remembered that he and Marcus hadn't really been very close, especially as they'd grown older. *But your parents*, Marcus had said when he'd heard of Brendan's decision to enter the Order. *Who's going to help them out? You're leaving Frankie stuck with everything.* Hadn't Marcus said that, sixty-odd years ago?

"But what have you been up to all these years?" he asked Marcus now. "What happened to you after I left?"

"I moved to Athol when they cleared the valley. Worked there for a while. Then there was the war. Then I came back, got married—Annemarie Scanlon, you probably don't remember her—and we had three kids. I sold insurance, thirty years. Annemarie died in '74."

Marcus paused and ran his fingers over the dash. He had tufts of white hair in his ears, Brendan saw. They made him look like an old cat. "Two of my kids live in Michigan now. One's on the West Coast. I live here." Marcus gestured toward a shabby white house across the square. "I've got a nice room there, and a nice part-time job—you know. It's just a life."

Just a life, thought Brendan. As if anyone's were ever that. He longed for details, but when he tried to imagine telling Marcus about his own life, he could see why Marcus had been so brief. It would take hours, days, for them to explain themselves to each other, and the telling would mean reliving everything. And who could stand that? Just surviving was work enough.

He felt tired, suddenly—enormously, overwhelmingly tired—and he wished he'd found Marcus a decade ago, when he'd still had some energy. His hands shaped a few signs in the air, the first signs of the Lord's Prayer, but he didn't realize they'd done so until he looked up and saw Marcus watching him curiously. "We used to hear you guys talked to each other with your hands," Marcus said.

"True enough," Brendan said, but he tucked his hands

under his shirt and willed them to be still. Bongo, who'd been watching them patiently, sighed and yawned and flopped to the floor and closed his eyes. Brendan wished he could lie down beside him.

"Nice dog." Marcus reached down and scratched Bongo's ears. "Yours?"

"My nephew's. He's the one who's driving—he went to get some coffee." Brendan was so tired he thought he might be asleep already, his eyes open but his brain completely disconnected. He struggled to keep the conversation going. "This job you have. What is it?"

But before Marcus could answer, Henry opened the door and stood before them with his hands full of paper sacks. "Hello?" he said. "Who's this?"

"This—" Brendan said, but it was all so complicated, how could he ever explain? Years ago, his abbot had told him that there were no true coincidences. There were lesser plans and greater plans, plans that might influence only the comets or a pair of paramecia. But every conjunction of events or people had a purpose, however small. Why had Marcus been sitting just there, feeding the pigeons just then?

Marcus shot out his hand and took over. "Marcus O'Brian," he said to Henry. "I was sitting here feeding the birds and I noticed Brendan watching me, so I came over to make a little conversation. And wouldn't you know, it's the damnedest thing. Brendan and I knew each other when we were boys."

"You're kidding," Henry said.

"No," Marcus said. "It's true." His hand still hung in the air, waiting for Henry to grasp it. "Brendan and his brother and I used to play together."

Henry's face paled. "You knew my *father?*"

Marcus looked at Brendan, who nodded. "This is Henry. My nephew."

"You're Frankie's boy?"

Henry grasped Marcus's hand. "I am."

"But we've met. You wouldn't remember, you were so

little—your father and I were in the service together, and I visited him and your mother a few times after we came home, before . . . didn't you have a sister? A little girl, curly brown hair?"

"Wiloma," Henry said. "You saw Wiloma."

Brendan leaned his head back and wished he were not so tired. Henry seemed to feel all the excitement at meeting Marcus that he should have felt himself, that he would have felt if his head had not grown so heavy that even his brace could hardly hold it up. The coincidence didn't seem to bother Henry at all. What kind of mind did he have? Brendan wondered. He had come to St. Benedict's for a routine visit, agreed to an unexpected trip, accepted the improbable gift of a van without a question. Now he accepted the appearance of this stranger who was no stranger equally easily. And yet it meant something that Marcus was here. It had to mean something.

Brendan let Marcus chatter on, filling Henry in on the details of how his family had known theirs, how he and Frank junior had done this and that, and how he remembered the very night Henry's mother and father had gotten engaged at the Farewell Ball. Brendan thought how he'd missed all of that. He'd been in the abbey when Marcus and Frank junior had been in high school; he'd been on his way to China during the Farewell Ball and had heard about it only years later, from his parents. He had never known Henry's mother, and it was strange to think that Marcus knew more of Henry's family than he did himself.

His throat was dry and sore. Quietly, interrupting the flow of talk, he said, "Henry? Did you happen to get some coffee?"

Henry looked down at the paper sacks. "Of course. I'm sorry." He dug out a steaming cup and offered it to Brendan. "You want something to eat? I didn't have much money left, but I got us some fried-egg sandwiches and a couple of Danish."

"Nothing for me," Brendan said.

"Marcus?"

"I'd take one of those egg sandwiches. If you've got no use for it."

Bongo sat up and drooled and whined as Marcus and Henry unwrapped their sandwiches. "Why, the poor thing's hungry," Marcus said. He plucked the egg from his roll and looked at Henry. "Do you mind?"

"I forgot," Henry said, looking abashed. "We've been driving half the night. Go ahead." Marcus tossed the egg to Bongo, who snapped it up and then wagged his tail so hard it thumped on the floor. Henry tossed him half a cheese Danish. "You lie down now," he said. "That's all you're getting." Bongo collapsed, licking his whiskers.

Marcus bit into his empty roll. "So, what are you two doing here? Not that I'm not thrilled to see you."

Brendan's left hand rose into the air and hung there for a minute before he was conscious of it. He was too tired to talk anymore. Henry spoke for both of them; to Brendan's surprise, he spoke clearly and well.

"Uncle Brendan never saw the reservoir," he told Marcus. "He left before the dam was finished, even before they'd cleared most of the valley, and he wanted to see what it looks like now. And he wanted to show me the place where I was born. Da—my grandfather, you might have known him—"

"Sure, I knew him. He was a fine man."

"Da had some land in East Pomeroy, outside the reservoir, that he gave to my father and Uncle Brendan—maybe you've seen it, if you visited my parents. We thought we'd go take a look at the part Uncle Brendan hung on to, if we can find it."

Marcus nodded. "That's nice land. That's a nice bit of woods."

Brendan raised his head. "You *know* it? Still? You know where it is?" It was meant, he thought. It was meant to be. He should have understood.

"Of course I do," Marcus said. "It's my job."

"What job?" Henry said. "You have a job?"

"Sure. I was just telling your uncle. I have a part-time job at the new reservoir Visitors' Center. Nice park—you ought to see it. Nice building, nice people. These kids fresh out of college put together exhibits about the valley's history, and what things were like before the reservoir, and I'm who they ask about the old times. I *am* the old times. They've dug up all these pictures and things and they want to know who the people were, and where the houses used to be, and . . . you know." Marcus laughed. "I have a desk there, nameplate and all. Not bad for an old coot."

"But the land," Brendan said. "My land?"

"It hasn't gone anywhere." Marcus turned to Henry. "Of course the cabin where your folks lived—that's been gone for years, someone bought that piece and logged it. But the chunk east of where the cabin used to be is still sitting there, untouched and as pretty as you please. I used to walk up there, wishing your father weren't gone and wondering what happened to the rest of your family—no one ever heard from your grandparents after they moved. Your grandfather was so furious at the way things had turned out that he turned his back on everything here. And then you kids just vanished after the accident . . . oh, it's nice up there. You ought to see it."

Henry's face was radiant with enthusiasm and greed, and Brendan groaned to himself. The land was how he'd lured Henry here, and he did want Henry to see it; he wanted to see it himself. But that wasn't all, or even most, of what he wanted. He wanted to see the water; he wanted, somehow, to see his lost home and his lost abbey. Henry said, "I know you're busy—but is there any chance you could take us up there?"

Before Marcus could answer, Brendan said, "We can find it ourselves. I'll recognize the roads."

"But this would be so much easier," Henry said.

"But—" Brendan said. It was wrong, all wrong—he didn't

want to impose on Marcus, and he'd wanted to see the reservoir alone. He'd had to have Henry because he needed a driver, but to add Marcus as well, as some sort of guide—he might as well go on a tour. He said, "And anyway, we want to see the reservoir, too. There are some places I particularly want to visit."

"No problem," Marcus said. "I'm supposed to go into work this morning and give a little talk to the Sunday tourists, but I'll just call and cancel, tell them I met some old friends. Then we could drive up the east side. There's a place near one of the gates, a little point where we can see the part of the reservoir that covers what used to be Pomeroy. It's right near your family's land—you can both see what you want."

Henry turned to Brendan. "'Wouldn't that be great? Who would have thought this would work out so well?"

He had no sense of curiosity at all, Brendan thought. No sense of wonder. For the first time since leaving St. Benedict's, Brendan felt overwhelmed. He had bribed Henry without thinking of the consequences, borrowed the van without thinking who might be upset, directed their way here without thinking what they might do when he arrived. He hadn't allowed for coincidences that might not be coincidental.

He closed his eyes and sighed and willed himself to accept whatever might come. This trip wasn't in his hands anymore and perhaps it never had been. He imagined the van as a skin-covered curragh, the road as an ocean, Henry and Marcus as his guides, and Bongo as the long-legged hound who led the monks to food and water on the first island Brendan's patron saint had found. He thought, I will see what they show me. I will go where they take me. He opened his eyes and said, "Wonderful. Lead on."

25

THE WOMAN AT THE DESK INSIDE THE VISITORS' CENTER WORE a light green blouse decorated with an embroidered patch. The patch reproduced the molded-plastic relief map mounted on the wall—green for the valleys, blue for the rivers, yellow for the hills—and as Wendy stood there, unable to think of what she wanted to say, her eyes wandered from the patch to the map and back. The woman seemed mildly pleasant, more or less patient. She touched the patch that had caught Wendy's eye and said, "Pretty, isn't it? It's a reproduction of the valley topography before they built the reservoir."

"Pretty," Wendy echoed faintly. Who were "they"? The patch made her head spin, as did the huge bumpy map and the displays and photographs lining the walls. There were pictures of men dwarfed by a half-built dam, trees stacked like bundled chopsticks, buildings being wheeled away on trailers. She thought of her own home vanishing by a similar sleight of hand, the house jacked up and moved and the weary yard sinking below a sheet of water that would cover all her past mistakes. For the first time since her mother's phone call, she had a glimpse of why Grunkie might want to visit this place. The reservoir, she thought, had sliced a clean cut through his old life and set him free to live another. She would have given anything for a similar close to her past.

"Is there something I can help you with?" the woman asked.

Wendy opened her mouth, still not sure what she wanted to say. Before she could speak, Roy elbowed past her and said, "We're looking for this land."

"What land would that be?"

"My friends' great-uncle," Roy began, but Wendy pushed him aside, furious at his interference.

"We'd like to go for a hike," she said. Her voice was high and cracked, with a hysterical edge even she could hear. She hadn't slept all night. The woman's unblinking eyes reminded her of Christine, and every time she looked at Roy she thought of Christine's words: that she took things, stole things, to make up for all she'd lost. Christine had been talking about Henry, but Wendy was sure the reproach had been directed at her.

Everything, at that moment, reminded her of everything else. The maps on the wall reminded her of how badly she'd gotten everyone lost, after Lise had finally relinquished the wheel: she'd chosen the wrong road from the snarl of highways intersecting west of Albany, and then, when she'd discovered her mistake just north of Troy, she'd chosen wrong again in her attempt to find a route to the Massachusetts Turnpike. While Roy and Lise and Delia slept and Win stared at the back of her head, dropping his lids each time she looked in the mirror and offering no help at all, she had wandered through the Berkshires until she'd stumbled onto the Turnpike by accident. At the exit for the reservoir, when she asked the tollbooth attendant for directions, she'd been so bewildered that she'd written the directions down carefully but somehow still written them down wrong. And so when Roy woke up and insisted on driving while she navigated, what should have been an easy half-hour end to their trip had turned into a two-hour exploration of Holyoke and Ware and a string of towns she had never wanted to see.

The towns had all looked the same and the road never went in the right direction. Roy said nothing about what they'd done and seemed determined to act as if nothing had changed. He had set his jaw and looked straight ahead and driven as if he were working, never once looking directly at her, never once touching her. When she had let her hand drift down to his thigh, he had twitched away as if he'd been burned. And now, in this building that had taken them so long to reach, he seemed to think he should spill their secrets to this stranger.

The woman looked from Roy to Wendy and back again, as if she were reading the tension between them. "Where would you like to hike?" she asked Wendy.

Her voice placed invisible quotation marks around the word *hike*, and her gaze sharpened as she took in Delia and Lise and Win, who stumbled wearily behind Wendy and Roy. We look like delinquents, Wendy thought, running her tongue around her sour mouth. There was a certain pleasure in being so grubby that her clothes no longer acted as a disguise.

"Along the east shore?" she said. "Sort of toward the north?"

"North? It's a big place. . . ."

The woman's face tightened when Lise plopped down on a chair and said, "This is ridiculous." The woman took a flimsy, crudely drawn map of the reservoir from the stack before her and tossed it down in front of Wendy.

"Here. Dotted lines are the hiking trails. Solid lines are the roads. Gates are marked with these small numbers—you can leave your car at any of them. No swimming. No fires. No hunting."

Lise sniffed and said, "Do we look like hunters?" which did not improve the situation. The woman's growing disapproval of them hung in the air like an odor. The walls were lined with all the information they might need, but the woman didn't offer any of it and Wendy was too worn out to ask. She realized, standing there, that they'd been crazy to come. Hurtling through the night in pursuit of their parents, hoping to find Grunkie on a bit of land along an enormous shoreline—Lise was right, it was ridiculous, and the way she'd acted with Roy was worse than that. The peculiar smile he'd given her when he'd opened his eyes had seemed so accepting, as if he believed that they'd both been lost in sleep and had committed only an unconscious bit of mischief, easily dismissed. The way he stood so coolly beside her now told her that he'd found a way to blame her for what they'd done.

She thanked the woman, folded the map, and left, with the others trailing behind her. In the parking lot she smoothed the map over the hood of Roy's car and stared at it. The lines swam in front of her eyes, and she might have given up right then if Roy had not dropped a hand on her shoulder and said, "Calm down. It's going to be all right." When she turned to him, she read a distant kindness in his eyes.

"Let's get focused here," he said. "Let's try and remember what we're doing."

Win was standing apart from the rest of them, with his eyes fixed on Roy's hand. "I'd really like to find my mother," he said quietly. Wendy stepped aside and let Roy's hand fall from her shoulder. "Sometimes she gets a little . . . disoriented, or something," Win said.

"That's true," Wendy said, relieved to think of her mother's behavior, which was always worse than hers. In this way at least, her mother was reliable. "Especially when she's around Uncle Henry."

"You're sure you want to interfere?" Roy asked.

She wasn't sure, now, that she'd wanted anything more than to escape from Christine's presence and sit next to Roy in the dark car, but she supposed that she and Win and Delia and Lise *did* want to interfere. They wanted to interfere with their parents' strange behavior, which was galloping away with their lives. Their parents were careless with everything, with their own lives, with each other, with them. Lost in the little towns north of Troy, crossing and recrossing a narrow causeway suspended a few feet above a lake, it had come to her that Grunkie was really dying. Her mother and Christine could neither help nor hurt him much; her uncle, by keeping Grunkie out of their clutches, couldn't save him from what counted. They were wasting what might be Grunkie's last days, and as she thought of him tugged this way and that by his niece wanting to save his soul and his nephew wanting to save his land, her sense of purpose returned.

She said to Roy, "Sometimes we *have* to interfere. Sometimes we're the only ones who know what's going on." Her mistake, she saw now, lay in calling her father. If she hadn't been so lost in her own daydreams, and so jolted by the panic in her mother's voice, she would have seen that she and Win could have driven their mother here themselves. No Lise, no Delia, no Roy. No mess.

Delia sided with her immediately. "We have to help however we can," she said, and although her face was pale from all she'd drunk, her silliness had vanished and her words were serious.

"Okay," Roy said. "So where are we going?"

Wendy drew Win to her, but he pulled his arm away. "I saw you, you know," he said angrily, as if she hadn't been aware of his eyes throughout their whole long night. He maneuvered Wendy away from the others and turned his back to them. "I saw you and Roy. And I saw that stuff in your bag, that you ripped off at the plaza. What's going on with you?"

"Nothing," she whispered. "I don't know." She could feel herself unraveling, the loose ends of her old lives sticking out in all directions. She smoothed the panic from her voice. "Let's just do this, okay?"

Win still stared at her suspiciously, as if she were turning into their mother before his eyes.

"I'm all right," she told him. "Really."

"Really?" he said, and when she nodded they bent over the map together. The outlines of the reservoir were similar to what she remembered of the maps their father had shown them: an elongated mitten, with a narrow western branch stretching north like a thumb, a short lobe like a wrist in the south, and then a larger, wider, eastern branch. The spot their father had shown them lay, she thought, along the eastern branch and near the top. Either of the two points jutting into the water might be the point near Grunkie's land.

"East Pomeroy," Win said. "Isn't that what Dad said the town was called?"

"I think," Wendy said. "But those old names aren't on here."

"We'll just have to wing it," Win said. "We'll hike in, take a look around. If they're not at the first gate we try, we'll try another."

"I could go back inside and ask that woman," Roy said. "She might know what we're looking for."

She might, thought Wendy. She might know exactly where East Pomeroy was, or used to be; she might even know the place where their father had once lived. But Wendy couldn't bear to face her again. "No," she said. "We can find it."

And so they drove north to the gate Win picked, and they found it without any trouble and parked the car and started walking. But they hadn't counted on the unmarked trails or the deer paths that crossed them or the exuberant undergrowth, and they hadn't expected the hills and streams and ridges that weren't on their useless map, and they hadn't realized just how exhausted they really were. Within minutes, they were seriously lost.

Wendy's shoulder ached from her bag, although she'd crammed the loot from the Thruway plaza beneath the seat. Win strode next to her, trying to look as if he knew where they were headed. She was sure they had strayed from the main path some time ago, and that the tiny overgrown trail they were following had been made by deer or dogs. Behind them, Delia was drooping and dragging her feet and sticking close to Roy. Lise trailed all of them and complained about her shoes, which were pinching.

"We ought to be heading to our left," Win said. "The water has to be to the left of us."

"I know," Wendy said. But every time the path looped to the left it bent right again a few yards later. They seemed to be traveling along the outlines of a knot, and she was sure they'd crossed their own tracks several times. She was hot and tired and thirsty and had nothing useful in her bag. A huge bird, a hawk or a heron, rose from a tree with a whir that made Delia shriek.

"See?" Win said. "See how he's heading left? He's heading for the water."

"So?" Wendy said. "What do you want me to do about it?"

Win gave her a disgusted look. "We should have gotten a better map. We should have asked that woman for some help."

Wendy could see no point in telling him how that woman had frightened her. "You want to go back?"

"Too late now. But how about we break our own trail for a while? If we cut through here, I know we'll hit the water." Win plunged into the tangle of dogwood and witch hazel to their left.

Roy drew up to Wendy. "Where's he going?" he asked. The hairs on his arms lay in smooth, soft lines.

"He's sure the reservoir's over there," Wendy said, forcing herself to meet Roy's eyes. She felt herself begin to blush.

"You think?" Roy said, but then Lise caught up with them and said, "I'm not going in there," and Wendy snapped, "Fine. Stay here," and stomped after her brother, pushing aside the branches and vines and no longer caring who was behind her. None of this would have happened, she thought, if Lise hadn't been so obnoxious in the car. And if Delia hadn't been so afraid of Lise, and if she'd had the sense to flaunt Roy instead of trying to hide him—the ground was dry, and the path Win was making was not so difficult after all. Branches whipped at her knees and thighs, but her shoulders and head were clear. Behind her she could hear Roy urging Delia on, and all she could think was that they were truly lost, the kind of lost where they would not be able to retrace their steps and where their only hope was to stumble forward into what they longed to find.

Win marched ahead of her, sticking grimly to his chosen direction. Christine's comment last night had stung him, Wendy knew, and so had her own behavior; he was so afraid of failing to act, or of acting as strangely as the women around him, that he was unwilling to admit to the confusion and fear she knew he felt.

They came out on a trail as smooth and wide as a sidewalk. The trail led to a wider dirt road; the road led to a clearing and split around a large wedge of grass. Craters lined the sides of the fork, and Win stopped and said, "Cellar holes. Look."

The holes were edged with bricks and draped with ivy and vinca and raspberry canes. Lise came up behind them and said, "We're here? About time." Then she plopped down on the grass and took off her shoes and rubbed her feet. Roy sat down as well, and before Wendy could move to join him, Delia threw herself down and rested her head in his lap.

"We're still friends," Delia said in response to Lise's frown. From the look on Lise's face, and from Delia's disregard of it, Wendy knew the charade she'd acted out with Roy was over. Delia must have realized that Lise couldn't do anything more to her than tell their parents, and that their parents were too distracted to care. Or perhaps she'd sensed the troubled current flowing between Wendy and Roy. Delia smiled at Roy and teased him quietly. But there was no mistaking the confident way she touched his arm.

Mine, that touch said, and Wendy convinced herself that Delia deserved him. Roy gazed over Delia's head at Wendy and stroked Delia's hair quite deliberately. Wendy felt that he did this not to be mean but to let her know where they stood. Which was nowhere, she thought, with a kind of calm despair; they were more than friends, less than lovers, connected through Delia and almost family. They were drawn to each other and weren't going to do anything about it. She couldn't imagine living with the wild surge of feeling that had filled her in the car. Then she couldn't imagine living without it. Grunkie, she thought, had cut that part of his life out like a wart. She had no idea what an abbey looked like, but she imagined a group of vaguely churchlike buildings surrounded by a wall. In the wall was a gate that closed at night, shutting everything murky and dubious outside.

She looked away from Roy and Delia to find Win peering at a small brass plaque set in the grass. "This was the Pomeroy Common," he called. "Maybe this is the place."

Their father, Wendy remembered, had said the cabin stood in East Pomeroy, and she wondered if he'd made some sort of mistake. But this land was low, and she'd had the impression that the land they were searching for lay along a ridge. And also there was no one here. But a ridge rose south of them, low and rolling, past the tall grass beyond the cellar holes, and the sky behind it had the glow and spaciousness of sky over water. Wendy pointed this out to Win.

"They could be up there," she said. "The reservoir's probably just beyond that ridge, and maybe there's some other way in that we missed completely, and that Mom and Grunkie and Dad and Uncle Henry took."

Win studied the map. "There's a gate below us they might have taken," he said.

What was wrong, Wendy realized, was that the land they were searching for shouldn't have been inside any of the gates. The gates marked the boundary of the reservoir's watershed, and it didn't seem likely that her grandparents could have had a cabin inside that line. From the corner of her eye she saw Delia drape an arm around Roy's neck. Lise stood up suddenly and strode over to Wendy and Win and flicked the map with her thumb. Her face was pinched and drawn.

"So where are they?" Lise said. "All this way, and they're not even here . . . are we just going to sit around all day?"

Lise was jealous, Wendy realized. She'd been jealous of her and Roy when she'd thought they were together, and now she was more jealous of Delia and Roy and upset at what she must have sensed of the conspiracy to fool her, and she was so lonely her only comfort was her sharp tongue. In the car last night, she'd complained about her mother—how, now that Kitty was losing the house and moving into Lise's apartment complex, she was all over Lise all the time and leaned on her for company and comfort. It wasn't fair, Lise had said. Her mother was counting on her too much because she couldn't count on Henry at all, and it wasn't fair.

But no one had listened to her. Delia had been drinking vodka and telling jokes and humming songs, and Roy had been listening to Delia, and Win had been asleep and Wendy had been so absorbed in the pleasure of sitting next to Roy that they had all ignored Lise, acknowledging her comments only enough to tell her she worried too much. Which she did, Wendy saw, but no more than she did herself, and anyway they both had reason to worry. She couldn't remember how and when she and Win and Delia had begun to band against Lise, but she knew they'd started long ago, even before their parents had shattered their lives. She wondered now if they'd shunned Lise because she was nasty, or if Lise had grown nasty because they'd shut her out.

"We think they might be on that ridge over there," she said to Lise, trying to speak gently and kindly. They had everything in common, she thought. Neither of them had Roy. "Or maybe just beyond it. They can't be far."

"Fine," Lise snapped. "Let's go. I swear, if I get my hands on my father . . ." She walked off, all by herself, through the waving grass.

26

B RENDAN SAID, SEVERAL TIMES, THAT HE WANTED TO SEE THE dam first, but Henry, with the enthusiastic backing of Marcus, overrode him. The dam would keep, Henry said. Although of course he wanted to see it, too, and they would see it, later— but the morning was so beautiful, perfect for walking, and he was so full of energy, and Marcus had said that if they went by the Visitors' Center they might be stuck there for a while. "And anyway," Henry said, "I want to see the place where I was born."

The words cloaked his real longing in a reasonable disguise, and Brendan was unable, as Henry had known he would be, to resist him. Henry hardly felt guilty about this at all. He'd done everything else that his uncle had wanted this whole long trip, and he could see no reason not to give in to the fierce excitement that gripped him.

"We'll be there in half an hour," Marcus promised. As they set off, pulling away from the shady square and heading east and north around the base of the reservoir, Henry was filled with a sense of well-being. He'd slept—not a lot, but enough—and he'd eaten and had his coffee; the sun cast a buttery light on the land. When he gazed in the rearview mirror he saw, not the battered face he'd been wearing for the past six months, but the face he'd had before his crash. The lines around his eyes only pointed up their sparkle. His hair wasn't gray but only attractively streaked; his complexion was rosy, not florid. He saw a man in the prime of life— young, still quite young, full of vigor and optimism. He'd gotten his uncle here safely and had had the great good fortune to meet a man who'd known his father. And although breakfast had dented his slim bankroll he still had twenty-two dollars left, which was almost enough to get them back home. He felt sure he could persuade Marcus to lend them a little more.

Brendan was silent in the back of the van and Bongo was asleep, but Marcus, sitting next to Henry, kept up a nonstop flow of chatter and directions.

"Take a left here. Then a right, at that light. This used to be farmland here, where those brown buildings are—they make computers in there. All these businessmen have moved here from the city the past couple of years, and you wouldn't believe the prices they're paying for houses."

Henry's heart leapt at that. An influx of wealthy executives, a rising real estate market—if his uncle's land had any view at all and even reasonable access, anything he did there would mint money. The land would come to him clean and unencumbered, the way the farm had in Coreopsis. But this time he'd know what to do with it.

"Turn left here," Marcus said, and then he started talking about the years before the dam was built and how, even before the acts authorizing construction had passed through the legislature, men from Boston had invaded the area.

"They were the slick ones, they were, and you can't tell me they didn't plan every step of it. We didn't have phones or electric then, and most of the roads weren't paved, and most of the farmers weren't doing so well and neither were the mills. Those men were like vultures—they smelled the weakness. They came sniffing around, sniffing out the greedy men and the failures and the widows, and they spread rumors that the dam was coming and that land values were going to crash."

Marcus's voice rose a little and he plucked at the loose skin on his neck. " 'Sell now,' they said, and they offered a premium to the first ones who did. Pots of money, more than some could resist. Then they went to the neighbors and said, 'See, so-and-so sold already for a good price. We can't offer quite as much now, but it's still a lot, more than you'll get if you wait.' They offered each round of sellers less, and pretty soon people panicked—and the diehards, the ones who'd held out until the rumors became a sure thing, they threatened them with eminent domain."

He pursed his lips and made a disgusted noise. "What can you do with men like that? 'We can take it anyway,' they said. 'And we will.' And they did. People like my parents, and your grandparents—they held out so long they got almost nothing."

Henry listened with half an ear, but Marcus's story seemed impossibly distant, like a fairy tale set in a time Henry couldn't imagine. The fact was—his daughters and Kitty had often accused him of this, and he'd had to admit they were right—the fact was that, despite his ability to imagine alternate lives for himself in places he'd never been, he couldn't imagine a scene without himself in it.

He tried to picture the valley during the 1920s, but he could see only flappers and gangsters, images from movies, nothing that squared with Marcus's tales or with what his parents and grandparents had told him. And he couldn't help thinking that those men from Boston had only been doing their jobs. He'd used the same tactics himself, on a smaller scale—in his glory days, when his developments had sold out immediately and the people who moved in were young and had small children and were thrilled with their homes, he had sometimes acted secretly to piece together his parcels of land.

He had never looked at land that was already advertised for sale. Instead, his talent had been to cruise the countryside in a mood as relaxed as a trance, waiting for the flash that would tell him *here, here, here.* A certain combination of topography and location would flash in the sun like a mirror, and he'd look at the land and see himself reflected in it. Then he'd start the slow, secret process of tracking down the various owners, and after that the even more secret process of finding out what those owners might want or need. And of course he'd approached those people one by one, cutting them out of the herd, and of course he'd offered large sums to the early sellers and then smaller sums to the later ones. How else could he have assembled his tracts at a reasonable price? Those men from Boston had only been canny, and he blamed his grandparents' bitterness on their inability to see what was coming and get out early.

He interrupted Marcus midsentence to say, "But you all knew it was coming—why didn't you just get the best price you could and go somewhere else?"

"Because this was our *home,"* Brendan said acidly from behind Henry's head. "Our families had been here for generations. Our lives weren't for sale."

"That's right," Marcus said, and he gave Henry an odd look. "What do you do for a living, anyway?"

Henry stiffened, waiting for his uncle to say something scathing about his real estate career. Marcus seemed old-fashioned, one of those stiff types who disapproved of development on principle, and Henry was anxious not to alienate him. When Brendan said nothing, Henry said, "I'm working in a corrugated-box factory these days, running a die-cutter."

To his surprise, Marcus broke into a huge smile. "Isn't that something, now. Used to be, there was a big box factory in Pomeroy that your father worked at in the winter. When they moved it to Athol, after the building started, he commuted out there. It's nice to think you're following after him."

"I didn't know I was." Henry looked in the rearview mirror and caught Brendan's gaze; Brendan dropped his eyes, leaving Henry to wonder why he'd never mentioned this. Then he wondered what else Marcus knew that Brendan didn't, or hadn't seen fit to mention.

They drove along the base of a long, low hill and crossed a river that was, Marcus said, one of the three that fed the reservoir. On the other side of the river was a quiet town that seemed very old. Henry turned where Marcus told him to, and the road, already small, narrowed further and became frost-heaved and rocky.

"You want to take a right at this fork," Marcus said. "Then you'll have to be careful—the last stretch is dirt."

Marcus knew about the place where his father had worked, Henry thought. Perhaps he knew more than that. "What happened to my father during the war?" he asked. "Did he ever say?"

"You must have heard that story before."

"Not from you. You knew him." Henry saw Brendan lean forward in his chair, as if to catch Marcus's words, and he remembered how Brendan had lain in the parlor in Coreopsis, telling him stories about the war in China. Those tales had come from the same time and the same war but a different place; although Henry had clung to them, they had never done more than circle around his father's war.

"I was *with* him," Marcus said. "But it's a long story."

"Tell me," Henry said.

Marcus drew his arms together in his lap. "War stories," he said sourly. "I hate war stories." But then he stretched his arms out on his knees and gazed into his open palms, as if the words Henry wanted were written there.

"Nothing went right for us," he began. His voice was distant and cold, and Henry saw that the skin inside Marcus's elbows was as crinkled and fragile as Brendan's. He checked his own arms quickly; the skin was creased but firm.

"We'd both joined the National Guard before Pearl Harbor, and our unit got called up in March of '42. They shipped us over to Oahu for training, and to serve as part of the base defense force. We didn't see combat until November of '43, when they shipped us over to the Gilbert Islands. A place called Makin."

"I remember that name," Henry said. "I used to have a map—" But before he could say another word, Marcus rushed ahead as if he couldn't stop.

"We didn't know what we were doing," said Marcus. "And our officers were as green as us. We outnumbered the Japs there ten to one and they didn't have any heavy guns, but we didn't know that—we got pinned down by a handful of snipers screaming curses at us and tossing lit firecrackers and yelling from the trees. We couldn't move. We couldn't sleep. We thought there were thousands of them. Some of us got so scared we fired into the dark, just to be shooting at something, and then the Japs would see where we were and start firing back at us. So we'd try to stay calm, but then a couple more guys would get hysterical and give away our positions again, and then the Japs would sneak up and pounce on our foxholes." Marcus paused for a deep, shaky breath.

"Is that what made my father so crazy?" Henry said. "Was he one of the ones who fired?" He couldn't really picture the scene, but he could imagine the shame: he'd been living with the shame of failure for months.

"No," Marcus said. "He did all right. But it took us four days to clear Makin, and by the time we were done, a Jap sub had reached the atoll and it sunk one of the escort carriers our last day there. A torpedo exploded the bombs in the hold and the carrier blew up. Men, planes, clothing, everything everywhere—hundreds of men were killed and almost all the rest had horrible burns. Then all the naval officers started saying how there hadn't been that many Japs on the atoll, and how we'd taken four days to do a two-day job, and that if we'd finished when we should have, the carrier never would have been hit. It was *our* fault, they said. Those men died because we didn't know what we were doing."

He paused again. "Pricks," he said bitterly, and then he went on to tell Henry how their unit had gone back to Oahu under a cloud. The plans for the invasion of Saipan had been under way by then, and the men were thrown back into training with no rest at all. No one believed they'd see action again so soon.

"What a mess," Marcus said. The Marine landings went badly; the tide was too low, the channel too crowded, the amphibious tractors and tanks got stuck on the beaches. Marcus's unit was landed two days later, to back up the Marines. They lost most of their equipment during the landing, and then one disaster had followed another.

"The Marines were moving north," Marcus said. "Through the center of the island. The commander threw us into the middle of the line, between the two Marine divisions, and he ordered us to sweep through this place called Death Valley." Marcus moved his hands in the air as he talked, sketching a map along the dashboard and windows as he tried to explain how the valley floor was bare of cover and how the cliffs along the sides were riddled with enemy gun positions.

"They made mincemeat out of us," he said, chopping at the air. "We couldn't keep up with the Marines on our sides, who were in much better positions. The line got bent like this," he said, making an arc with his hands. "Us in the middle, almost a mile behind the Marines on our flanks. The Marines had to wait for us and the brass had a fit. The commander—a Marine, of course—was telling everyone we couldn't fight, or wouldn't fight, that we were inferior. Useless, he said. Too old, poorly trained. Our officers didn't know what they were doing and turned tail when things got tough.

"We *didn't* know what we were doing, and our officers couldn't lead horses to water, but we *fought*. We fought hard. And all we got for it was shit."

His voice rose, cracked, quivered, and Henry realized how old Marcus was, and how long ago all this had happened.

"We were stuck in some places for days. Men dying all around us, all of us worn-out and hungry and thirsty and running out of supplies and ammunition, no one helping us and everyone saying what a bunch of no-good failures we were. We couldn't link up with the Marines on our flanks for a week. You can't begin to understand the kind of tired we were. In the end we lost as many men as the Marines, but the Marines got all the glory and we took all the blame.

"The story got into the newspapers and there was a big investigation. The Marines said the Army guys were bums, and the Army said the Marine commanders had given the Army troops the worst jobs and sacrificed them. Everyone was arguing about who should have commanded who and how, and they all lost sight of us. All the men we'd lost, all the men who went home missing arms and legs and eyes— that counted for nothing. The men who'd acted like heroes weren't heroes. They were the guys who'd been too slow at Makin and been responsible for the sinking of a ship, and then too slow again at Saipan."

Marcus smacked his hand against the dashboard. His hand was wrinkled and spotted and gnarled and had no more strength, Henry guessed, than a child's, but the vinyl shell was brittle and it split in a sudden star of cracks. "Damn," Marcus said. "I'm sorry."

"Don't worry about it. It's not mine. No wonder my father was bitter." That was the point, Henry thought, of this bloody story. That his father had been falsely blamed for something he couldn't help. He thought he knew how his father had felt.

"Of course he was bitter. We were all bitter. But bitter wasn't what did your father in."

"No? Bitter is hard on a man. . . ."

"It was the last day," Marcus said. "When they announced that we'd taken the island. I was with a mopping-up operation further south—but your father was with the troops at Marpi Point."

He paused, as if Henry would know what he meant. Henry had to admit that he'd never heard of the place.

"How could you not have heard of it? Don't you read?"

"I was a little boy," Henry said. "I was a baby."

Marcus shook his head. "It was horrible. It was famous. The Japanese civilians who'd been hiding in caves during the invasion gathered on the cliffs at Marpi Point when they heard the island was lost—the Japanese soldiers had told them that the Americans were going to torture them if they surrendered. Our troops set up a PA system, and they got interpreters to tell the crowd that the fighting was over, that we had food and water waiting for them and that they were safe. It didn't do any good. Your father told me they lined up on the cliff and jumped off, a hundred feet onto the rocks and the surf below. Men pushed their children in front of them. Women jumped with their babies on their backs. People stood and bowed to the American soldiers and then held grenades to their stomachs and pulled the pins. The water below the cliff was so full of bodies that the Navy boats couldn't move without running over them. Your father stood there, screaming at these people not to jump, and they jumped and jumped and jumped. He saw . . ."

Marcus cleared his throat and stopped. When he continued, his voice was quiet.

"He said he saw a boy just your age jump into the water holding his father's hand. He was never the same after that. He had malaria, and terrible dysentery, and he'd lost a lot of weight—they sent him to the New Hebrides with the first wave of troops to be rehabilitated. But he never got better.

He couldn't sleep. He couldn't eat. When they finally shipped him home, he was in worse shape than when he'd left Saipan. And then he got here and saw the reservoir, and somehow the water here reminded him of the water there, below the cliffs . . . I don't know. No one can really understand who wasn't there. I was there, and I can't understand."

Henry heard everything Marcus said, but much of it passed over his head. He saw the scenes Marcus had described, but he saw them distantly, as if in a movie, drained of pain and blood and sound, and he could no more imagine what his father had felt than he could imagine himself in those places. He said to Marcus, "My father would never tell us what had happened there. My mother told us he was hurt in a place we couldn't see."

"True enough," Marcus said, but then he closed the subject completely. "That's enough," he said. "That's just enough of that. It makes me sick to talk about it." He looked up from his hands and out the windshield. "Go slow here. These ruts are terrible. Do you recognize anything yet?"

Henry peered into the trees surrounding the van. The road looked like a hundred other roads he'd explored; the trees were just trees and he still didn't know their names after all these years. Willows he recognized because they signaled water, and maples because Kitty had planted one in their backyard, but otherwise trees were either things to cut down to make way for buildings, or things to preserve to enhance the value of a lot. Fifty feet ahead of him, the road was blocked by a yellow gate.

"Pull over here," Marcus said. "Anyplace is fine."

Henry parked and looked around. He thought he sensed something in the woods to his right, a flash that was either memory or his old, skilled recognition of a likely plot. "We're here?"

"Pretty much."

Henry twisted around on his seat and looked at Brendan, who hadn't said a word throughout Marcus's story. "Isn't this something?" Brendan's eyes were shut and his face was very white. "Uncle Brendan? You okay?"

Brendan cleared his throat twice and said, "Fine. Just a little twinge."

"What do you think? Do you remember this?"

"I never saw it. Or if I did, it was never like this—I was in the monastery before this road was built, long before your parents moved out here. I never saw the cabin."

"It's gone now," Marcus said. "You want to get out?"

Together, Henry and Marcus lowered Brendan's wheelchair to the ground. Bongo jumped out and darted past the gate, his nose half an inch above the ground as he followed some irresistible scent. A trail cut into the trees, twenty feet or so before the gate, and it wound up the gentle slope and then vanished. The slope, Henry saw, was the tail end of a long ridge running diagonal to the road.

Marcus pushed Brendan's chair close to the trailhead and said, "Your land starts about a hundred yards in, I think— on the top of the ridge, running north and east. The section your brother lived on is at the far end of the parcel. You can still see where it was logged, even though it's growing in. I wish there was a way to get you up there."

"It doesn't matter," Brendan said. "I just wanted to know it was still here."

"But it's *gorgeous.*" Henry turned to Brendan and Marcus, aware that his mouth was stretched in a childish grin. The parcel was remarkable, he could tell already—elevation, good drainage, obviously plenty of water. And if there was a view of the reservoir from the top of the ridge . . .

"I'd like to go down to the water," Brendan said quietly. "Is there some way we can do that?"

"No problem," Marcus said. "This road runs right to the water's edge, and it's not that bumpy—I can push you down."

"Would you mind?" Henry said. "If I just did a little exploring? I'll only be a few minutes, half an hour at most. I want to go up on the ridge."

Marcus frowned. "You don't want to come with us?"

"Let him go," Brendan said. "It's going to be his, and his sister's—he might as well see it."

Marcus shrugged, and then he took a pencil stub and a small notebook from his shirt pocket and sketched a rough map for Henry. "Look for the boulder, here, to the left of the trail, near the three birches—the boundary runs right near it. The far end, where your folks' place was, is marked by the beginning of the logged area."

"Great. I'll just be a little while." Henry stepped back to the van and changed his shoes for the sneakers he'd taken from Kitty's, which made his feet feel light and youthful.

"We'll be down at the water," Marcus said. "It's not very far. Come get us when you're ready." He stood quietly for a minute, his hands resting on the back of Brendan's wheelchair. "You know, your parents . . . ," he said, but Henry was off before Marcus could finish his sentence.

He didn't want to think about his parents anymore: not about his father struggling over steamy islands or watching people crash from cliffs, not about his mother chain-smoking by the radio or about the mornings when he and Wiloma had followed their parents through these woods, these very woods, on this trail or another, winding gently down and left toward the shore where the reservoir lapped at the rocks. The story Marcus had told him changed nothing—all these years he'd thought that if he knew what had happened to his father he'd understand what had happened to his own life. But the story was only a story; his parents were still dead.

The water was close, he remembered suddenly, just down the road and beyond that curve, and a small wooden dock jutted into the water. There was a shed someplace, where his father had rented a boat. He climbed with firm, strong steps until he reached the boulder Marcus had described, and then he stepped across that invisible line and thought, *Mine*, as his foot touched the springy moss. *Mine, mine.* He climbed higher, admiring the widely spaced old trees. A road cut through here might spare the best of them, preserving an authentic woodland feeling. Buyers were always willing to pay more for that.

At the top of the ridge he turned and saw the reservoir shining below him. Islands dotted the water—*Hills,* he remembered his father saying morosely. *Those used to be the tops of hills*—and the shoreline was ruffled with points and bays. Around him as far as he could see stretched green woods, his woods. He hardly thought at all about how half of this would be Wiloma's or how none of it would be his until his uncle died.

Somewhere, not far away, the trees thinned to young undergrowth and exposed his parents' cabin site, but he couldn't make himself look for the clearing. Someone else owned that land now. It was gone and so were his parents, but so, too, was the sad and dispirited creature he'd been these past six months. He felt a great surge of exhilaration and hope, and a conviction that his earlier selves had nothing to do with him now. With some energy he could turn himself into someone else. Without hardly knowing it he began to whistle, and his sneakered feet picked their way lightly along the path.

The condominium complex he'd imagined earlier faded away and he saw houses instead: modern, cedar-sided, with huge windows facing the spectacular view. Homes for the computer executives, spaced on large lots and linked by a narrow, curving lane. He could see the development's slogan already, the carved wooden sign that would span two tall pillars: "Any Closer To The Water—And You'd Be In It!"

Near the water, near a dock and shed that were either the ones he remembered from his childhood or replacements of them, Henry saw Marcus and Brendan beside a bunch of aluminum rowboats. They were facing the water; Marcus stood next to Brendan with his arm straight out, pointing at something in the distance. Bongo stood up to his chest in the water, drinking thirstily.

"Hey!" Henry called, full of excitement, drowning in plans. "You guys!" They weren't very far away, but they couldn't hear him.

27

WILOMA AND WALDO OVERSLEPT, AND IT WAS AFTER TEN BE-
fore they finished breakfast and headed for the dam. Wiloma
wished she'd never touched the margaritas Waldo had ordered. Beyond the fact that she felt queasy now, and beyond
the ridiculous ways she and Waldo had behaved, she disliked
the film of irritability and suspicion the drinks had left behind.
The day was beautiful, but the light hurt her eyes and made
Waldo look pale and pouchy. He was as kind and thoughtful
as he'd been throughout their drive, but now his kindness
seemed calculated and she found hidden motives in his every
word.

When they walked into the Visitors' Center, he said, "Why
don't you let me do the talking?" Her first impulse was to
say no; then she caught herself and wondered what she
feared. There was nothing he could do legally to get her share
of Brendan's land, and she was long past the point where
she'd give him something just because he wanted it. Except
that her behavior last night seemed to prove she wasn't—

she'd been more susceptible to him than she would have believed. When she realized this, she also realized that it wasn't Waldo she feared, but her feelings for him. She let him do the talking after all.

The woman at the desk was grumpy. "Up to no good," she was saying to a young man who stood behind her. A group of rude kids had apparently just passed through and she hadn't liked the looks of them. Waldo interrupted her complaints to greet her, and she turned to him with a brusqueness that made Wiloma's heart sink. But within a few minutes, Waldo had charmed the woman completely.

He spread his maps out on her desk and told her how interested he was in the history of the reservoir; how his wife here—*his wife?* Wiloma thought—actually belonged to one of the old families from one of the lost towns; how they were hoping to find a piece of land that her family had once owned. Without ever mentioning Henry or Brendan, without ever giving the least impression that they were desperately seeking a runaway or that anything was wrong, he managed to convince the woman of the urgency of their quest. They'd come all this way, he said. They'd been thinking about this for ages. It would mean so much to them if they could just find this place. . . .

The woman responded warmly; Waldo was irresistible when he tried. The woman pulled books and maps from the shelves around her, called over one of her assistants, and bent over Waldo's maps, listening to what he said. In half an hour she'd solved their problem as neatly as a jigsaw puzzle.

"Here," she said, drawing pencil lines on the map that showed the valley before the reservoir was built. "The old Auberon farm was right around here." Wiloma bent over the map and stared. That box outside the village of Pomeroy was where Brendan and her father had grown up and where Da and Gran had spent much of their lives. With a smile of triumph the woman pulled over another map, a new one with the reservoir in place. "If you compare these two," she said, indicating various lines, "you can sort of imagine where the water lies over your family's old place. The other parcel you were talking about is here."

She moved her pencil north and east and pointed out a spot just beyond the blue lobe of water. "Of course, the village of East Pomeroy doesn't exist anymore, and that land's been incorporated by another township. But it's right here, just outside this gate. There's someone here who can tell you all about the area and what's happened to it, one of our local historians. Marcus?" She turned to the man sorting photographs behind her. "Where's Marcus O'Brian? Isn't he supposed to be in this morning?"

"Called in a little while ago," the man said. "He told me he'd run into an old friend, some guy he hadn't seen since they were kids, and he was taking him up the east side to look at something. He's not coming in."

"Too bad," the woman said to Waldo. "Marcus knows everything about this area—he's really quite fascinating. You'd enjoy him. He's almost eighty, and he grew up in the valley himself. He's one of our living resources."

Wiloma looked at Waldo. Almost eighty; almost Brendan's age. Was it possible the old friend he'd met was Brendan? "You've been so helpful," Waldo said. "Really. I don't know how to thank you."

"You just enjoy yourself. Have a nice day." The woman was flirting with Waldo, Wiloma saw, as if the two of them were alone. Waldo touched the woman's hand and then began rolling up his maps. The woman pulled another, smaller map from a corner of her desk. "It's easy to get where you want to go," she said, indicating a route. "Just follow this."

"Thank you," Waldo said again, and they left. Outside he turned to Wiloma and laughed. "Wasn't she something?"

"She gave you what you wanted."

"What *we* wanted. Who would have believed it would be this easy?"

Off to the side, a few hundred feet away, the dam curved across the water like a huge sleeping snake. Wiloma couldn't tear her eyes from it, and Waldo's gaze followed hers. He said, "You want to take a look at that first? Before we head out?"

She shuddered, remembering the feelings it had raised in her last night. She remembered, too, what Christine had said—*I have to see your uncle as soon as possible*—but she hung back from telling Waldo about Christine or about why she needed to get Brendan home so quickly. She said, "Let's just get this over with. I want to get Uncle Brendan away from whatever craziness Henry's got going, and the sooner we get that van back to the Home . . ."

"You're right. Let's go."

The woman's directions were perfect, accurate down to the last turn, but still Wiloma was surprised when they took the final fork and saw the van parked there on the dirt road. She caught her breath as they drove up and parked behind it, and she was conscious of feeling a little cheated, as if the search hadn't taken long enough.

"But they're not here," Waldo said. "It doesn't look like anyone's in the van."

They climbed out of the car and looked around. A trail entered the woods and ran up the hill, and Waldo looked at the map the woman had given them and said, "I think your uncle's land is up there."

Wiloma looked into the trees. Her uncle's land—and near it, touching it, must be her father's land and the cabin in which she'd been born. She leaned back against the Saab, momentarily unable to breathe. She remembered this land, she remembered everything about it. The cabin sat high on the ridge back along its length, and in the winter the water had been visible through the leafless trees. A narrow path ran down from the ridge, through the flatter land to the shore, and where the shore jutted out in a small point there was an old wood dock on which she and her mother and Henry had sat. There were turtles under the dock. There were small silvery fish that swam in schools. In the woods there were violets and larger flowers her father had named for her when he'd come home: lady's slippers, columbines. The trees were dotted with oval woodpecker holes.

Waldo walked over and put his arm around her waist. "You okay?"

She struggled to speak. "It's just . . . It's just . . ."

"I know. It's beautiful here. No matter what happens, you shouldn't sell this. It's your family's home."

This surprised her so much that the tightness eased in her chest. "I know," she said. "I know every inch of this place— I know just what it looks like up there. But I didn't expect you to realize what it means to me."

He shrugged and picked at some mud that had dried on the car. "I'm not such an asshole. Not all the time."

"Why did you drive me here?"

"You seemed like you needed some help," he said, but then he dropped his eyes. "Okay, I was maybe a little interested in this place, what you and Henry were planning to do with it, and I was thinking maybe there was a way I could be a part of whatever you did. And also I was afraid maybe you'd want to give your share to that church of yours, and I wanted to keep you from doing anything foolish. The kids ought to get this someday, not some group of fanatics."

She let that last comment pass. "I'd never give this away. This is important."

"So was the place in Coreopsis," Waldo said quietly.

"I didn't give that to anyone," she snapped. "I let Henry *use* it. How was I supposed to know . . ." She sighed. "You're right. That was a mistake."

"That's all I wanted—to be sure you didn't make another."

She moved away from his arm, fighting the urge to lean into him. "You don't need to worry. I'm not as stupid as you think." There were lines on the ground near the van, she saw—parallel lines like the tracks of snakes.

"Look," she said. They walked over and inspected the tracks, which led from the van to the gate and then vanished.

"Brendan's wheelchair?" Waldo asked.

"Must be." She patted her hair and tried to gather herself together. *The entire secret to life,* she remembered from her Manual, *is not to be distracted. Focus on what's important.* "Let's go."

But above them, in the distance, they heard whistling. Just a few notes, the fragments of a tune—loud, broken, cheerful. "What's that?" Waldo said.

Wiloma looked up and behind them. She couldn't see anyone, but she would have known that whistle anywhere—that was Henry, who let out unconscious peeps and chirps when he was happy and thought he was alone. He had done that even as a little boy, when he'd been all she had to cling to.

"Henry's up there," she told Waldo. "That's his whistle. He must have Uncle Brendan with him."

"There's no way. You couldn't get a wheelchair up that path. And anyway, these have to be Brendan's tracks."

"Maybe so. But that's Henry up there."

Waldo looked up the hill and down the road. "Here's what we'll do. I'll go find Henry. You follow the wheelchair tracks and find your uncle. We'll meet back here. Okay?"

"Okay," Wiloma said, although the idea of being separated dismayed her. She watched Waldo vanish into the trees, and then she turned down the road and walked past the gate.

The road was rough, dotted with puddles and rocks. The snakelike tracks vanished and then reappeared and then vanished again. A flicker flew past with a whir of wings, and a flock of chickadees rose from a witch hazel at her approach. She walked quickly, intently, trying to focus on her uncle, and she was rewarded when she came around a curve. The trees thinned and then stopped abruptly at the edge of a clearing, and in the distance, where the clearing opened onto a pebbly bit of beach, she saw her uncle next to a man who was pushing a rowboat into the water. A dock stood nearby, and a shed next to a group of other boats. She supposed this was a place from which fishermen set out. A dog pranced between Brendan and the man putting in the boat, and she thought she recognized it as Bongo.

She opened her mouth to call out to her uncle, but a noise distracted her. Behind her, from the ridge, she thought she heard voices calling, and she turned and ran her eyes along the trees. From this clearing—oh, she remembered this, remembered how she'd been able to look up from here and see the cabin winking through the forest—she could see the whole length of the ridge, angling back from the reservoir. She saw the trail carved along the top, and a flash of blue she knew to be Waldo's shirt. That was Waldo yelling, calling her—or perhaps he was calling Henry. That flash of white, there, farther out along the ridge—was that Henry?

She waved her arms over her head, hoping to attract the attention of one or both of them. She heard more shouting—Henry? Waldo?

". . . doing here?" she thought she heard, and then "What?" She strained her eyes and ears. That blue flash *was* Waldo, moving very quickly now, and the white flash standing still was Henry. And they were not, either of them, calling to her. They were shouting at each other.

She closed her eyes for a second. "Idiot!" she heard.

The word carried down the ridge and across the clearing to her, but she couldn't tell who had yelled it and she turned her back on both men. They were hopeless, useless. She took three cleansing breaths and fixed her eyes on the place where her uncle sat. Then she squeezed her eyes shut and opened them again. The wheelchair was empty, outlined against the reservoir and the floating green islands, and from the point across the small cove to her left she thought she heard still other voices calling. The rowboat drifting away from the shore had two men in it, and a dog.

28

IT WASN'T EASY, GETTING INTO THE BOAT; AT FIRST, BRENDAN had thought they'd never manage it. Marcus had tugged Brendan out of his wheelchair easily enough—that was simple, that was only a guided fall—but the boat's lip had seemed insurmountable until Marcus, his hands under Brendan's armpits, had looked up and said, "Say—we have company. Maybe we can get that woman to help."

Brendan had recognized Wiloma emerging from the trees, and as he did, the vague wish he'd formed to set out on the water, the half-joking suggestion Marcus had made that they borrow one of the boats and go for a row, had crystallized into a fierce desire. He couldn't imagine how Wiloma had followed him here, but he knew her presence meant the end of his adventure and he wasn't ready to go back. Not to St. Benedict's; not, particularly not, to whatever strange ceremonies Wiloma had planned at her house. He had seized the side of the boat in his hands and, with a strength he hadn't had in years, hauled his torso in. Marcus, who acted as if this were a lark and they were still boys, had laughed and flopped Brendan's legs over the side and then eased Brendan's crumpled form onto the seat in the stern. Then he'd stepped in himself and pushed the boat away from the shore. At the last instant Bongo had slipped in, wet and dripping, and now he sat on the floor between Brendan and Marcus, his toenails scrabbling with each movement of the boat.

"Where to?" Marcus asked. He rowed with small, hesitant strokes, the blades barely breaking the surface, but the water was so smooth and calm that they moved along quickly. Wiloma, on the shore, had broken into a run; she stopped near the empty wheelchair and called to Brendan and then, when he didn't answer, turned and began shouting to someone on the ridge. Henry, Brendan supposed; they must have found each other.

"That woman's calling you," Marcus said.

"That's my niece. Henry's little sister."

"No." Marcus squinted through his glasses. "Not Frankie's little girl—what's she doing here?"

"I don't know."

"We better go back."

"In a while," Brendan said. "In a few minutes. Not yet."

He looked past Marcus, at the three islands closest to him. They were lined up in a jagged row, like the islands his patron saint had found on his voyage across the sea. The Island of Sheep, where the sheep were as big as cows and as white as clouds; the Paradise of Birds, where the trees were covered with talking birds instead of leaves; the Crystal Island, as clear as glass, pierced by a hole through which the curragh had slipped. There were birds thick around these islands, but no floating icebergs and no sheep, although Bongo sat gazing over his shoulder and looking as wise as the hound that had led the saint and his men to safety.

He hadn't expected the reservoir to be so beautiful. His father's bitter stories had made him imagine it as shallow, weedy, and dark, shadowed by the mist of deception that he'd sensed for himself as a boy. One of the reasons he'd joined the Order was that he'd heard the monks gathered at night and prayed for the preservation of the valley. Politics had failed, he remembered, and so had pleas and complaints; the men from Boston had baffled his parents' neighbors and confused them so badly that they argued over details when they met. But the monks within the enclosure walls had acted with one mind, which he'd wanted to join. He said to Marcus, "I can't get my bearings. Those islands there—what were they?"

"You know." Marcus lifted his oars from the water and pointed. "That one on the left, there, that's the top of what used to be Blueberry Hill. The one in the center's the top of Hollaran Hill, and the big one on the right is what's left of Mt. Pomeroy. Your parents' place was in the gap between Blueberry Hill and Hollaran Hill—remember? We can row right over it."

They still weren't very far from the shore; when Brendan turned he could see Wiloma clearly, and he thought he could even make out Henry in the distance, among the trees. Blueberry Hill, Hollaran Hill. What was Wiloma doing here? He supposed she had heard about the missing van and had grown anxious; she fussed over everything and always had. A fish jumped from the water near the boat and left an arc of glittering drops in the air. Bongo snapped his jaws at them.

Brendan said, "Could you row us over toward the right a little? If we could head just to the left of Mt. Pomeroy . . ." The monastery had lain between Hollaran Hill and Mt. Pomeroy, in the rich land through which the Paradise River had run.

"You're the boss," Marcus said. "What a day—isn't this weather something?" He rowed a few strokes, facing the shore and the ridge while Brendan faced him and the islands.

"Say, I think I see your nephew up there on the ridge. He's an odd one, isn't he? He doesn't seem like his father at all."

"It was hard for him," Brendan said quietly. "Being orphaned." The war story Marcus had told had shaken him badly. In the van, bumping up the rutted dirt road, he'd seen the accident that had cost Henry his parents as he'd never seen it before.

The inside of the old gray Plymouth is dark and quiet. Frank junior and Margaret haven't spoken since they left the dance; Frankie, sodden with drink, picked a fight with two acquaintances and then stormed out to the car. Margaret wouldn't have followed him if she'd had any other way to get home. But the hall was eleven miles from their cabin on the ridge and the rain was falling hard.

She sits next to him silently, only saying, "Slow down. Please?" when he twice takes a curve too fast. She is wearing a white dress and thinking about the months to come, wondering how she will pull him out of this dark mood he can't seem to shake. And Frankie—Frankie is thinking how much he'd like to close his eyes and rest. Just rest: neither plagued by nightmares nor haunted by his dead companions and his memories of what lies beneath the reservoir. He is only thinking, not planning, but his foot is heavy on the accelerator and when he heads into the last curve on Boughten Hill, Margaret shrieks and so startles him that his hands leap from the wheel. Even as the car stumbles over the edge of the road he is trying to find his way back.

But that couldn't be right, Frankie couldn't have left the world like that. Marcus couldn't have meant for him to infer that from the story he told. Marcus, he saw now, was meant to bring him to this place. And while he was glad Henry was up on the ridge, exploring his parents' land, and even glad that Wiloma had found her way here, he could not, for the moment, concentrate on anything more than the boat's slow movement toward the place where his abbey had been.

He imagined the buildings still intact beneath the water,

although he knew this wasn't so; his father had told him that everything had been razed. But still he imagined that beneath the water lay the garden surrounded by the stone-walled cloister, the dormitories looking down on the garden, the stone chapel, the flowerbeds, the fields, and the high enclosure walls. His whole life seemed to lie there, in the silent community he'd had for a decade and had never been able to reconstruct. He saw, now, that his decision to leave the Order had really been formed when he'd left this place, and that the grim days in China had only served as his excuse.

His faith in monastic life had broken during the nights when he and his brothers had prayed so fervently for the preservation of their valley that it seemed the whole place might take wing. Even Father Vincent had joined in, despite his warnings about the danger of praying for specifics. This was different, he'd said; although their prayers sounded like petitions, they were really appreciative worship of a beloved place. The sophistry of that argument had been evident to Brendan, but he'd pushed aside his qualms while they chanted the first lines of a dark psalm over and over again.

Save me, O God, he remembered, *for the waters are come in unto my soul. I sink in deep mire, where there is no standing: I am come into deep waters, where the floods overflow me. I am weary of my crying: my throat is dry: mine eyes fail while I wait for my God.* What could resist the power of all that prayer?

Anything, he'd learned. Any group of men with a plan.

He bowed his head and tried to pray again, and that was how the children saw him when they first came out on the shore. The cove that separated them from the point where Wiloma stood with her hand on Brendan's chair was very narrow; no sooner had Wendy seen the chair and her mother than Win pointed toward the water and said, "Isn't that Grunkie? In that boat?"

254

"That's Bongo!" Delia said. "That dog."

"But that isn't Dad rowing," said Lise.

They were so tired and discouraged that they hadn't spoken for more than an hour. The distance from the old square over the hill to the water had been deceptive, and they'd lost the trail entirely and had to wade through a bog tufted with club moss and sphagnum. Wendy had lost her bag in the bog; the strap had snagged on a jagged stump, throwing her to her knees. When she'd turned to disentangle her shoulder, Lise, who'd been following right on her heels, had stumbled and stepped on Wendy's arm and then, in a motion so clumsy Wendy still couldn't believe it, had leaned against the stump for balance and pushed the bag off and into a pool of water that seemed to have no bottom. They'd lost half an hour fishing about in the pool with sticks, but the bag was gone and so were Wendy's wallet and the blank-eyed dolls.

After that, Wendy had given up hope of finding anyone and had begun to wish only that they'd somehow find their way back to Roy's car. Roy had ignored her; all his energy had been taken up with Delia, who had collapsed on a tussock of bent grass and refused to go any farther until Roy promised they'd head home in an hour or two. Lise had cursed Wendy for being fool enough to bring her bag along, and Win had grown so pale and tight-lipped that he'd frightened Wendy. And yet here they were, separated from their mother only by a sheet of smooth water, separated from Grunkie only by another, larger sheet. Those sheets seemed, at first, like nothing.

"Wendy?" her mother called across the water. "Win? What the hell are you doing here?"

"Christine sent us," Wendy called back, unable to think of another explanation.

"What?"

"Christine," Wendy said again, and then, "Where's Dad?"

Wiloma pointed toward the wooded land behind her. "Up there. With your uncle Henry."

Lise dragged Delia a few feet forward. "Can you see him? Where is he?"

"I can't see anything," Delia said. "No, wait—there's someone in a blue shirt up there. Is that Dad? Or Uncle Waldo?"

Win came up to Wendy and rested his arm on her shoulder. "We found them," he said. "I don't believe it." His voice was tired and puzzled.

"*You* found them," Wendy said. "We never would have gotten here without you."

Win shrugged as if his navigation had been nothing, but she could tell that he was pleased. "So we found them," he said. "Now what?"

She didn't know. Her mother and father and Grunkie and Uncle Henry were all here, and all of them appeared to be safe, and she couldn't think of a single thing to do. Her mother called, "How did you get here?" and she called back, "Roy!"

Roy, Wiloma thought. Who was Roy? On the shore across from her she saw Lise and Delia, who must have come with Wendy and Win; a fifth person stood near Delia, a boy with long hair and legs in black jeans. Was that Roy? She dimly remembered Kitty complaining about some hoodlum Delia had been seeing, but this boy didn't look so bad and it seemed a miracle that they were here at all. Last night Christine had said they were sleeping—except that, Wiloma remembered now, those had not been Christine's words exactly. When she'd asked for Wendy, Christine had said it was very late and that she could talk to Wendy in the morning. Not a lie exactly, but a deception all the same. Wiloma felt a prickle of anger at Christine, but she pushed it down and concentrated on her delight at finding the children here. Between them and Waldo, Henry wouldn't stand a chance; whatever strange plan Henry had in mind was doomed.

Win called, "Mom? Are you all right?" and she heard the

fear in his voice. He and Wendy worried so—they acted as if she were always on the verge of breaking down again, as if they didn't understand how the Church buoyed her up and kept her safe. "I'm fine," she called, and on the opposite shore Win turned to Wendy and said, "I guess she's okay."

"She's all right," Lise said impatiently. "But can't you hear Dad? I don't know who he's yelling at."

"Probably our father," Wendy said. "Mom must have sent him up there after Uncle Henry."

"Wonderful," Lise said bitterly. "Thanksgiving all over again." Wendy remembered the two men fighting at a holiday dinner years ago; something about the one development they'd worked on together. She and Lise had been children then, and the fight had terrified them.

"I wish we had one of those boats," Win said, pointing to the row on the opposite shore. "There's no way for us to get over to Mom, except to walk back into the woods and see if we can find the mouth of the cove and cross over there."

Wendy looked down the cove, which cut back so deeply that she couldn't see its end. The shore of the point where their mother stood ran parallel to them. "This must be the mouth of a river. A stream must come through those trees."

Win followed her gaze. "I guess."

Wendy looked again at the sheet of water separating them from their mother. "It's so narrow. And it's so warm out—we could just swim it."

Roy left Delia's side and came over to Wendy and said, "No," even as Win's eyes lit up. "Why not?" Win said. "It's so shallow—it's nothing."

"It's a bad idea," Roy said. For a second, Wendy let herself think that he was protecting her. Then he said, "Delia and Lise won't go for it—Delia hates the water. And we ought to stick together. It won't take that long if we walk."

Win ignored him. He had already stepped out of his sneakers when Delia walked to the edge of the water and began shouting toward the boat. "Grunkie!" she called, waving her arms. "Grunkie! Hi! It's me!"

Lise joined her. "Grunkie! Come back!"

Brendan had kept his back toward Wiloma and the sounds Henry was making in the distance, but when he heard his nickname he craned his head over his shoulder and saw Lise there, and Delia and Wendy and Win, lined up on the shore and waving at him. For a minute he thought he might be dreaming. He hadn't seen them all together in years; Wendy and Win took turns coming to visit him with their mother, and although he'd seen Lise only yesterday, before that he hadn't seen her or Delia since Delia had left for college.

Years ago, Kitty and Wiloma had sometimes dressed up all four children and brought them to St. Benedict's for Christmas. They'd crowded into his room, squirming and squealing and restless, holding cards they'd made from red and green construction paper. All up and down his floor, his friends had strained for glimpses of them; all year long he'd held the vision of their last visit in his mind. And now here they were, as tall and straight as young poplars on the shore. It was wonderful, wonderful; Wiloma must have brought them with her as a surprise to him, and he was grateful to her and then embarrassed that he'd left her behind. Somehow she'd understood that he wanted his whole family here with him; she hadn't been chasing him, she'd come to join him. He leaned over the side of the boat and waved to his family with both arms, and just then, just when Marcus, looking alarmed, pulled in his oars and said, "Be careful!" Bongo recognized Delia's voice and leapt to his feet and barked.

He was a big dog, and his toenails hadn't been clipped in a long time. His feet spun on the aluminum and he fell heavily, rocking the boat; Brendan, unbalanced and twisted toward the shore, slipped over the side and into the water so quickly that his greeting was still on his lips. His head rose above the water once, but his glasses fell off and he could see only colored shapes. The water wasn't cold. His family was all around him, and Marcus had rowed him just to the spot overlying his abbey, and he sank easily, gratefully, down into the silky water, past a school of minnows that scattered, past a pair of trout who eyed him kindly, past the waving weeds and toward the glimmering stones. Surely that was the chapel below him? And the cloister, the garden, the great wall against which he'd leaned as a child, listening to the monks within? And there were the fields and the grazing cows and his family's farm in the distance; and the sky was blue and his brothers were chanting and his family spoke softly to him.

He thought of Roxanne, the one person at St. Benedict's he'd failed to say good-bye to; he felt her warm hands on his legs. Then he thought of all the kind people who'd leaned from their cars and spoken to him as he sat on his lonely corner. He heard Bongo barking above him, fish breathing water below him, and he thought of the tale his abbot had told him before he'd sailed for China, of a man who heard a voice in a dream that told him to set out on a journey. The man obeyed the voice; he traveled far and had many adventures. But when he reached his destination, he found only a stranger who told him the treasure he sought was hidden back in his own house. *That's the way it works,* his abbot had said; he'd said that only a journey to distant lands could reveal what lay buried at home.

In the water, which was warm and pleasant, his hands shaped the words for his abbot and then for his brother and Jackson and Marcus and the little boy in Henry's half-built house. Then they fluttered and snapped as the water made its way inside him. Horrible, to lose the air; horrible to be sinking from the light the way the families on the Saipan cliffs had sunk into the rocks and waves. The darkness was overwhelming, but against it he saw plums—fleshy, succulent, sweet—arcing over a wall and into his hands. His limbs felt weightless and liquid, all their pains dissolved. Finally, he thought. Finally, I have come home.

Henry, so oblivious that he hadn't seen the boat leave the shore nor heard his daughters and his niece and nephew calling to Wiloma and Brendan, suddenly became aware of the shouting below him and saw that his uncle's wheelchair was empty. He looked away from Waldo, with whom he had been arguing, and he said, "What's going on down there?"

Waldo took his hand off Henry's arm. "Those are our *kids*. On that point across from Wiloma. How the hell did they get there?"

Henry looked at the four children, all of them, along with a stranger, facing the water and shouting something he couldn't understand. He saw Win step out of his clothes and hurl himself into the water, swimming toward a small boat in which sat a man—Marcus?—and a dog that looked like Bongo. The boat was rocking from side to side, although the water was glassy. Wiloma, he saw, was standing with her arm on Brendan's wheelchair. Her mouth was open in a circle.

"Where's my uncle?" he asked Waldo. Waldo had accused him of kidnapping Brendan, and the idea had made him so furious—kidnapping, when he'd gone so far out of his way to help his uncle, when he'd done everything his uncle had asked—that he'd accused Waldo of ruining Wiloma's life. And then Waldo had brought up Coreopsis, taunting him again with his failure, and Henry had retaliated by telling him what he planned for this land, and the two of them, once again, had almost come to blows. But now, in the light of Brendan's disappearance, they stood quietly and tried to figure out what had happened.

"Maybe he's in the shed," Waldo said. "This sun—maybe he wanted to get some shade."

"Without his chair?"

"We better go down."

"There's a path here. A shortcut." Without thinking, Henry found his way to a trail he'd known as a child, which led down the face of the ridge and cut directly toward the shore. As they descended they vanished from sight among the trees, and when Wiloma turned around to cry for help, they were gone.

Bongo stood with his front paws on the side of the boat, barking loudly at the water that had swallowed Brendan. Wiloma closed her eyes and then opened them, thinking Brendan might somehow miraculously reappear if she willed it strongly enough. When he didn't, when she saw only the barking dog and the rocking boat and Marcus stabbing his oars into the water as if he could fish Brendan out, she bent her head over the wheelchair and threw up. She couldn't swim and neither could Henry; Da had never let them near the water and had refused even to let them wade in their shallow pond. Her own children swam like fish, she had made them take lessons very young, but she had never been able to learn herself and all she could do now was wipe her mouth and then listen as a strange wail, which seemed to come from outside her, filled the air.

Her son splashed through the water, as naked as a fish, but she watched him without either hope or fear. There was no chance that he'd get to Brendan in time, she thought, and no chance that he'd drown trying—the sun was warm, the water was calm, and Win was very strong. He'd swim out and back and nothing would change; he'd continue drifting away from her, growing more and more distant each year until he was gone entirely. He was gone and Brendan was gone and Wendy was leaving; Henry and Waldo had vanished. She had nothing and had brought this on herself.

She had allowed herself to believe that her uncle was dying and that Henry had kidnapped him; she had let her panic overwhelm her and push her into a corner where this was the only possible outcome. She recalled the words of her Manual: *We see what we believe as surely as we believe what we see. All the thoughts we have ever had exist even when we do not think of them, just as rain exists on a cloudless day.*

She made herself think of Brendan's Spirit floating up from the reservoir and merging into the Light. He was transiting without her or Christine or the Healing Ceremony, but he was only lost if she believed he was. She saw her son swimming toward the boat, as if he still believed he might help. She watched him hang on the boat, catching his breath, and then dive once, twice, three times, returning empty-handed. The old man in the boat reached down and helped her son from the water, nearly tipping the boat over in the process. She saw Win rest his head on the old man's knees, as if he were crying.

She could not spare a glance for the children on the opposite shore, who stood as if they'd taken root. Wendy meant to swim out with Win, but the looping, wordless wail that had poured from her mother's throat paralyzed her. Even Delia's voice, when she finally heard it, seemed to come from far away. "I shouldn't have called him," Wendy thought she heard Delia say to Lise. Delia's face seemed to have shattered into unrelated parts, which Wendy could focus on only separately. A swollen eye against glinting water, a nose against a background of trees, a mouth among the rocks. A pair of sandpipers hopped behind a pair of knees, and in the shallows Wendy saw a set of shimmering shapes that resolved into a school of minnows. The minnows were lined up with Lise's eyes, which were fixed upon the water.

"I called him, too," Wendy heard Lise say woodenly, and then Delia wailed, "Bongo!" as if Bongo were something more than a dog, as if they could blame a dog. Delia fell to the ground in a tangle of hair and tears and arms and legs and cried so hard that Lise sat down and twined Delia in her bony arms until no one could see where Lise ended and Delia began.

Roy stood near Wendy with his hands over his eyes; he said nothing when Wendy stepped out of her shoes and began walking toward her mother. The water looked like a broken mirror, the edges facing the sun lit up and the trailing surfaces shadowed. It rose to her ankles, then to her knees, and then her thighs. Perhaps Roy never noticed that she'd moved. The water rose to her waist and then to her chest and she leaned into it, ready to lift her feet from the bottom and swim. But Win had been right, after all—the water in the narrow cove never rose over her head, and at its deepest point she was able, by stretching her neck and her legs, to keep her toes on the bottom and the water below her chin as she parted the glittering fragments with her hands.

29

F ROM THE "LETTERS TO THE EDITOR" OF THE *PARADISE VALLEY*
Daily Transcript:

March 29, 1938
Dear Sirs:

*Yesterday, when our towns formally ceased to exist and the
Commission took over our valley by eminent domain, marked
the end of our twenty-year struggle to preserve our homes. We
have all received notices asking us to vacate our properties.
Our train has ceased to run; our churches have ceased to
hold services; our fields lie fallow and those buildings already
abandoned have been razed before our eyes. Meanwhile the
embankment rises higher each day, and the politicians in Boston gleefully anticipate the completion of the dam and the
filling of the reservoir.*

*And so it appears that, after all, we must go. A few more
town meetings, the closing of our schools and post offices and*

clubs, and then those of us remaining must leave. Who can calculate the damage done to us? Ten years from now, when the people of Boston turn on their taps, who among them will sense the lives that were destroyed to provide them with water? Who among them will even know that such a place as the Stillwater Reservoir exists? They will drink thoughtlessly, perhaps imagining that their water comes from a source closer to home, and if they should look at a map, they will not connect the great blot in the center of the state with the liquid filling their glasses. In a decade or so the blot will seem to have been there always, and no one will remember that beneath it once lay a community.

Newspaper reporters from other parts of the state swarm here now, suddenly perceiving what they choose to call ''the tragedy of the valley residents.'' They ask us for interviews. They photograph our abandoned buildings. Where were they, one wonders, when this tragedy might still have been prevented? Where were they during the hearings that decided our fate? I would urge you to send these vultures away with the contempt they deserve.

Frank B. Auberon, Sr.
Pomeroy

Part V

Old Men's Tales

30

THE NIECE," THE OLD MEN SAY, AS THEY DO EACH WEEK WHEN Wiloma swishes through the pneumatic doors. She brushes the snow from her jacket and boots and sets down her carton of books. In the common room the windows are dressed with sprays of spruce and holly and a large artificial tree bristles in a corner. "The niece is here," the old men say, and they sit straighter in their chairs.

They never call Wiloma by her name; she is "the niece" as Henry is "the nephew" and Wendy and Delia and Lise and Win are "the children." A legend as florid as any saint's life has grown up in the six months since Brendan's journey, and in it Wiloma and her family have been reduced to nameless characters. Roy doesn't exist in the legend; Waldo surfaces only rarely. Brendan, as Wiloma once foresaw, has become a hero to his old companions.

Spencer, Charlie, Kevin, and Ben; Wallace with his clouded eyes; even Parker with the electronic box in his throat where his larynx used to be—they're glad for the food and books she brings, glad for all her help, but what they really want is to talk to her about Brendan. They want to tell her how they were present the day he broke out, and how they knew he was planning something outrageous.

"Brendan was cunning," they whisper in their shattered voices. "He bided his time."

"He stole the keys," they say, holding up their own twisted hands in imitation of his. "He tricked Fred Johannson and stole the keys and convinced his nephew to drive the van, and then he took off on this journey. . . ."

They want not to hear what happened but to repeat their versions of what they want to have happened. In some of the versions, the encounter with the police cruiser at the 7-Eleven has turned into something just short of a shoot-out, with Brendan defying the officer from the van as the nephew roars out of the parking lot. In others, the Home's quiet search has turned into a statewide manhunt. There are versions in which Brendan meets a beautiful waitress who takes him home for the night, and others in which he and his nephew sleep in the fields like tramps.

"He went back to his family's land," say the men. "He made his way back home."

The administrator has told them that Brendan died in his sleep. Peacefully, painlessly, they've been told. At his childhood home. Buried near his family. And so the men, who don't know that his body has never been found, nor that his childhood home is long gone, accept the official version of Brendan's end and embroider the rest of the journey instead. They crowd more and more details into each telling, although no one could have accomplished so much in so little time. They tell stories of meals in lovely restaurants and dancing girls in bars, offer scenes in a boat and in the mountains and in several different hotels. There are evil bikers whom Brendan confronts, a reunion with a long-lost brother, a contest involving three questions and a knife. And yet in all these tales, no matter how fantastic, there is always this kernel of fact: the trip is always Brendan's idea, Brendan always the instigator. Bitter and hard to swallow, but true. Wiloma has had to let go of the idea that Henry kidnapped him.

Waldo brought her that news first, before she was in any shape to hear it. "It's not like you think," he said on the shore of the reservoir. He and Henry had emerged from the trees together, after it was too late for them to help. She had raised her hand to strike Henry's face and Waldo had caught her arm.

"Brendan talked him into it," Waldo said then. "He took the keys to the van and told Henry they were allowed to borrow it. Henry just did what Brendan asked. He just drove."

"I just drove," Henry repeated.

He stared at the water, stupid and stunned; he looked at her and said, "He fell *in?*" When she nodded, he sprinted for the van. Running away again, she thought, and so she was amazed when he returned a few minutes later with a tangle of colored silk ties. Days later, he told her he'd rescued them from Kitty's closet at the start of his trip; the girls had given them to him, he said, and he didn't want Kitty to throw them out.

But that day on the shore they seemed to have come from nowhere. Henry knotted the ties in a useless rope, not looking at her or his daughters, not looking at the water, watching his hands and knotting, knotting, until Win finally rowed Marcus back to land. Afterward, after that bleak, lost sequence of hours punctuated by policemen and divers and wailing sirens, Waldo told her that Henry sat the whole long afternoon with his hands tangled in the ties.

She can't remember this. She remembers Wendy, dripping wet, emerging from the water. She remembers Waldo leaving and then coming back with strangers in uniforms, Win sitting so close that she could smell his hair, Lise and Delia clinging to Roy. She can't believe Henry was left by himself except for the few minutes Waldo could spare him. But Waldo says this is what happened. He says Henry only drove, only did as Brendan asked. He says the only words Henry said that afternoon were, "I can't swim. I never learned how." Should she believe what Waldo says? The tales the old men tell her are based, in part, on the smooth story Waldo told the administrator: lots of omissions, no lies. Waldo's version of Henry's words probably reflects the same unconscious adjustments.

The men have no tales for her today; many of their rooms are empty. But upstairs, on Brendan's old floor, she finds Parker valiant in red plaid, rolling his wheelchair back and forth as he impatiently waits for her.

"I want to show you something," he says, tapping the face of his watch. The box through which he speaks reduces his voice to a raspy squawk. "But we have to go now. Can you take me down to the library for a little while?"

Wiloma has things to do at home and knows she ought to get going, but she has made a rule for herself since she saw Brendan slip below the water: on her weekly visits here, she tries to do whatever the old men ask. She doesn't give them advice; she doesn't try to change their lives. If they want liquor or cigarettes or chocolates wrapped in foil, she brings them and never says a word about what's healthy or not. Parker's color is bad today; he'd be better off in bed. When he says, "Can we go?" she nods and says, "Yes."

Down the corridors, down the elevator, out into the green basement hall—she can just make out Roxanne through the window in the door to the whirlpool room, massaging the legs of a man whose face is hidden. Strange sounds emerge through the open library door down the hall. "Wa-ka-*wa*-kee," Wiloma hears, or something like that. A woman's voice, clear and passionate. "Wy-a-*wee*-no, ko-*tay*-nu."

"Latin?" she asks Parker. She steers his wheelchair around an empty florist's carton sprouting frills of green tissue. "Is that Latin? Or is it Greek?"

"Neither," he rasps. "That's the prayer group in there—that woman's received the gift of the spirit. But listen to the rest."

As the woman's voice rises and then fades, another voice comes from a hidden corner. A man's voice, cracked and worn, says, "Let us offer up a healing prayer for the soul of our brother Brendan, who departed this earth six months ago today."

"That's Ben," Parker says. "He promised us all he'd do this."

"You knew about this? Don't you want to go in?"

"I'd rather listen from out here. Those prayer people make me nervous."

Ben's voice cracks but then steadies again. "O Lord," he says, "we ask you to be gentle with the soul of our beloved brother, who underwent many trials on his journey to you. We ask you to forgive him his small trespasses, and to welcome him into the peace of your presence. Although we could not be present at the burial of his body, we join together today in praying for the repose of his soul."

There is a rustle inside, and then a murmur. When Wiloma cranes her head around the doorframe, she sees that all Brendan's friends have somehow produced white sprays of freesia from their pajamas and robes. The long stems sprout paired buds near their bases and open flowers at their tips. Kevin, leaning against his walker, seems to have caught his stems in the zipper of his warm-up jacket. The blossoms jut out from his stomach as if they have grown there. Wallace, propped up next to Kevin, leans over and tugs the flowers free.

"Praise the Lord," Ben sings out, and the men with the flowers repeat this after him. The outsiders, the prayer-group members who have come to lead the service, shuffle about uneasily. It is clear that the old men have caught them by surprise. "Praise his works, his ways, his days," Ben says. A minute of silence follows, and then the men, perhaps responding to a signal from Ben that Wiloma can't see, toss their flowers all at once toward the center of the room. The arched stems hang in the air for a minute and then fall onto the table awaiting them. When they land, Wiloma releases the breath she hadn't realized she was holding.

The flowers remind her of the story Christine told her when she came back from the reservoir. When she limped home, grieving and lost, Christine said she'd performed a Healing Ceremony that morning in Brendan's absence. She'd recited the passage from the Manual, she said, and burned the mistletoe in a porcelain bowl. As she was mixing the ashes with birch extract and powdered minerals, she saw a flash signaling Brendan's successful passage into the Light.

"And there was a smell," she told Wiloma. "A little like andromeda—you know those waxy white flowers on the shrub out back?"

The andromeda near the kitchen window was in bloom on the day that Brendan died, and Wiloma suspects that Christine only smelled the fragrance through the screens. This is the woman, after all, who lied about the children: Wiloma hasn't forgiven her for that, and they haven't seen each other since that night. But still, Wiloma can't account for the flash Christine saw, any more than she can now account for the soft fragrance filling the library. Freesias are deeply scented, she knows; perhaps the fragrance is only natural. But it is deeper and stronger than she would expect from a handful of blossoms, and it carries to her the conviction that Brendan's Spirit is finally safe.

That night, when Wiloma goes home, she tries to explain to her son what she saw: "The men at St. Benedict's had a sort of memorial service for Grunkie today. They ordered a box of flowers from somewhere and each of them held a few stems. When they offered them up at the end of their prayer, it was like . . ." She looks at Win's face, which is closed and suspicious, and she reels her words back. "It was nice," she says lamely.

Win might as well be in another country; since Wendy's disappearance he has spent most of his time at school and the rest frantically assembling information he has gathered from colleges in California. If he could go farther, Wiloma knows, he would; if he knew how, he'd keep running across the water. If he could figure out a way to enter college early, he'd do that, too. Meanwhile he waits for his freedom so palpably, and with such fear that he'll never get it, that Wiloma feels forced to behave in front of him.

She knows that, despite his longings, he won't leave until he thinks she's all right. Much of her energy, these days, goes into convincing him that she is. She does much less with the Church. She never brings Church people home. She makes real dinners for him and watches TV with him at night, instead of reading pamphlets in her room. But still he is thin and tense and very unhappy, and although he hardly ever mentions Wendy, she knows that he misses his sister and resents her for leaving him here alone. When Wiloma looks at him, she is haunted by her last days in Coreopsis, alone with Da after Henry had fled. She wants more than anything that Win should not feel trapped in the same way. Christmas is still several days away, but she decides to give him his best gift early.

"I got a job," she tells him. "A real one. I'm starting right after New Year's Day."

"You did? Not with the Church?"

"At St. Benedict's," she says. The relief spreading over his face is so visible that it stings. "I've been spending so much time there I thought I might as well make it official. They hired me as an aide."

Win's face falls a bit. "The money. They can't be paying you very much . . ."

"It's enough. Your father's going to pick up your tuition when you're ready, and he's willing to help out with the mortgage here—it's enough, it's more than I've had. I'll be fine."

"Really?"

"Really."

The knowledge that she finally has a job brightens Win's mood considerably. He starts to tell her about Stanford and

Berkeley and UCLA, flashing photos from college brochures and telling her about the soccer scholarships he may get if he plays well next season. She listens as attentively as if his plans were not almost wholly the result of his need to run away from her.

The house seems very silent when she finally lies down in bed. She hears the babble of the prayer group and the gentle whisper of the flowers soaring through the air; she sees Brendan, as she does each night, slipping through the water as Henry tries to save him with a web of good intentions. She tries to picture Wendy slipping out the door, but all she can see is her slim back, turned away from everyone on the day of Delia's wedding. A slim back in a dull green dress; she left the dress behind along with all her other clothes.

"Mom," said the note Wendy left on the refrigerator. "I've gone on a trip. I don't know when I'll be back, but I'll be fine."

During all of July and the first weeks of August, Wendy hardly ever left the house. She had lost her museum job— some business about a few missing dolls, some irregularity Wiloma never got straight—and she paced around like a restless cat. Waiting, Wiloma had thought. For college to start, for the summer to end. Grieving over Brendan, perhaps; maybe worried about her. But at the wedding the look on Wendy's face had warned her that something else was also going on.

"I'm fine," Wendy writes, on postcards that do no more than tell Wiloma what part of the country her daughter has just passed through. The postcards come from Montana and Oregon and Wyoming and Idaho; Wendy writes that she has been waitressing and cleaning salmon and baling hay. Wiloma worries about her all the time, and yet part of her also feels a deep satisfaction at Wendy's escape.

When Wiloma finally falls asleep, she dreams of the day she graduated from high school in Coreopsis. She dreams that she took her diploma in one hand, her suitcase in the other, and walked boldly out of the building and into the world.

31

IF WENDY WERE SLEEPING SHE MIGHT DREAM OF HER MOTHER, but she's still wide-awake. For months now she's been hitchhiking from place to place, keeping the Rocky Mountains between herself and her old life. Keeping odd hours, shedding old ways. Kalispell, Dillon, Coeur d'Alene; she's drawn to small cities and towns contracted to their cores, fading and failing places where the only inhabitants are people who've always lived there and haven't yet run away.

The edges of these cities and towns are abrupt, and between them lies more space than she ever imagined. The sky is so enormous that sometimes, as she waits for a ride for the better part of a day on a road that stretches from nowhere to nowhere for miles, she can see mountains—Cascades, Tetons, Absarokas—floating in the distance like a promise. Everything seems promising here, even the men who pick her up in their cars and trucks and warn her that she ought to be more careful. They look nothing like the men she knew at home. They remind her how easily she could be hurt, but none of them have hurt her. When they ask her where she's from, she makes up stories.

"Michigan," she says. "Just outside Lansing." Or San Diego, Arizona, Baton Rouge. In bars she tells similar stories to the men with whom she dances, and once in a while—on four occasions now—she has let a man bring her home. Twice, when she found work and a man she liked in the same town, she has shared a roof for a couple of weeks. She has yet to want anyone as fiercely as she wanted Roy, but she has almost stopped hearing the echo of Christine's voice.

Tonight she's in a bar just outside Spokane, watching couples dance to a raucous band. Stephen, the out-of-work carpenter sitting next to her, was leaning against the wall when she first walked in. One of his legs was bent, the sole of his work boot pressed against the paneling. His hands were jammed into the pockets of his jeans, and the sleeves of his shirt were rolled halfway up his forearms. He was staring moodily at the spinning dancers, tapping his earthbound foot to the beat, and when she strolled up and asked him to dance, he said yes immediately. On the dance floor he led her firmly through a two-step, which she'd begun to learn in other towns in other states. His open palm, pressed against her back, was dry and strong.

After the dance he smiled down at her and said, "You're not from around here, are you?"

"No," she said, and she touched his bare forearm. "Would you like a beer?"

For a minute she thought she might lose him, that she'd moved too quickly or misjudged the loneliness and longing she thought she saw on his face, but then he smiled and shrugged and said, "You surely can." Now they're sitting knee to knee on a pair of stools at one end of the bar. He started buying, after the first round; a pitcher of beer sits between them and she keeps his glass filled. He was married once, he tells her. He is twenty-eight. His two little girls are in Boise with their mother.

When he mentions his daughters his face clouds, and Wendy does something she has learned to do in the past few months, which almost always works. "Do you have any pictures?" she asks.

He reaches for his wallet. Inside, in plastic sleeves, are stiff school portraits of a gap-toothed girl with blond hair and glasses and an older girl with a brown ponytail. "The little one's Dora. She's in first grade this year. Nancy's in third."

"They're gorgeous. Beautiful girls."

He smiles at her then, smiles at the pictures, smiles back at her. "So are you," he says lightly.

She lowers her eyes. She knows she isn't beautiful; she is only young. As young as her mother was when she met Wendy's father; younger than Sarah was when Wendy's father fell in love with her; younger, even, than the women her uncle used to chase. When she thinks of how nearly she missed understanding what this gives her, she closes her eyes for a second and then sips at her beer. The beer flowers inside her, loosening her joints and her brain.

Stephen slips the wallet back into his pocket. "Where are you from?" he asks. One finger lightly strokes the soft flesh below her elbow.

"Here and there. I've been traveling for a while." Below the bar his knee just touches her thigh, and soon he is telling her about the cabin he has in the woods twenty miles away. How snug it is when it snows; how his woodstove heats the whole place; how beautiful it is at dawn.

"I love it up there," he says. "If I didn't have that place, I'd go crazy."

"You're lucky. Having a place like that." The dim light shadows his face, carving it into hollows and planes. In the morning it may only turn out to be another face, but right now it is everything she thinks she wants.

"What about you?" he says. "Where are you staying?"

"I don't know. I just got into town this afternoon." She gives him the slow smile she has learned only recently, and his hand tightens on her arm. She knows he believes he's been hit by luck. For a second they hover on that fine edge from which the evening may fall either way, and Wendy thinks of all the times since Delia's wedding when she's been similarly poised.

The wedding was held in a rented garden at the art museum: very pretty, very subdued. Lise—not Wendy—was Delia's maid of honor, and when Wendy kissed Delia and wished her luck, Delia looked at her feet. After the ceremony, Wendy wandered over to the pond by herself. The ducks that dotted the sleek surface were feeding on something invisible, upending themselves so abruptly that their heads turned without transition into fat, pointed tails. The sight transfixed her, and she found herself muttering, "Heads. Tails. Heads. Tails," like a gambler gone mad with a quarter. Her mother's life, Delia's life. The life her great-grandparents had led more than half a century ago. She could choose, she saw. She could live any way she wanted or in several different ways, carving her life into sharp, separate parts the way her great-uncle had. Massachusetts, China, Manitoba; Coreopsis and then St. Benedict's. He had moved a lot for someone meant to be bound to a single place. She moved from the pond to the hedge to the gate, from the gate to her house to the road.

Stephen splits the remains of the pitcher between their glasses. It is well past midnight; the dance floor is densely crowded. Couples lean into each other down the bar and along the walls, pursuing the delicate negotiations that will bring this Saturday night to the close they all want but haven't dared hope for. In the bathrooms, she knows, men are checking their wallets for the rubbers they think they remember putting in there a week or a month ago. Women are adjusting their underwear and consulting with their friends. The pay phones near the door are busy; there are parents and spouses being deceived, baby-sitters being begged to stay until morning. Within this desperate last-minute whirl, Wendy feels perfectly at home.

THE FORMS OF WATER

Home is what you dream of, she remembers her mother saying. *What everyone does. But you have to learn that your only true home is in the Spirit.* Of all her mother's mottoes this now seems the most false: that the body is nothing, the body is dust, the world is made up of our ideas. Stephen leans over and cups her chin in his fingers and kisses her lightly. His cabin will be spare, she knows, clean and dark except for the glow from his woodburning stove. Stephen will be considerate. Her home, she thinks, is in her body, from which she learns everything.

When Stephen whispers, "Would you . . . do you think . . . I have this cabin and if you need a place to stay . . . do you want to come home with me?" she forces herself to hesitate for a minute, as if all that has happened between them has been his idea. He's forgotten that she first asked him to dance, that she touched him first, that she bought the first drink. She looks into the mirror behind the bar, as if she is weighing his invitation. She waits until he strokes her fingers with his. Then she says, "Well, I guess."

At the door, Stephen wraps his scarf around her neck. "It's cold out," he says. He smiles at the size of her backpack and sets it aside as he helps her dress. The backpack holds everything she owns, clothes and shoes and a few books, the sprig of mistletoe she stole from Christine and the list of rules she once kept in her closet. The list reminds her of Grunkie, who lived by so many rules they formed a Rule.

Once, visiting him with her mother, she'd asked him about those rules: "Are they like punishments? Or like the warnings on the playground list at school?" She'd been eight or ten then, still in love with his smiles and the warm approval in which he bathed her. At Christmas, when she and Win and her cousins poured down the pale halls to his room, he'd given them crisp white envelopes filled with pressed flowers and leaves and then promised prizes to those who named the plants correctly. His rules, he told her, were neither warnings nor punishments. They were suggestions that shaped a joyous

281

life the way an empty bucket shaped sand. They were nothing in themselves, he said. They became what you filled them with.

So far she hasn't managed to fill her own rules with anything, and if it weren't for him she would throw her list away. What she remembers of Grunkie is the way he turned to her and Lise and Delia when they called his name, the way he smiled and raised his arms before he fell. She is sure he smiled, and sure his smile meant something. And somewhere in the back of her mind, she is aware that he drowned six months ago today.

Stephen stands behind her, easing her arms into the sleeves of her coat and then folding himself around her like another garment. She wonders how her mother and Delia could stand to give up all this wildness. She wonders how Grunkie could live so long without having this even once.

Stephen turns her around until she faces him. "All set?" he asks.

"All set," she says.

Soon she'll have to leave his cabin and begin her travels again, but for now she likes the dent in his chin and the way he holds her. When he opens the door, she sees snow piled up on the parked cars, as white and solid as if it had never been water.

32

It IS ALSO SNOWING IN MASSACHUSETTS, WHERE HENRY SITS IN a cabin even smaller than Stephen's. One room, four windows, a simple porch, and a steeply pitched roof. Marcus, who helped Henry build this place, has told Henry it sits a hundred yards from the site of his parents' old cabin. The windows frame segments of water and sky similar to those Henry saw as a child.

Across the cluttered table from Henry, Marcus peers at some yellow papers. He has pushed aside the cards and the cribbage board, as he often does when he visits; he comes for a drink and a friendly game, but he ends up telling stories. A pair of bricks may set him off, or an iron hinge, an ancient scythe blade, one of Henry's family mementos. He has a tale to go with the picture of Henry's parents at the Farewell Ball, which is tacked to the south wall. He has anecdotes related to Da's newspaper clippings, which hang from a corkboard on the north wall, and more to go with Da's "Letters to the Editor," which frame the window facing east. Lately he's been telling stories about the papers he now holds in his hands.

The papers come from the briefcase Henry received from Da when he first left Coreopsis; the same briefcase he took from Kitty's closet at the start of his journey with Brendan. As soon as the cabin was finished, he hung the pictures and the clippings on the walls. Then he leaned the briefcase against the table, where it sat until the night Marcus idly picked it up and ran his fingers over the leather.

"Used to be everything was made like this," Marcus said. "You don't see tanning like this anymore." Marcus slid his fingers inside and commented on the firmness of the stitching. Then he asked Henry what he'd left in the small interior pocket.

"Nothing," Henry said. The briefcase had never been more to him than the shell surrounding the relics Da had left him, and he'd emptied it carelessly. But Marcus said, "There's something here," and then fished four sheets of paper out. A pain shot through Henry's chest, as if he'd swallowed a seed.

"Your grandfather's handwriting," Marcus said. "I think. Do you know what these are?"

Henry bent over the brittle sheets. The writing was cramped and jagged, the pen strokes so shaky that each letter appeared to be fringed. He could not be sure Da had written the pages, nor could he tell where the pages were from. He told Marcus he'd ask his sister what she knew, and then they waited for her answer for two weeks. Still, he counts himself lucky that she writes to him at all.

In July, after Waldo sold the house out from under him, and after Delia announced she didn't want him at her wedding, Henry had packed his few belongings and then gone to visit his sister. He had nothing, he'd told her then. His job had vanished, his kids didn't need him, he had no place to live. "I'm going to take off. Make a new start somewhere."

He'd heard the self-pity in his voice, but he hadn't been able to correct it.

The children had been at Waldo's and her house had been empty and quiet. She had a spare room, he knew: the place where she'd intended to bring Brendan. For a minute he wondered if she might offer to take him in.

"Again?" she'd said. "You're leaving *again?*"

Her voice had been so bitter that he'd been completely surprised. "What *again?* It's not like I've ever gone anywhere." At that moment he'd believed his words absolutely. He was fifty years old and he'd never been anyplace interesting; all his travels had been in his dreams.

But Wiloma sat down at the table and wept, and when she could catch her breath, she said, "It's not like you've ever stayed. How could you leave me alone when Da was dying? Where were you when Brendan drowned? You've never been here, you've always been off with your stupid projects." Then she told him a story about Da's last days, which he'd never heard before. "There was a book," she said; she went up to the attic and returned a few minutes later with a faded, red-bound volume. "This was all I had to get us through it." She handed it to him. "Where were you?"

He couldn't remember. Driving, he supposed; that was what he'd always done when he was troubled. He drove Kitty to Niagara Falls, he drove back and forth along the lake, he drove to his new apartment and around the site of his first development. He held Wiloma's book in his hands and remembered driving very fast and going nowhere. But she couldn't have thought he meant to abandon her.

"I don't know where I was," he said. A wave of guilt swept up from his stomach and then was pushed aside by anger. "Maybe I was around and you didn't want to see me. Like that night before Brendan and I took off—how come you wouldn't even say hello?"

"I always talk to you when you're around," she said. "When was this?"

He reminded her how he'd stood in front of the community center window and waved at her, how she'd looked right at him and then turned away. "I hate it when you do that," he said, and all the pain of that moment hit him again. "I hate it when you ignore me."

"I didn't see you. Really. I don't remember seeing you at all."

And that might have been true—at the reservoir she hadn't seemed to be aware that she never looked at him. "That's worse. That you can't even see me."

She couldn't seem to answer him. She looked over his shoulder, out the window, into the trees. Then, finally, she looked at him. "Where are you headed?"

Of course she wasn't going to offer to take him in. "Massachusetts," he said. Of course he would have turned down her offer, had she made it. "I want to spend some time on the land Uncle Brendan left us. That's all."

Wiloma had let him hold her precious book, but at that she snatched it back from him. "Don't you *touch* that land. It's half mine, it's mine as much as it's yours. If you think you're going to pull some business like you did with Coreopsis—"

"No business. I just need a place to stay for a while, until I figure out what to do."

She had folded her hands in her lap. "I can't stop you. When has anyone ever stopped you from doing anything?"

Her neck had rings around it, he saw, and her hands were as creased and worn as his. He gestured toward the book. "Could I borrow that—just for a while? I'd like to have something of Da's with me."

She'd let him take the book, which he now keeps on the floor by his cot, but he hadn't been sure when they'd parted if she'd forgiven him and he's still sorting out in his mind the acts for which he needs to be forgiven. For a few months he'd heard nothing from her, but then she started writing him letters after she learned that he'd finished the cabin. Cautiously friendly, guardedly open; letters in which he can feel her pushing herself to be kind to him. Guilt may be driving her, or pity or love; or maybe the letters are only a duty her church says she has to perform. Whatever they mean, he is grateful for them. She sends news of Wendy and Win and tries to answer the questions he asks.

Four sheets of paper, he wrote in his last letter to her. *Lined, like they came from a notebook. The handwriting's hard to read, but it looks like Da's. What do you think they are?*

Her answer arrived this morning, and now he reads her letter out loud to Marcus. He skips over the parts about the kids and about the job she plans to take, and also the lines where she asks him, for the tenth or twelfth time, why he's wasting so much time on these old things. *The past is the past,* she writes. *You can't change it.* And yet each time she writes him she seems to heal a part of their old estrangement.

"Listen to this," he says to Marcus. " 'Those must be from Da's notebook. After Gran died, but before Da was so sick he couldn't hold a pen, he used to scribble things in this notebook with a speckled cover. He never let me see what he was writing. Then one day, after you took off with Kitty, I found the notebook under his bed with some pages torn out. All the pages left in it were blank. Maybe he stuck the ones he'd written in that briefcase before he gave it to you. But why would he give those to you and not to me?' "

Marcus reaches for the letter and reads the passage for himself. Then he asks, "Why would he?"

"I don't know."

Marcus shakes his head and pours them both a drink. "Might as well add it to your list." His tone is mocking but affectionate.

The list Marcus is talking about occupies the back pages of the notebook Henry has been filling: unanswered questions, things to follow up. There are forty or fifty of these. They have to do with his father and the tale Marcus told in the van, which he hardly heard at the time; with Brendan's request that they visit the dam before the land, which might have changed everything had he granted it; and with a score of other things related to Brendan's last journey. Who were those people camped out in the house in Coreopsis? Why did Jackson stay in his garage? What happened to the broker in Buffalo who was caught robbing all those banks? And where did that army of uprooted men come from, the men who knocked on his door when he still lived with Kitty and wanted to shovel snow or clean gutters, the carpenter's helpers and plumber's assistants who hung around Coreopsis Heights begging for work and who now seem to be everywhere, their lives as twisted as his?

The rest of his notebook is filled with the stories Marcus has told, the information he's gleaned from books and maps, and the fragments he's been able to reconstruct of the tales Da and his father and Brendan told. Henry writes in this notebook every night, the act of writing so new, after years of dictating to willing secretaries, that his pen still stutters on the pages. Sometimes he feels like a monk himself, shut inside a medieval cloister and patiently copying manuscripts no one will ever read. Even Marcus, who delights in uncovering obscure facts and useless details, sometimes looks at what Henry's doing and shakes his head.

"If you're going to spend your time like this," he says, "why don't you put in some more stuff about everyday life before the reservoir? Why don't you write a real history of what happened to the valley?"

What he means, Henry knows, is *Why don't you put in some more stuff about me?* He can't answer that; he knows that's the question everyone else at the Visitors' Center wants to ask as well. The bookshelves at the Center are lined with pamphlets full of facts. What day the men in their fancy suits first came into the valley; their names and ages and occupations; who said what at the endless meetings; what houses were razed and in what order. But the heap of paper he's accumulating has a logic of its own, and he thinks that if he can understand it, he will understand what he's doing here.

Marcus moves to the window facing the water. "It's really coming down out there. We'll have six inches by morning."

"You'll stay over?"

Marcus nods. He often spends the night on Henry's extra cot; the path to the cabin is rugged and he has nothing to rush home for. Henry reminds himself to set the alarm clock, so he'll have time to drop Marcus off. A load of sheet-metal stampings is waiting for him at the place in the valley where he sometimes works, and he's so grateful to have his license back that he almost enjoys loading the pallets, unloading boxes, driving rickety trucks full of metal parts over bad roads. When he returns from his run to Springfield, he may stop at a bar and have three beers. No more—if he has four, he knows he'll start to feel misunderstood. When he has four, he ends up telling other lonely drunks how he has come to be living like a hermit.

I messed up my marriage, he will say in a small voice. *I took something that belonged to my sister and I ruined it. Then I took my uncle on a trip and couldn't save him when he had an accident. Then I came here.*

He will tell this over and over again, to anyone who will listen, and no one will understand how he has given up almost everything and gotten so little in return. No one will praise him for his sacrifices; no good luck will fall in his lap and no letters will arrive from his wife and daughters, begging him to come home. Wiloma told him that Delia threw out the framed copy of the Farewell Ball photograph that he sent as a wedding present. Lise won't answer his letters. No one seems to understand what a struggle it is for him to walk these acres every day and resist the urge to change them.

He rises and stands by Marcus, near the nail from which

dangle the knotted ties that didn't save Brendan. It's too dark for him to see the reservoir, but despite that he sees his uncle floating below the water and then all he might build on this land. Buildings would block out his visions of Brendan, as they have blocked out everything for years. The temptation to build is terrific; if he had money, he might not be able to resist. But he has no money, and no prospects for getting any.

What he has, instead, are the stories that fill his notebook— the ones Wiloma and Marcus have told him, the ones he remembers from Da and Brendan and his father. When he looks out the window, he sees families jumping off the cliffs at Marpi Point, plums arcing over a wall, Da dying while Wiloma reads to him about snow and water and clouds. He sees Roxanne moving her hands along Brendan's legs and Marcus shooting into the night, just to be shooting at something. On Makin, Marcus has said, Henry's father had been brave but he had not, and he had been one of the men who shot at nothing.

Henry wonders if he may be shooting at nothing himself. He might be writing Latin verse in his notebook, for all the good it will ever do; no one will read it, no one will care, his lost family is only one among a million. The words with which he tries to preserve them are only words, no more likely to survive than the words Da scribbled so long ago. And yet Da's words lie on the table, on the pieces of paper that Marcus has set down, and Henry walks over and makes himself read them again.

The pages, worn and brittle and stained, contain no astounding insights, no solutions, no revelations. They contain no generalizations, no overview of life in the valley before the reservoir, no statistics, no assessments, no blame. Nine short paragraphs, written in a wavering hand and widely spaced. The words are Da's, but as Henry sits down and begins to copy them, the voice he hears is Brendan's.

THE FORMS OF WATER

The Paradise Valley was 13 miles long and 4 miles wide at the base. The eastern branch, where we lived, was less than a mile across. Our nearest neighbor, Timothy Dana, made excellent cheese.

We had pigs, cows, and chickens at our place. We raised berries, potatoes, apples, corn, and four kinds of winter squash. I had a pig each year, a pet crow, three black Labs, and Flossie. Flossie had to be put down in 1911.

I met Eileen for the first time outside the feed store in Pomeroy. Her hair was as dark and shiny as Flossie's coat and parted in the center. She wore it in two long braids, wrapped twice around her head like a crown. Her eyes were blue and her feet were small. She was standing with her father that day.

Her father had a red face and enormous shoulders, but I was taller than him. He never stopped hating me. He brought Eileen and her sister and his wife over from Ireland when Eileen was four, and he worked at the sawmill. He was jealous of our land—we had a large place even without the woodlot, which I bought in 1926.

Brendan's birth went very easily, but there was a blizzard when Frank junior was born and the doctor couldn't get to us. Neither could my mother or hers or any of our neighbors. Frank junior was breeched and Eileen was in labor for two days. She told me to do what I did with the calves, but when I reached to turn the baby, I couldn't get my hand inside. I tried to turn him with my fingers. When he came out he was folded up like a lamb, bent at the waist with his legs against his chest, his face on his knees, his feet and arms over his head. I thought he was dead at first. Later he was a good-looking boy. Eileen was sick for a long time, and we had marital relations very seldom after that.

The apple trees in the orchard were planted before I was born and were 51 years old when we left the valley. We had Winesaps, Jonathans, Granny Smiths, and a yellow kind Eileen made good pies from. I can't remember the name of those. The petals fell off the trees in the spring and floated on the pond and scared the cows. That was the pond where Brendan almost drowned.

My father let William Benson keep his beehives under our apple trees. In return, William gave us some of his honey each year. The honeycomb was brittle and delicate, and I kept the wax in my mouth after I sucked the honey out. The wax had no real flavor, but it smelled of apple blossoms and something else, maybe pollen.

Frank junior used to follow Brendan everywhere, but he didn't follow Brendan into the abbey and I was grateful that I'd been left with one son—the right one, even; Frank was the hardy one. Now I wish he'd followed Brendan in. Brendan looks awful but at least he's alive. I should have made Frank come to Coreopsis with us.

Our neighbors were Timothy Dana, whose family had lived in the valley forever; the Bourdins and the Gendreaus, French Canadians who came down around the time my grandfather did; and the Gregorys, who came from Ireland when I was a boy. And the monks, of course. On quiet spring evenings after a rain, we could hear them chanting when we went to milk the cows. The whole valley lay under a mist. Some of the shrubs were hinting at green, and the fields had thawed and turned black. The willows were yellow near the pond. The colors seemed very bright against the mist, and through the air, so softly we could not be sure we heard it, came the sound of the men chanting to welcome in the night.

Barrett

8/93